Teaching Little Fang

Teaching Little Fang

Mark Swallow

M

MACMILLAN LONDON

First published 1990 by
MACMILLAN LONDON LIMITED
4 Little Essex Street, London WC2R 3LF
and Basingstoke

Associated companies in Auckland, Delhi, Dublin,
Gaborone, Hamburg, Harare, Hong Kong, Johannesburg,
Kuala Lumpur, Lagos, Manzini, Melbourne, Mexico City,
Nairobi, New York, Singapore and Tokyo

A CIP catalogue record for this book is
available from the British Library

ISBN 0-333-54210-X

Photoset by Rowland Phototypesetting Limited
Bury St Edmunds, Suffolk

Printed in Great Britain by
Billings and Sons Ltd, Worcester.

The publishers and author are grateful for permission to
use material from BBC Monitoring – Summary of World
Broadcasts and from 'And Now In China' © *Washington
Post*, April 29, 1989.

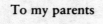

To my parents

one

Grandfather smashed his chopper into the wall about six inches from Little Fang's head. Squirming in his bed, Fang wriggled deep to seek some protection from the quilt as Grandfather wrenched the axe free and hacked and hacked again. Hysterical noises slaughtered the morning silence until, finally, the butcher crashed down the mortal blow. Fang twitched and slackened beneath the covers. He would rest in peace at last.

Emerging an hour later from the bedroom he shared with Elder Sister, and wearing a blue track suit and green canvas shoes, Little Fang went to the family's tap in the next room and began washing his face vigorously; three times he peered over his flannel to observe Grandfather still squatting over the bloodied victim and drawing on a cigarette.

'How long today, then, Grandfather?'

'Oh, quick, very quick!' He had been waiting for the question. 'A minute until the key wound and death at one minute fifteen.' Grandfather stroked the bird's feathers and mud flaked off on to the cement floor.

This backyard slaughter, the usual Sunday morning reveille, was always followed by such an exchange. Grandfather charted his health against the time he took to kill the weekly chicken and today's result was the best for a while (excluding an illegal killing last month). It confirmed his own opinion that he was holding dotage at bay. (His ears were another source of comfort for it was said that the owner of ears whose tops hung down and looked dry was soon to die: Grandfather's were goblin-sharp and sappy.)

'Mother gone to market yet?'

'Two hours ago, boy.' Fang boggled at the thought. An energetic forty-three-year-old, she had started selling dyed wool at one of Yanzhou's free markets on Sundays. Her success had been instant, especially among the peasants who lived in the surrounding countryside. Proceeds from her colourful balls now doubled her salary as a mathematics teacher at No. 2 Middle School.

His toilet completed, Fang drew the sword from its scabbard by the front door and, inspecting the blade, went out into the late October morning, which offered sunshine and the winter's first real fall of snow and a freezing Siberian wind.

Spatters of blood and chunks of plaster lay at the foot of his bedroom wall. Standing in the middle of the yard, he held the weapon upright in front of him and concentrated on concentrating on nothing for a minute. Then he began the elaborate swordplay which had him dancing to all corners, alternately darting and holding a pose. The handle's long red tassel swirled after a sword flash and then hung motionless against his taut body before snapping into another lunge.

After five minutes he went to the woodshed to collect a flail. Holding the central staff with both hands, he began to rotate the batons which hung on chains at each end. He swivelled them faster and faster – above his head, behind his back and around his ankles – gracefully bending his trunk to and fro.

The batons were whirring at full speed when he mistimed a move and the heavy wood slammed into his hip-bone. He shrieked. A minute later the other end of the flail (which he knew from his dictionary to be called a 'swingle' in English) smashed into his shin. Fang yelped and, tears in his eyes, threw the flail back into the shed, picked up the sword and hopped indoors to examine his wounds.

Grandfather was now in a squall of feathers, plucking the chicken and stoking the fistfuls of plumage straight into the stove. There was a hideous cackle from the eye of the storm as Fang pulled up a chair.

'How many?'

'Two, Grandfather – one bruise, one cut.'

'Foolish boy! Burn the flail! The sword is all you need!' A feather gusted up his nose and he sneezed expansively over the chicken.

Fang pressed his wet flannel over the flap of skin. Another bloody Sunday! He couldn't be bothered to defend the flail against the sword yet again, but Grandfather never tired of the topic and, hunched over his prey, he appeared to be vital proof of the power of the martial art of the sword: his tiny frame was still strong after eighty-odd years, almost all of which had been spent swishing his weapon.

He had only recently consented to practise a more leisurely form of *tai chi* (unarmed) after a terrifying incident in which one of his daughters had lost half an ear. The upshot had been a moving ceremony attended by his six daughters (including heavily bandaged Third Daughter) at which he had presented his sword to Little Fang. There had been one last, unprogrammed, flourish which had had the women fleeing for the woodshed.

Fang had been impressed by the gift and tried to show his thanks with diligent training. But he refused to abandon the flail which had belonged to his father – and which infuriated Grandfather as a bastard form of martial art. It was even more difficult to justify his occasional use of the dumb-bell which he had bought for chest expansion. Grandfather took both as great insults and they spiked his pleasure at the natural skill Fang had immediately shown with the sword. For his part he had been diligent with his own unarmed *tai chi*, being caught with the sword only once since, on the occasion of his fastest-ever Sunday slaughter.

Fang returned to the bedroom and querulous sighs from Fu, who turned her face to the wall and humped the quilt more closely about her shoulders.

'So noisy and so selfish, Little Brother.'

Fang said nothing audible in reply and, picking up his gloves and coat, left her be. He stepped carefully around Grandfather who was now squatting by the door, hacking the chicken to bits. Wheeling his bicycle down the track to the main road, Fang passed a neighbour who was returning from market with a bushel of bean shoots strapped to her rear-wheel rack.

'Cold, eh, Little Fang?'

'Cold – but Sunday!' he replied.

The woman laughed. 'What's the difference?' A pig squealed in another backyard as he mounted the bicycle, an old Flying Pigeon. He was unable, immediately, to think of any spectacular difference. More blood perhaps.

He headed down the gentle hill to the centre of Yanzhou, shadowing both brake levers as he passed the sand factory. Lorries were apt to stick their bulbous snouts out into the bicycle traffic completely unannounced. Two people had died in collisions over the past year and Fang had gone over the handlebars once himself. (Of course they would never begin to be able to get to the next depot on time if they had to wait for a break in the droves of cyclists. The logic was tough, but everyone understood it.)

After the roundabout at the bottom of the Baihao Hill Road, Fang joined the slow-moving masses heading east along the city's main Harmony Boulevard. A Russian-made saloon with grimy net curtains across the rear window swung straight out of another compound, horn blasting. Everyone else braked, but Fang – the little rebel – thought he had enough speed to overtake the slowly accelerating car. His reckoning was correct – just – and he won an angry fist-clench from the driver.

He raced along the wide, gritted road, playing the 'lane game' and drawing reproving glances as he shimmied through impossible gaps in the traffic. Others had to brake for him all along his route but Fang went faster and faster. He shouted a greeting to a family friend who had wife on the back and child perched on the handlebars – the small family vehicle. We are both traffic criminals, he thought, shooting on past a red-and-white-striped police kiosk in which two officers sat talking behind their sunglasses.

He soon reached a modern block no different from six others looming in dreary sequence around it except that his friend Qiao lived on the top floor. Locking the Pigeon, Fang ran up the concrete stairs, flushing out two large cats from piles of refuse on consecutive landings, then hammered on the flimsy front door.

Qiao drew him in by the elbow and immediately put his arm around his shoulder as they walked through the flat. Qiao's mother, a great vase of a lady in a head-cloth, looked up from her cabbage washing and nodded. Fang glanced into the living-room where the family's magnificent avocado-green fridge stood next to their twenty-two-inch colour television. Before envy could curdle his expression he noticed Qiao's father pottering about on the narrow veranda at the end of the room.

'Hello, Old Qiao!' he shouted. The portly cadre turned and

peered out between two pot-plants to wave a welcome through the glass divide.

The boys had been lifelong friends despite a dispute between their parents many years ago (Fang had given up trying to get details of *that* out of Mother) and now a shared passion for learning English had reinforced their relationship. These weekly sessions in Qiao's tiny but well-appointed room were a most important part of Fang's routine: they provided Sundays with some focus which saved them from the fuzzy frustrations of all other days.

'And how are you today, old fruit?'

'I am very well thank you, Mr Fang. Slept like a log in fact.'

Qiao opened a packet of biscuits. Of course, they had to speak English at 'English Corner' — an iron rule which rather limited topics.

'We must strive to improve our speaking abilities,' said Qiao after a while. He looked as serious as usual at this time of the week.

'All work and no play makes Jack a dull boy! Be sure to remember this, Qiao.' Fang easily dredged such phrases from his memory of the fusty textbooks of their schooldays and he could get away with a bit of teasing at English Corner because Qiao acknowledged him to be the more fluent speaker. Fang regretted he was unable to let this run over into other days of the week because he was bettered in other fields: Qiao's family had money and contacts and Qiao had a classy girlfriend too.

And although Fang slightly resented leading him through the corridors of idiom down which he had tripped alone months ago, Qiao was his only fellow-traveller and he would go on leading him. You needed fellow-travellers in Yanzhou. Fang could not afford to lose him. The only other allies were the BBC and Voice of America — fair-weather friends, hardly dependable in the northern wastes of China.

It was an alarming thought which gave rise to questions like why was he studying English anyway if its only purpose was to have stilted conversations on Sundays. He didn't like to think too hard about exactly where it was leading but his blindest article of faith was that his beloved English would carry him to somewhere or something utterly splendid.

There was still an hour before the BBC programme which

formed the centrepiece of their meetings. Some weeks they warmed up with Radio Peking's English-language service but the pace of learning it offered was much too slow for Fang. And today, rather than endure a third lesson on how to buy stamps in an American post office, he preferred to keep their conversation going.

'I wonder if the flax mill is holding dance party this year,' he said.

'I shall get some tickets if so for us,' said Qiao.

'Smashing idea. Mother is becoming worried that I have no girlfriend – the dance party might applease her.'

'Applease, Little Fang?'

'Yes, applease. Look it up. I cannot explain every new words for you.'

'Well, what about Miss Ping?' Qiao referred to a classmate who had taken to casting sheep's eyes at Fang during their last year at college. 'Why do you not inviting her?'

'Nooo! Too shy! And remember, she has not got one word of English. Oh no, Miss Ping is not the girl for Mr Fang!'

'Mr Frank Fang . . .'

'Thank you – Charlie Qiao! Well remembered indeed! She is not the girl for Mr Frank Fang!' (They had christened each other last Sunday.)

Fang thought of Miss Bo, Qiao's girl. She didn't have English either but she had so much else – so brazen and bold. Qiao said she wore lacy finger-mitts in her home, and lipstick, and high heels.

'Maybe', said lecherous Charlie, 'we can finding someone for you in here . . .' He produced a glossy calendar, picked up by his father during some business trip to southern China, and admired the models. Watches gleamed on their naked limbs and their bodies appeared to writhe against the incomprehensible glitter of Hong Kong at night. The tip of the new Bank of China nuzzled April's breast and June seemed to be straddling the Bond Centre's roof.

They then examined some photographs of an evening's drinking a fortnight ago. Flushed faces leered out of the garish interior of Little Luo's parents' home – no, that was the restaurant: they'd gone to their home afterwards, laughed uproariously and seen to a case of lukewarm beer. Luo had got himself married that summer. He and his wife – yes, that was her, a miserable-looking girl – were living with his parents until a flat came up. They didn't expect to wait more than eighteen months. Only then, said Luo, would he set about having a child.

He had spent much of the evening detailing the family-planning procedure by which he was going to 'avoid overpopulating the parental home'. There had been shrieks of laughter about contraceptives and Fang had even noticed the wife's shoulders shaking with what had to be mirth as she washed up in the next room. Luo had also made great show of not drinking the last inch of beer from his bottles: such forbearance was said to ensure a male child. In fact he left about half a bottle.

Contraceptives! Fang found them fascinating, terrifying and amusing all at once. There were those – and Qiao was almost certainly among them – who had managed to pull off some premarital sex, but the practical difficulties were great and Fang had never heard of it happening with anyone other than the girl you were down to marry. So what, really, was the point?

The point was that it had been 'done' – by Qiao, by Luo and, if the rumour were true, even by Podgy Peng. But not by Fang – that was fact. This failure (it had even prompted him to buy the odd bottle of expensive Three Bulls beer which claimed certain properties) was another reason for maintaining and strengthening bonds with Qiao who was generally admired – and who claimed to have been much more than admired.

They had often tried to discuss sex at English Corner but, since Fang had a little vocab but no experience and Qiao vice versa, success had been limited. Rootling around in the college dictionary that spring they had turned up 'penis' but it had not given rise to much useful discussion.

Qiao began fiddling with his radiogram as the hour approached. These were always nervous moments before they found out whether the BBC's Hong Kong transmitters would have the spunk to beat off Radio Moscow. Today the reception was very bad and they were only just able to hear what they were missing: a programme devoted to 'Business English'.

This compounded Qiao's disappointment because Business English was his favourite. Indeed business was the reason he wanted English and, like most of their classmates, he aspired to a job in the Yanzhou Foreign Trade Bureau. Unlike most of them, however, he was bound to get one. And then, he hoped, he would be exposed to edifying contacts with the plump foreign businessmen they had seen being ferried about the city; swooping off to factories and mills around Yanzhou; swooping back to the one acceptable hotel for banquets of sea cucumber, tortoise and scorpion. Eventually, Qiao assured Fang, there would be business trips abroad.

Fang was not taken with the idea, and not just because he knew he was hardly Foreign Trade material. He hoped he was living at a time when 'cultural exchange' was bringing more important contact with the West; the Dragon was creeping down from the mountains, learning to like having its belly tickled after so many centuries alone. Fang had no idea how he would get himself caught up in such thrilling developments but he had enjoyed agonising fantasies – day-dreams and night-dreams – set on a sheer white American campus with steak for lunch and great-haunched blondes asking to be taken to drive-ins every night. A VOA series on 'student life' was supplying further details – when he could hear them.

He could not, however, see any prospect of getting to America yet. But he was young (well, twenty) and hopeful that something would come up – or come down from Peking where he had heard from Brother-in-law that there were now all sorts of scams and schemes for going abroad to study. He'd even said some students never came back.

Although Fang was always greatly rocked by his dream, he had revealed it to no one, not even Qiao. If an opportunity arose he didn't want any competition – however feeble.

After another hour of conversation (Fang had to remind Qiao yet again of the difference between the active and passive moods during his otherwise passable account of an evening's petting with Bo; at one point Fang agreed to let Qiao revert to Mandarin because he was so eager to establish who was doing what to whom) they went to play football in Liberation Stadium, stopping to slurp up a bowl of noodles on the way.

The pair were quickly absorbed into the usual game, which

was one of several going on. Their former classmates knew all about English Corner but no one had applied to join because Frank and Charlie were known to be streets ahead of any other English-lover in Yanzhou.

Fang had never been able to apply his martial art co-ordination to football and he really didn't enjoy it, so he was relieved when snow began flecking the weak sunlight and the game petered out. He pedalled back up the Baihao Hill Road, head lowered against the sharp flakes, past the queue outside the city's cinema, and wheeled his bike into their yard. As he shoved open the door, he longed again for the day they would all move into a block like Qiao's.

In the warm kitchen-dining-sitting-room, Mother greeted him with the quiet deference which seemed to be acknowledgement of his role as Man of the House, but which was entirely undercut by the glint in her eye. It unsettled and diminished him and, at this stage (or at any stage), Fang did not need to be diminished. He smiled back uncertainly, failing as usual to meet her eye.

The round table was laid and Grandfather already in position, smoking a rank Golden Weasel cigarette and clearly expecting to spit again in due course: his bile jar was half full at his side. Fu was combing her long hair in the mirror with those exaggerated movements which always annoyed Fang. She was so self-regarding. Her tall and slender figure made him feel as anxious as ever. If Mother could threaten him with an eye, Fu did it with her whole body; it was an unspoken challenge he did not know how to meet. Family feelings! They grew stronger and more complicated by the month.

Throwing his gloves down on the chest of drawers, he looked at the technicolour-tinted portrait of his 'dead' father which lay there under a sheet of glass. The kindly face was so familiar that Fang could never believe how little he had known him: slight smile, square jaw, clear brown eyes made lighter and even more perfect by the hazelnut hue of the photographer's paint. Father, who had gone away just before supper in February 1975 – and never come back.

Big Fang? No, he had always been Little Fang too, not because he was especially small but because he was so lively

and sharp – despite his limp – that it had never seemed right for him to graduate from Little to Big or Old, even when he was able to dandle another Little Fang on his knee.

And there was he, a moon-faced infant in his high-chair, bib dotted with what looked in the photograph like egg or splodges of chicken soup but which were really Chairman Mao badges. He had usually worn four but Mother pinned on more when they went out. (Fang had come to see this as proof that the largest babies, the ones with the biggest bib space, were the most patriotic. Chairman Mao retards you! Long live the Great Helmsman!) Fang was staring up his own nostrils reflected in the glass top. He took his seat.

The three of them raised their chopsticks in unison as Mother laid out the food on the round table: bean shoots, cabbage, pork fat, cow tendons, crab-apples swimming in their sweet tinned juice – and shallow-fried chicken. Grandfather stabbed at this last plate to claim his victim's head.

Fang ate hungrily and silently, avoiding Fu's chopsticks and her glances. She seemed to hover in wait over each plate, eager to do battle with Little Brother who was, of course, trying to get more than his fair share of the meat dishes.

'Anything happen at market, Mother?' she asked with more insolence than interest.

'No, Fu, but very busy. Peasants everywhere.'

'How much?' Another of Grandfather's habitual Sunday lines, followed by raucous sucking on a splinter of carcass locked in the vice grip of his sticks.

'Fifty yuan – a very good day, Father. The snow made them rush for my wool.'

'You should take it more easily,' said Fu, proceeding according to custom. 'Let the boy go instead of wasting his time with all that English rubbish.'

'Shut your mouth, Elder Sister. What did *you* do all day?'

But this was a very bad question. 'Wrote to Husband, visited Aunt, walked in the park. It was my rest day. Why do you complain about that, O Constantly Resting One?'

She made so damn much of her sinecure at the People's Liberation Army sanatorium. The one time he had seen her at work she had been making cotton swabs at the rate of one every five minutes. Fang mouthed 'swab' at her across the table, drew hard on his beaker of beer and forced his eyes between the converging beams of Mother and Grandfather to stare at the yellowed wall. But he was too late.

'When *do* you hear actually?' asked Mother.

'By the middle of next month – as I told you last Sunday.'

'Ah, so long! Too long!' said Fu. 'What until then?'

'I will profit from the time by improving my English so that I can use it in my eventual job whatever it might be,' he replied with effortful dignity designed to repay Fu some of the fury she had aroused in him.

Fang's eye sought out a small scroll hanging next to the kitchen clock. It bore one Chinese character, painted with the usual calligraphic flourish, and its meaning was that much-vaunted quality: tolerance.

The Sunday pattern had included these regrettable career questions ever since his graduation from technical college (Yanzhou's 'university'!) four months ago. It always reminded him – as if he didn't remind himself often enough – that the very best he could hope for from the job-assignment official was something like Second Translator at the flax mill. A factory floor was at least as likely.

Although graduates were usually assigned more demanding work, there was always the social factor and Fang's family 'back door' contacts were famously poor: a 'capitalist roader' – rehabilitated okay, but that's not much good if they've never found you – for a father; an eccentric grandfather who could not be prevented from wandering (every wander disastrously lowering their stock in some quarter of the city); a mother whose instant business success had aroused bitter envy which she had exacerbated by not apparently noticing at all.

And then there was Fu. Her high-handed demeanour had been the jewel of his misfortunes: the whole city must have known by now that she was unwillingly biding her time ('stuck in the sticks with the hicks', as she put it) before getting the necessary residence permit to join Husband, a fabulously wealthy taxi-driver in Peking. These were Fang's millstones and this evening they were really crushing.

When rice had been served and flicked down their throats they turned to watch their spluttering black-and-white television: a documentary about sugar-beet followed by an excellent love story from glamorous Guangzhou in the far south. Its dénouement, however, was spoiled for Fang by his having to tackle Grandfather by the door. There was an unpleasant scuffle – dangerously close to the sword. Not content with hawking up a jar and a half of bile since supper, the old buzzard had tried to sneak out for a late-night constitutional. These were strictly prohibited by Mother.

Then a neighbour called in to pass on an hour's gossip and check up on all the shouting. This particular woman was known in the alley for making more noise than a hundred ducks and she was in good voice tonight. Fang sealed himself in the bedroom trying to fall asleep before Fu could come in and start clattering her cosmetics. In this he failed – she was clearly determined to get her own back for the morning – and Fang lay awake under his quilt for two hours, troubled and dissatisfied and quite certain that, for the best day of the week, Sunday in Yanzhou was miserably dreary.

two

6 November 1988

One minute forty – but it was a young one and the snow is now very deep so Grandfather took it all right. Kept on and on at me about the sword, offering to show me some more moves. But I'm not falling for that one. Wily old slasher!

Two more bad mistakes with the flail: a bruise on last Sunday's cut and a graze on the shoulder. No one sympathetic. Too cold to hold the dumb-bell.

Fu being quite bearable all of a sudden. Period probably over and she has heard that her residence permit may have started being processed already – plus the news that Brother-in-law is coming down to stay for a few days. Where will I sleep? Woodshed?

English Corner not bad. Qiao had got this 'art book' from Podgy Peng – full of naked Westerners. The breasts on them! Reception was bad again but it perked up for the BBC World News afterwards – mostly about Africa, loads of new words. Should listen more often – I'll try to get it on my transistor. It went right over Qiao's head!

He thinks his Foreign Trade job will be landed by the end of the month. One of the cadres there, a big one, dropped in. Imagine! A courtesy call! Qiao's life will be a glide. Of course he packed me off immediately so he could go and pour tea and peel apples. Well, who wouldn't?

Went down to the stadium but couldn't be bothered to play. Bright day but big wind. Bicycled around. Saw Miss Ping but she didn't spot me. Crowds of peasants in for market, plump and shoving like beasts. But they're certainly colourful – better than the drab lot round here – and they really go for the wool. I saw one family arrive in a trailer drawn by a brand new Komatsu tractor with Eldest Son on a Yamaha or Suzuki behind. He had a pig trussed up and squealing between his legs! They say that some of them have built two-storey houses with patterned tiles – on the outside! Rich pigs! They should be building statues to Deng Xiaoping out there in the stinking countryside.

Mother made more than seventy yuan out of them just

like that. She could barely take time off to *look* at me. She's
sharp down there – and has to be. The old hag selling plastic
handbags in the next stall tries to shout her down but
Mother yells loudest. No wonder she doesn't feel like saying
much back here. Grandfather knocked over his jar before
supper. Deliberately. Sunday! Some day!

Fang tipped back on the stool and pushed his plastic-covered
notebook away, shunting Fu's pots of cream. She was out
visiting some very loyal schoolfriend. He looked at himself in
the dressing-table mirror. Flat face.

Why did he document such tedium? He should do it in
English perhaps, to put off prying eyes, but then he might lose
some of the finer points of his frustration. He clung to his
diary along with the belief that life was inexorably improving
– a process so achingly slow that only by referring to past
notebooks could he notice it at all. But every little counted
and he didn't want to risk a halt by stopping the writing.

The leaders' encouragement of individual initiative was
most convenient for Fang's purposes. It provided a frame for
his brightly painted – but formless – picture of the future.
Opportunities would arise.

Nevertheless he was careful not to appear too ambitious. A
big tree catches the wind and all that and, anyway, to bang
on about his plans at home seemed plain insensitive: both
Mother and Grandfather had been disastrously crossed by
history; it had done them in as effectively as any sand lorry.
In fact it seemed that their apparent fearlessness in the face of
public opinion nowadays was due to the past: no one could
hurt them like history had.

Mother's first term at university in Shanghai had coincided
with Mao's decision to replace the curriculum with the single
command, 'Bomb the headquarters!' So she had found herself
pushed aside by students charging out of their dormitories to
'do revolution' on anyone who stood for anything except
Mao, Mao, Mao. The campus closed and because of her
background she was denounced as a 'puppy of a running dog
of imperialism' and sent to Qinghai's brutal countryside for
labour reform. Within a year she had met Father who was
living near by in one of the re-education centres for rusticated

intellectuals (known as cowsheds) with his own dying father. The couple managed to marry but another official decision had soon separated them, attaching Father to a medical unit in another province. Fang knew little beyond that, except that his parents didn't see each other for three years until another posting decision let them collide and live, tremblingly, a normal married life for four years. Then, with the political situation growing wilder still (Fang could remember detecting a new sense of terror in their home), Father vanished. There was little more to add to that.

A member of the 'stinking ninth category' (Mother was dubbed an 'intellectual' because of Father), she had been too frightened to follow up her enquiries with the local political commissar and had concentrated instead on hiding her grief from Fu and Little Fang.

After Mao's death in 1976 and the peace which followed on the fall of his cronies, the Gang of Four, the family had been moved to Yanzhou. Grandfather and his third daughter joined them soon afterwards – when he had found it impossible to go on living in the house in which his wife had died. She had broken her neck when a 'little revolutionary general' of the Red Guard shoved her down the stairs harder than intended. Oops!

Fang's feelings towards Mother were complicated. He knew her life had been blighted by history (which had at least allowed time for his birth – a first lucky hand from his own benevolent fate?) but he just could not accept the idea of a young life, Mother's life, disappearing in this way (a disappearance almost as absolute as Father's). And it was no more conceivable just because it had been repeated millions of times in that foul decade. The barbaric tyranny of one fat old man, drunk at the wheel of the sand lorry.

Just as his own hope made him feel guilty, he felt that unlike Mother and Grandfather he had no reason for his frustration and anger; and that, as they grew, these feelings were separating him from his own generation as well. This frightened him. He thought of the expressionless faces of the cyclists forever jamming on their brakes; of Mother's friend who had broken his leg last week falling down a manhole, left open overnight; of Mother arriving bright-eyed at university and being knocked aside by Red Guards in their new armbands running the other way. How could he be so sure he would avoid the sand lorry? He couldn't – but he was.

three

He would miss English Corner which was regrettable; but he hadn't been to Baihao for at least eighteen months and Mother would like to know the latest fridge prices. Fang decided to go with Fu to meet Husband off his train the next Sunday.

And she didn't seem to mind. In fact she had been more like a dove than a dragon in her most recent contacts with Fang. It was as though she were out to do a last-minute deal to get his co-operation during Husband's visit. She seemed very nervous about this, the first he had paid them since the wedding; then he had not been impressive, inevitably failing to live up to her descriptions of his wit and beauty. Fang had watched the smart young groom very closely that day as he faced Fu's human dowry; he was like the naïve car-buyer who suddenly has to reckon with insurance bill, tax disc, the huge running-costs behind his gleaming new Toyota (no previous owners — Fang was pretty sure).

But since that day in the spring Husband had landed a job in a Peking taxi firm which immediately made him a figure of more consequence. Besides, he would bring presents. Fang had never felt more like co-operating with Fu.

As they left home that cold, bright morning, Mother pressed a string bag of over-ripe pears into Fang's hand. The fruit was already breaking up against the mesh but Mother wouldn't hear of a bus ride being attempted without provisions. Brother and sister walked down the hill to the bus stop at Fu's brisk pace. She had tied an orange scarf around her neck and bright lipstick showed off her rose-bud mouth. She wore Husband's last gift, a Peking puffa coat, which wasn't so long that it hid her fashionable jeans, also from the capital, tight against her legs. Fu was an admirable travelling companion. If only she would talk to me a little!

But under the bus shelter where the shapeless females feasted on her there was no need for speech to make her statement clear: I'm no country girl, Peking is calling, Husband is a taxi-driver and my jeans are stone-washed. Leaning on the metal barrier Fang caught the whispered reply: 'Proud, proud girl . . . will bring no joy to her family!'

Sand lorries were rumbling around in the compound opposite. A small boy lashed his whip at a sparrow which had just alighted on top of the anti-spitting campaign poster. Fang dribbled a length of phlegm on to the road, hoping to show the other bus folk that he was as gutsy as his sister; hoping also to win her attention — but failing there. Instead he tried to talk to a pretty little girl whose hair was arranged in three erect pigtails. She squealed and ran back behind her mother, peeking out as from behind a huge fan.

Spotty Zhang passed by on his bicycle and waved, obsequious as ever. Then a famously strong *tai chi* teacher called Biao stopped at the kerb and Fang drew himself up for some manly conversation.

'She's looking good today.'

'Yeah, thanks, Biao. Losing some of her freshness perhaps — what do you think?'

But even he, even Mr Yanzhou, failed to catch Fu's eye and then had to move off with undignified haste as a minibus drew up. Fang shunted his way forwards, Mother's pears collapsing against his leg.

The co-driver was yelling out the destination although everyone knew it and there were already far too many people for the aged vehicle. But he was bound to be in business with the owner of another which would soon arrive.

And as Fang shoved juicily towards the door, with string bag in front of him, he calculated how much these road bandits made on the round trip, each day, each week and, finally, he speculated on their staggering monthly wage. His mind easily provided the usual icons of wealth which Co-driver would possess and the packet of Marlboro 100s in his breast pocket confirmed his socio-economic group. The private sector! Daily contact with Baihao had made this man a Yanzhou tycoon at thirty.

Fang stepped up into the minibus and, as he looked behind him to check that Fu would also make it, clipped his head hard against the door catch. They took a double seat on the sunny side. That was fine but Fang's legs were pressed into his chest because he was over the rear wheel-arch. He forced down the collar of his padded coat with his chin and prepared to mention the problem to Fu. It would be unbearable to be stuck here like a honeypot for three hours. But however accommodating her present mood, he could see she would not swap places. Her legs were longer anyway.

Fang concentrated instead on an old woman's flustered entry. She had just managed to yank her arm inside when the door crashed shut and was now plumping herself down on the plastic engine-cover at the front of the minibus. Lighting a long cigarette (two Golden Weasels joined together it seemed) she arranged her possessions around her, having to stamp a deformed four-inch-foot on to one sack which beat with life and threatened to move off down the aisle. Sitting on the engine your buttocks will be roasted before your bird's, thought Fang, with the malice he really wished on Fu.

By the time the engine fired every male passenger had lit a cigarette. To Fang's horror, Fu now did so too. This was blatant provocation: only the elders of her sex were allowed to smoke (some compensation, it seemed, for the agony of their feet, crumpled and broken by years of tight binding before the Communist Liberation in 1949). But Fu had no such excuse. She flashed her liberated glare at the men and exhaled expertly into Fang's face.

'That old baggage may have bound feet,' she muttered, 'but the rest of this lot have got bound minds.'

As a rule, Yanzhou minibuses sounded broken but hurtled along and got you there in the end. This one, however, had obeyed the rule once too often: it reached the top of the Baihao Hill Road, almost level with their alley, and then stopped. The engine ground out a final orison and billowed white smoke. An hour and a half after leaving home, Fang and Fu were rolling back into Yanzhou.

The driver went into deep mourning and spent the next dangerous seconds tugging miserably at a swathe of electrical wires which hung from the dashboard, like a knackered horse's nervous system. Their accelerating descent did not seem to concern him.

The passengers could only gasp: anything more explicit would have been to criticise the driver which was quite out of order because he was a licensed expert. Fang could feel a tremendous conflict between each passenger's will to save his or her skin and the will to save the driver's face. Even Fu held herself in, softly seething.

Co-driver, however, felt his own position permitted intervention and, encouraged by a natural cockiness, he yelled at the driver. When this failed he wrenched up the handbrake himself.

Their screaming stop was drowned in the lengthy foghorn blast of an articulated sand lorry which shimmied massively to avoid them. Three cyclists who had been cadging a lift on the lorry's rear bar were flicked across the road to end their ascent in the snow-filled ditch. As they climbed out (Fang recognised one as Spotty Zhang returning from his chores), an army jeep coming the other way forced them back into the ditch with a powerful spray of slush.

By now Fu's fury was visible – as delicate beads of sweat on her upper lip. She lit another cigarette. The driver, who had recovered somewhat, released the brake and performed a clever reversing manoeuvre which involved a hard wheelspin to the right and had them thereafter rolling forwards down the hill.

Everyone gasped with relief – relief disguised as admiration. At the bus stop those travellers who had missed the first bus were jamming gleefully into another, much newer and Japanese. Fang felt like joining Fu in furyland but since she would offer little companionship even there he decided to maintain a bland grin which might at least contribute to her anger.

Co-driver announced that another vehicle would be along in a minute – and so it was, with him behind the wheel, a fresh Marlboro between his lips. It was immediately clear that he would get them to Baihao in very good time, for he drove exactly as Fang cycled. Whenever a passenger declared the wish to alight at one of the little townships *en route*, Co-driver would flip an upturned palm expectantly back over his shoulder: since only the footbound old lady and two others had the wit or the supplies to cross it with enough cigarettes, he bothered to stop only for them.

This high-handed approach did not make for the best atmosphere in the minibus as more and more people missed their destinations, but there was never any question of mutiny: they were going far too fast for that. (At one point they swerved to avoid an elderly peasant who was digging a small hole in the middle of the highway, just over the brow of a hill. The bus flattened his little pile of broken tarmac and his lunchpack, but this disturbed neither Co-driver nor peasant.)

Lurching through the suburban roundabouts of Baihao, Fang felt excited. But it was a throwback to childhood and gave him no pleasure now, just more frustration. What good was it to nurse discontent if you couldn't even transfer it intact from Yanzhou to Baihao? Fu could: her disdain now looked even more refined; the curl of her mouth had achieved a better insolence. Baihao might be three hours out of Yanzhou but it was still forty-eight hours from Peking. Such a hick to be so excited! His legs were numb.

The large bus depot admitted any sort of vehicle and they shunted a horse and cart to get into a berth. Hordes of people poured into the railway terminus across the square. Fang discovered what time the minibus was returning (confirmed, rather, his expectation that it would leave just as soon as it had another fee-paying full house) and set off after Elder Sister who was already easing through the crowd to the station concourse. The arrival of another bus delayed him. Everyone was looking up and laughing at its roof which seemed to boast a shaggy, quacking fringe: two triumphant youths laughed down in reply for they were riding into town on a mattress of dying ducks. Fang chuckled and shoved on.

At the station entrance he looked up again and noted with approval an empty alcove in the brutal façade: Chairman Mao had taken his last train out of Baihao. He saw Fu and was reaching out to grab her sleeve when a passing peasant rammed his thigh with a large cardboard box. Fang folded with pain and by the time he could stand upright Fu had slipped on. Most people bore their ungainly loads aloft and caps were knocked askew by trembling elbows but Fang met more low-level obstructions which smashed into the fresh wounds from his martial arts. In the crush of blue and khaki coats the queues stood like breakwaters. Most travellers waved letters of reference from their work units to enable them to buy tickets.

He caught up with Fu again under the timetable and together they discovered that the Peking train, number 340, would arrive exactly an hour later than they had thought. They pushed through to the waiting-hall where hundreds of people seemed to have settled permanently. Those without seats had staked claims to the cement floor with sheets of *People's Daily*. Those without *People's Daily* stood and, in the most congested areas of the hall, they stood on one leg as if playing some unamusing party game.

Greatly unimpressed, Fu marched up to the nearest bench and swept away the horizontal legs of an old man whose toothless mouth yapped in (justified) annoyance as she sat down. There was no other obvious place – certainly this grandpappy wasn't going to give another inch – and since Fang did not dare create one, he went back into the sunny square.

Reaching a more peaceful herbaceous area in the middle, he was pleased to find another vacant Mao-plinth. But then, feeling vaguely threatened by a group of conspiratorial youths with tycoon hairstyles, Fang pressed on towards a row of shop fronts on the other side of the square.

Here traders had set up trestles on the pavement. Someone was even selling games of what Fang identified as pool on a pair of turquoise felt tables. Despite the evident difficulty of playing in coats, several young people had hired cues and were stabbing away, frequently firing balls out into the delighted audience.

Along from there Fang found baskets of cassettes bearing southern Chinese names; one even had an English subtitle, 'The Madonna of the East' – but it was far too expensive. Of course, they still had to sell the works of Xu Li, one of the People's Liberation Army's famous cheerleaders, even though she was now a sort of 'unpop star'. The trader had loaded these tapes into one basket at the back of the display.

Fang saw T-shirts with blotchy Western names prominently printed: Lee Cooper, Harley Davidson, Commercial Union Insurance. One man was holding up a pale blue shirt with 'ICI PHARMACEUtiCALS' printed on a gentle slant across his belly; his girlfriend nodded approval – as did the vendor. Six yuan changed hands in an instant. Quicksilver. Fang liked the look of all this and suddenly understood something of Mother's commercial passion.   •

From a little further down he heard music of the dance party sort and went to investigate. A loudspeaker had been nailed to a sapling, the wires running above the pavement and in through a hole in the shop's door frame.

Fang peered past the posters in the window to see a man with wet-look hair performing an undulatory dance before a girl who was sitting back to front on a chair and laughing.

'Sexy girl,' said Fang aloud, a breach of self-control which surprised him. He had just noticed the packet of Marlboro in the dancer's pocket when he was spotted himself.

'Want some style, friend?' the dancer shouted.

Fang stood in the doorway of what he now thought was a barbershop. It smelt of beer and soap.

'Well, I was just thinking . . .'

'I can blow it back, spike it up, whatever . . . but you must make your hair work!'

The girl looked up at him and – shameless enticer – smiled. As she stood up, however, her face assumed the nonchalance which he recognised only too well and she stepped slowly away through plastic streamers into a back room. The barber was still looking enquiringly at Fang, who glanced at his watch and decided to accept the offer.

'What's the price?' he asked as he was being prepared: five yuan – more than he had ever spent before on almost any part of his body (even three months of acupuncture treatment for asthma had cost a mere six yuan) but the suggestion of a 'new image' wasn't entirely unpleasant.

The hairdresser – perhaps even stylist but certainly not barber – worked quickly. With meek encouragement from the trapped Fang he revealed that, yes, he was manager–owner of the shop and could earn 200 yuan a month if he worked long hours. And he did because there was great demand for a place to listen to music, drink beer and get a weekly blow-dry.

Weekly what? Fang was amazed by such male vanity, which he had only ever imagined in the wildest of Western cities; but he was far more thrown by the sight of his own scalp now bristling into a nest of spikes.

'You haven't the body', said his new friend, touching him

lightly on the ear, 'to make a wave worthwhile but I've got some satisfactory elevation for you, eh?' Fang nodded unhappily. At least the shoots would lie low in a few minutes.

But the stylist – hypnotist even – had squeezed something from a tube into his fingers and now, with both hands poised to descend, he questioned the mirror, 'Gel? Fifty cents extra.' He was down on Fang immediately, fixing the spikes in glistening permanence. Then, as the sheet was pulled away and this amazing head joined the same old body, Fang shook with indignation and horror and acute embarrassment. Quiver, shiver, clatter went his spikes.

He paid the smiling (mocking?) entrepreneur and returned to the station as quickly as possible. Number 340 was due in two minutes and there was excited milling around at the exit. By the time it came in Fang had still not found Fu. The first arrivals soon emerged squinting into the sunlight and there, almost immediately, was Brother-in-law.

'Hong Wei! Over here!' called Fang. But as the stocky little taxi-driver waved in recognition – it was recognition wasn't it? – Fang gulped on a new breaker of embarrassment at having to welcome him in place of adoring wife – and all spiky too!

'Little Fang, I'm pleased to see you. And Fu?'

'She's here – somewhere. Don't worry. Good to see you!' They looked at each other and smiled and looked at each other again; and then Fang realised he could escape his discomfort by attending to Hong's luggage. Although encouragingly bulky, it did not give any hint of the Hitachi portable television which Hong had said might come their way – a disappointment which would make Grandfather wild.

Fang winced at a sharp clip on the shoulder.

'Terrible boy! Where did you get to? Slipping off and – aah! – Little Fang, what has happened? What did they do?'

'He's here, Fu – Husband's here!'

Pathetic to watch, Hong Wei was manoeuvring his upper body, trying to intercept Wife's appalled examination of Little Brother.

'Fu, dear wife,' he murmured.

She looked quickly at him.

'Hello, Husband. So you've arrived.'

She took his hand but continued her scrutiny of Fang. He knew she was just doing this to avoid having to show Husband her emotions, or to hide her renewed disappointment over his greasy little face. Surely this new hairstyle did not merit quite such attention. Fang felt fluster approaching and was relieved when she turned back to Hong – poor squat Brother-in-law – who was still beaming up at her. Lost for alternative vocabulary, Husband breathily exclaimed, 'Yes, Fu, I've arrived.'

Fang's exotic new head shook with some grateful sniggers as he gathered up Hong's bags. Elder Sister would be gloriously exposed now that he had arrived and her disillusion had begun anew. Sweet melon lips, bitter melon heart. But Fang couldn't relax either: she would take care to home in on his spikes again. He should not score points off Hong. They must serve each other in the common struggle. His alliance with Fu had not lasted long.

To an outsider, without Fang's insight, the young couple looked happy enough, from behind: Hong swinging his little pigskin valise contentedly by his side as Wife led him across to the buses. Fang took the strain and bundled after them. They quickly boarded a full-sized charabanc which seemed likely to leave soon because they took some of the last seats. But it was state-run: the fare would be lower but the rub was to wait for the driver and his mates to finish their hand of cards – waiting for a Full House. This would have taken a mere twenty minutes had not Hong shouted at them to get going. The outburst was uncharacteristic (both Fu and Fang looked at him in surprise: he must have been greatly strained by his trip) and served to prolong the poker by another fifteen minutes. It also brought stern glares from the passengers who had caught the twang of a Peking accent in the ill-mannered shriek.

'Country people – so gormless!' said Fu, passing judgement in her practised stage whisper. She seemed impressed by this display of spirit from Husband but he was now depressed, low in his seat with ears glowing orange.

'Good journey, Brother-in-law?' asked Fang after several minutes' silence.

'Not bad. Slept well, ate lots. There was even a foreigner in our carriage.'

'A foreigner? Westerner or black?'

'Western foreigner – young, tall, with yellow hair and blue eyes.'

'Where did he get off?'

'I'm not sure. Could have come all the way – eh! there he is now, coming out of the station!'

Fang launched himself across the aisle, punching one of Fu's small breasts in his eagerness to get a glimpse. But he saw nothing blond in the crowd and Hong was no longer sure himself.

'Gone! Maybe I was wrong . . .'

As Fang tried to regain his seat the bus started backwards and he steadied himself with another hand which found its way hard into Fu's other breast.

'Get off me, fool!' she shrieked. 'Not once but twice you've done that to me! Always clumsy, always stupid and now . . .', she let her malice explode, 'uglier than ever before!' Snatching his spikes, she tugged as hard as she could.

Thanks to the costly gel Fang slipped free but the blood was surging to his face. Everyone stared at a point, so many points, above his forehead and he boiled with fresh embarrassment. Fu screamed on, 'Like a rodent – greasy, prickly, ugly!'

A cocky little runt in front of Fang brought tears of laughter to the eyes of his several relatives with some pertinent comment and then, from behind, there jerked the gloved hand of a hag who had apparently been dared by her crass friends to touch a spike. There must have been a minute of general giggling. (Fang noticed that even the rear-view mirror was full of the driver's mocking smirk.)

But then Hong suddenly leaned forward in his seat and laid a restraining hand on Fu's arm.

'I think it's sharp, Fang, very sharp,' he declared. 'Like the young men in Peking.'

This intervention transformed the situation. In one comment Hong had raised Fang's stock with Fu, convinced Fang that he had taken a wise and stylish step and – selfless Hong! – confirmed the spectators' worst suspicions of his origins. A grand ally this! Fang recovered his composure, relieved to hear the peasants gradually reapplying bovine intellects to their habitual concerns – the next graze and who was rutting whom.

Having forced his shoulder behind that of the large lady at his side who was taking up more than her fair share of the seat (and who had somehow managed to sleep through the entire matinée), Fang closed his eyes. He tried to coax the colour out of his face and to watch the late afternoon's light patterns play on the insides of his eyelids. At first this soothed him, but then he began thinking of the foreigner: could it have been him Hong had seen in the crowd? Anything seemed possible in Baihao nowadays. Fang had been born just three hours from civilisation! Why could he not have been reared in some more distant reach of the province where ambition was stillborn and dreams quickly choked on dust and droppings? The hickdom of Yanzhou was not quite far enough away from temptation.

He had forgotten the fridge prices for Mother; he reached suddenly under the seat but, no, the pears had been left in the minibus. He looked over at Fu and Hong. They were talking quietly. He envied them their peace. He envied everyone their everything.

The bus crashed on through the shadows, blasting its horn continually at peasants who were getting back on to the road after another day's earth-scraping. They tugged their bicycles out of ditches or squeezed into bulging metal trailers pulled along by farting rotavators. Fang managed to laugh at one such chauffeur who was quite obscured, but for his smile, by the black exhaust trail rushing back into his face. Why should he be smiling? Not because he had escaped ambition but perhaps because he was seeing it satisfied. Sordid peasant ambition!

Great hills of grass were being inched along by donkeys whose semi-conscious masters casually flicked whips in their eyes. Fang prepared for himself the countryside clause of the Sand Lorry Law: 'When two motorised vehicles are on collision course, the smaller is obliged to swerve to the nearside kerb, no matter how many cyclists it disconcerts, injures, maims or kills. Nevertheless, shiny government saloons bearing Men of Great Face can expect all other vehicles of whatever size to acknowledge their right of way irrespective of any deaths this causes among the people.'

He slept for the last hour and was awoken by Hong at their

stop, the first in Yanzhou. The driver suggested they get their
own baggage down from the roof, shirking his task which was
shifted then, by one further remove, on to Fang's shoulders.
But as they coughed against the fumes of the departing
bus and shuddered in the cold night, Hong became more responsible about his baggage, relieving Fang of almost half
of it.

The pair of them walked slowly back up the Baihao Hill
Road a little way behind unencumbered Fu who hummed a
soft and infuriating tune.

'Do you think that foreigner did get to Baihao?' asked Fang.

'Could have. I'm pretty sure it was him I saw. Someone on
the train could speak some English and he told us the young
man wanted to teach or something.'

'Teach! Teach what? Teach where?' Fang was amazed.
Baihao now seemed to have a foreign language institute as
well as pool and blow-dries. Would the Americans open a
consulate there too?

'Don't know, but they teach everywhere these days. They
even had one at the taxi firm before I joined. The little bastard
had made off with three months' pay by the time they realised
he'd been teaching them German not English. You should see
the number of them in Peking . . .' He was speaking in the
lazy big-city way which Fang loved and despised by turns.
Bragging Brother-in-law!

'They're no good compared to the others, though,' he continued.

'The others?'

'The other foreigners you can get in your cab. You must
know the saying "You can always fool a foreigner"? Well, it's
still true for most of them – but the young ones, they really
guard their money. Disgusting! They don't play the game at
all, try to pay with People's Money, never tip, try to speak
Chinese! Idiots!'

'What about these others then?'

'Tourists, big-hotel folk – "American dumplings" they're
called – fat and thick!'

'And rich?'

'Yes – and rich!' Hong smiled like a highwayman in the
dark.

Fu managed to hold open the gate and they struggled into the yard. Mother was silhouetted in the doorway.

'Hello, Mother-in-law. How are you?'

Hong wisely respectful and so aware of his duties: already rummaging in his sack for . . . instant coffee, special hardback accounts book for her Sunday trading, Great Hall of the People dried fruits and – lovely gesture – battery-driven bamboo-scoffing panda from Peking Friendship Store. The expense! It was thrilling.

Each of these gifts was produced with a whinny of pleasure from Hong and gales of delight from Mother. All doubts about Son-in-law were being blitzed by this bounty. And Fu purred with quiet joy, no doubt expecting further tokens in the privacy of 'their' bedroom – now off-limits to Little Fang, who was given an English translation of Lu Xun's novel *Wandering*. (That's the trouble with having a reputation for bookishness: you never get anything else.)

But then, from the corner, there came a hawking.

'And for old sir, of course, a bottle.' Hong handed over the expensive rice wine without looking at Grandfather who acknowledged it with a sideways volley into the bile jar.

Hong hadn't been able to face the old devil since a string of firecrackers had exploded across the bonnet of the car as they arrived at the wedding. It had been by far the most terrifying moment of Hong's easy life and he seemed to expect further atrocities whenever they met.

Grandfather, for his part, referred to Hong in his absence as 'Peking Half-Man' or 'Chauffeur Ponce' and scarcely bothered to refer to him at all in his presence.

'Television?' he snarled as he padded back to bed. 'Didn't bring the bloody television!'

four

The next evening saw Fang sitting in the tiny security office at the gates of the Yanzhou Heavenly Tinned Foods and Preserves Plant.

Podgy Peng, a former classmate, had landed the pick of the temporary jobs between graduation and career assignment: helping his idle uncle manage the idleness of gatekeeping. Uncle was absent as usual but his swivel-chair was amply filled by Peng who rotated gently, evidently very happy with his lot. To his surprise and delight, this new position (which was as yet unofficial but which held some prospects within Heavenly Tinned Foods generally) had brought him unprecedented popularity.

Fang had been interested to observe the change in the plump features which had incurred years of numbing abuse through school and college (and surely deserved years more). Shedding its punch-bag timidity, Podgy's face was now as eager as a muntjak's while his body had acquired an extraordinary perkiness which lent some form, even proportion, to its bulk. He had a new, foraging enthusiasm for life which amazed his tormentors and dissuaded them from prodding and teasing quite as mercilessly as before.

Peng's sabbatical from derision had several causes but a sudden increase in personal charm was not one of them. No, the main reason was his access to this office which was warm and central, always open and well stocked: the gatekeeper, who shared his nephew's greed, managed to divert huge tins of mandarins and jars of preserved crab-apples into the office filing cabinet. The classmates also enjoyed watching everyone entering the compound dismount on passing the office — for this was the traditional sign of respect paid to a gatekeeper.

To cap it all, Podgy had somehow acquired one of the city's most elaborate radio-cassette machines, which he wisely brought to work each evening. It flashed and pulsed now, a clear sign through the window that the Podge was in and entertaining as usual.

The small room was effectively filled by the filing cabinet, the metal desk and the vice-gatekeeper, but this evening it also had to accommodate Littles Ling, Chang and Wong – respectively cramming mandarins, burning chestnuts on the stove and sitting like the dull dog he was on an upturned wastepaper-basket in the corner.

Fang had fled there from a deteriorating after-supper situation at home (the Peking Half-Man was about to melt or explode under Grandfather's searing abuse: either way it was going to be messy) and now Qiao squeezed in too, just released, he claimed, from the magical grip of his girlfriend's legs. Peng was delighted with the attendance and determined to make the most of it.

He derived a certain fame, like any enthusiastic and brisk eater – especially one with a decent girth – from farting. Forcing tears of amusement from the audience every time, these eruptions had to be considered among the gatehouse's major attractions. Of course Peng overplayed them, chivvying every last gas bubble out of his talented sphincter, but somehow it was impossible to get bored with these delightful horrors. Why was it so funny?

This evening he took advantage of the end of his Richard Clayderman tape (another thing going for Podgy's social club) to introduce the idea of marketing his chief asset.

'It would be too easy,' he said in his breathless way. 'We just get the keys for Processed Peas, stoke me with bean shoots and pop me on top of the filler. If the timing's right we could do forty cans in ten minutes.'

'And call them "Peng's Pongs", I suppose,' said Fang.

'But who would buy them, Podgy?' whined Wong, who was as usual taking everything seriously. (He could never afford to look bored because he rightly suspected he was admitted on sufferance anyway.)

'We wouldn't market them, idiot. I'm talking commercial sabotage. Remember that report in the paper about supermarket blackmailers in Taipei? Well, we just do some nifty substitution in the packing-room and slip a note to the manager telling him where to leave the money – or else!'

'Very dashing, Podge. And would you be doing the pick-up?'

'Look Qiao, this would be a team op. You can't expect me to fill that role too.'

Ling belched and then hunched over a new can of lychees to stop Chang's raids.

'You'd better mind you don't gloop a buttock through the filling hole because Peng's Processed Arse Meat might be a hit with the consumer – and then you'd be in real trouble,' said Chang.

Podgy quivered. 'Yes, I'd have to be very careful with the machinery, you're right.'

Fang suddenly realised the fat git was being serious. 'Hang on, old man,' he interrupted. 'Aren't you overestimating your charms? Yours is an aural product – you should not expect to be remembered by any other sense organ. Recognise the limits of your fartistry!'

Peng grimaced as they laughed. He had come so far lately but he just couldn't stop them laughing at him. And it was true that his farts rarely smelt. In fact everyone suspected he forced air into his colon unnaturally and since another newspaper story had detailed heroin-smuggling methods across the Strait of Formosa there had even been speculation that he swallowed small bags of air with his breakfast noodles.

Qiao lunged at Podgy with an empty crab-apple tin, saying he was eager to start production, but the anxious fat man managed to wedge his chair firmly under the desk. The cassette had ended again. Fang felt a blast of gloom as he realised, not for the first time, that this little gatehouse, with its hot air and banter, was the place where time passed most swiftly in Yanzhou – where the drips on the forehead lost some of their pain. Even his English studies dragged by comparison these days, so divorced from reality were they, surreal in their optimism; like trying to fill your belly by drawing pictures of cakes.

He bit forlornly into another crab-apple: tasteless. Peng was trying to trump the silence in his usual way but the effort was bringing nothing but blood to his face. Wong had raised himself from the bin and he was hovering around the stove (still trying to get close enough to roast his first chestnut), when the door suddenly flew open, satisfactorily crushing him back into the corner. It was Liu Wei.

'You're never going to believe this,' he shouted, gripping the side of the desk to catch his rushing breath, 'but there's a foreigner in town!'

'So? What's so great about that?' said Ling, hands on belly, crotch occupying prime position next to the stove door. In the past year they had often discussed sightings of chubby businessmen being chaperoned in government Toyotas. At first thrilling, these had long since lost appeal. The world's cautious response to Yanzhou's official opening to foreign investment (and, most laughably, tourism) hadn't satisfied the graduates.

'Another fat baby in a government pram, I suppose,' said Ling.

'No, this one's real! He's tall, yellow hair, blue eyes, and young! On the minibus today!'

Liu was still panting for breath, convinced that his story was worth telling. Fang for one agreed.

'Who saw him?' he asked.

'I did! I was on the bus from Baihao today and he was right there – in the same bus!'

So dear Hong had been right! The Westerner must have spent one night there and then come on. But if Baihao hadn't held him, what chance had Yanzhou?

'Well, what did he say?'

'Why's he come?'

'Where's he going?'

'I didn't really talk to him that much,' said Liu. 'He was right up the front and . . . well, my English is so bad. I was sort of shy . . .' They jeered in disbelief at the loss of this unique opportunity. 'But he spoke some Chinese, very badly. He told the driver he wanted to be a mouse.'

'Eh?'

'What?'

'Instead of teacher. He meant to say teacher but he pronounced it wrong. And I got in a smile at him when we arrived. They told him to go to the Dong Lan.'

Frank and Charlie leapt up and, rather to Fang's embarrassment, yelled, 'Let's go!' simultaneously in English. The others grabbed their coats which had fallen on top of Wong. He too struggled to his feet. Podgy thrust his chair back and looked up at Fang in urgent appeal. Was his time up already? Fang registered the moment but was too excited to care.

'See you then, fat man! Thanks for everything.' The social club's door slammed behind them. Podgy had had it coming.

In retrospect, their journey across the city really marked the high point of the evening.

They bicycled so manically that it took just ten minutes from the gates of Heavenly Tinned to the hotel (which now seemed quite divine too), even with Liu clinging on to Fang's baggage rack. But there the gatekeeper burst out like an articulated sand lorry and stopped them dead. He hadn't got to where he'd got by sleeping on the job. The Dong Lan was one of Yanzhou's most sensitive barriers and he was proud of his position. They could, of course, have ignored his shouting and continued through to the hotel entrance but he would have telephoned the reception desk before they even got there – and probably Public Security as well. And they'd never have made it across the lobby anyway, all visitors, especially their sort, being required to fill out meddlesome little chits (name; work unit; why visiting whom; time in; time out; and some space for 'receptionist's observations').

Protesting in the falling snow, Fang had made up some story about wanting to give a message to one of the waitresses but the gatekeeper hadn't bought that.

Much later now, Fang was recounting the events of the evening to Hong and Mother (Fu and Grandfather were in their respective rooms). Brother-in-law was clawing himself back to some conversational confidence after the pillage of the early evening. They sipped hot tea and blew the leaves across to the other side of the mug. It was a soothing noise but Fang was still excited.

'I asked the gatekeeper whether it was true about a young foreigner coming to the hotel and he gave me one of those hard Great Proletarian Cultural Revolution looks,' (Fang didn't like to mention this in front of Mother but now he couldn't stop himself) 'as if to say "Danger Zone, Head Off". Then he pretended his shift had only just begun and tried to get round us that way – you know, suddenly all friendly, sorry not to help – saying he hadn't heard anything about any new arrivals. Like hell he hadn't! What harm was there in telling us?'

'Orders is orders,' said Hong who had had a 'good Cultural', qualifying as a driver in the PLA just a week before the fall of the Gang of Four. (This had further endeared him to Grandfather.)

'But Yanzhou is an Open City now, Brother-in-law. The State Council has decreed it.'

'Sometimes, Son, you seem to think that just because someone works for the Government they must be evil, ambitious party men . . .' She glanced at Hong. 'But some of our city's best people work for the Government. I really don't think you should carry around this naïve view that authority is necessarily anti-progress and corrupt. This is the Eighties you know, Deng Xiaoping's decade.'

'Quite, Mother, that's just what I'm saying – this *is* the Eighties . . .'

'Well, I think you should open and reform yourself a little more carefully – let the Government tell you how fast to go. If you can't get into the Dong Lan, then there must be a very good reason. Western morals . . .'

'Go to Peking, Little Fang, and you'll see what problems the foreigners bring. Personally, I think there's something in the Government's fears about spiritual pollution . . .'

'That phrase! Brother-in-law, please don't use it. What spirit? What is there left to pollute in this stagnant pool? Inertia is killing all the little fishes!'

Hong looked startled by this outburst and Fang was suddenly alarmed he might have inadvertently quoted the Great Helmsman; this could have been brainwash slopping out of his memories of middle-school 'history' classes. Well, you could use Mao to justify anything – he'd suspected that for a while now.

Politics! Poor old Hong probably thought he had left them behind in Peking but there were some nights when Fang suddenly felt bloody niggled about something or other, and this was one of them. Hong yawned and plugged his mouth with a Double Happiness sweet left over from the wedding.

'Looks like Peking boy and talks like Peking boy,' he trilled, stretching back to scrape his grubby nails against the wall.

'I don't any more,' said Fang, reaching for his hair. Mother sniggered: she had been no ally over the spikes affair; indeed, her censure had been the last straw.

An insistent scratching came through the bedroom wall. Fu was clearly getting impatient! Images of love-making filled Fang's mind; they were never far off, always pulsing on the periphery of his consciousness trying to get in. He could certainly imagine Fu in action: she seemed to be made for it. (Was this a natural fraternal thought?) But Hong Wei? His second yawn in a minute! He seemed to be holding back from this next storm, the sexual tempest. Nothing of the gifted lover about him! Probably thought he was coming down to the provinces for a rest!

Hitching his trousers up over a heavy waist, Brother-in-law got up, bid them good night and waddled into the boudoir. Fang could only look forward to another night with Mother and Grandfather on the brick-based, under-heated bed which occupied the third and final room of the house. His brief attempt at sleep in the woodshed the previous night had failed completely though the time had certainly not been wasted: he had crept out to that frozen nook with torch, pocket mirror and fruit-knife and, sitting there on the edge of the old smelting furnace amidst coal-dust and shavings, Fang had put paid to those pricey frivolities which had caused him nothing but trouble – the Baihao spikes.

In the end Mother's judgement, when combined with Fu's hate-filled opposition, had easily outweighed Brother-in-law's favourable assessment. Fang's fruit-knife might have been blunt but it did the trick (and had also managed to put the wind up that week's hen when its nervy clucking had threatened to bring Grandfather out on night patrol).

Mother went next door, her voice climbing ominously against Grandfather's for a time before they both fell silent. Fang forced himself through *Yanzhou Daily* just in case any column should have been bold enough to mention the new-comer. None was. Washing and undressing quickly, he dived under the covers next to the frail old grampus. The bile jar was on the sill and the tight knot of wire around the window catch had not been tampered with. Mother shifted restlessly at their feet.

'Night, Mother.'

'Good night, Little Fang. He's asleep?'

'Like a baby dragon.'

But Fang was to lie awake for another hour, grabbing at the day's images. It had had frustration; every day had that. Life is frustrating and then . . . we die. 'Frustrate and rule!' the leaders might say. And how well it worked. But today had also had some tantalising hope about it – and that was very welcome to the equation. In Yanzhou unknowns were better than knowns.

He thought, finally, of the sword resting there by the front door. In six hours or less, he would be outside again, slashing at another morning with Grandfather's blade.

five

Other sightings of the foreigner were reported by the graduates over the next fortnight. He had eaten in the Noodle Palace, walked in Moon Park and been shown round No. 1 Middle School.

Most encouragingly, for it suggested a lengthy stay, he had been seen buying a bicycle, a brand-new Forever at 260 yuan. (It was said he had paid for it with crisp new Foreign Exchange Certificates which the bandit assistant had immediately swapped for the grubby popular currency, effectively doubling his money.) Apparently — a word Fang was having to use often these days — every other human activity on East Street had ceased as the foreigner took a practice ride: it was as though an oyster had started walking sideways in a colony of crabs.

But, Fang's informants complained, all too soon the Forever was bundled into the back of a Toyota and he was swept away by the Government Men. They cosseted him everywhere. A young interpreter, recently allocated to Yanzhou, had been given the foreigner as his special responsibility. He was predictably conscientious in his work.

For all Fang's delight about Yanzhou apparently bagging this big-beaked bird, this oyster, he was growing a little concerned that he had not set eyes on it, despite patrolling the city centre by bicycle every afternoon and rigorously following up every clue as to the creature's movements.

He was particularly frustrated to hear that Qiao had actually been introduced. Needless to say he had somehow got on to good terms with this strait-laced Interpreter Li and had therefore been allowed to engage the visitor in some small talk at the park gates.

He was from Delaware. After initial panic that the foreigner was French, Qiao had been reassured by the accent which was pure VOA. The young man was twenty-three, rather shy and awkward and, said Qiao, probably missing his motherland.

Interpreter Li had soon moved him on like the foreign dignitaries they saw in news footage from Tiananmen Square.

'Didn't you even get his name?' the jealous Fang had asked at the next English Corner.

'Yes – Ja Ke Ell Yot.'

'It's Jake! You should pronounce it Jake.' Fang knew the name from VOA's student life series: a Jake had been dating a Chrissie.

But learning a few details didn't help at all. Bad luck poisoned Fang's next week too. Although the American now seemed to have met the entire Yanzhou workforce, visited every factory and every institution, and paraded down each street, their paths had still not crossed. Fang's routes were extending markedly each day. He even began doubling back unexpectedly. He visited the department store so often that the shop girls started giggling. In one morning he bought a cabbage at six separate cabbage outlets.

And yet he had nothing – except cabbage – to show for his effort. Cabbage and frustration. Even Fu was now claiming to have seen the American ('the ugliest thing – no, the second ugliest thing – I've ever set eyes on') and from the post office came rumours of public readings of Jake's cards home before they were put into the Baihao bag. That Jake had become an obsession didn't surprise Fang but it was odd that it had happened without their actually meeting. He struggled to keep it in proportion, and failed. His unconscious was really perking up now too, posting unhelpful images to mock him further.

'The twenty-seventh person to come round that corner will be Jake,' he found himself telling himself on Peace Street or Harmony Boulevard. Fang had always had a thing about three times three times three but now he was spending an hour a day counting drab Yanzhou shoppers.

He dreamt he was climbing in the mountains of Guilin which he knew from a painted scroll at home: he was carrying his sword; as he reached a crossroads in the steep goat-track he met Jake, beautiful in silk robes; Fang hailed him in best BBC English but no matter what he said, or how well or how loudly he said it, the American didn't hear, or ignored him, and walked on by – up, it seemed, to the summit where there was someone else: Qiao, and another – Qiao and his girl were making love for Jake on high.

By the following Sunday Fang had become afraid of meeting his friends because they seemed to have worked out the purpose of his constant street beat and would come rushing up with news of more sightings – so many now that Fang should reasonably have been suspicious (not that reason was any longer part of his armoury). Only Podgy Peng avoided aggravating his depression because he hoped to win Fang back to the now beleaguered social club. (During his evening swoops through the city centre Fang had often looked in past the radio-cassette machine to see the Podge and Wong miserably scoffing chestnuts together.)

When he arrived for English Corner, which he had had to steel himself to face, Qiao quite yanked him in off the landing in great excitement.

'Have I got a surprise for you!' he said, hurrying Fang past the parents who were about their usual Sunday tasks. His hopes were now so unhinged that Fang was certain Jake would be waiting in the bedroom.

'Danananaaa!' said Qiao, in Mandarin, as he flung open the door. The only other human form in the room was the Mao bust which Qiao always said he kept as a joke (but really as a sop to his diehard father).

'Dananana what?' said Fang.

'Danananaaa brilliant news – that's what,' said Qiao staying in Mandarin.

'What brilliant news?'

'Ja Ke wants to teach in Yanzhou!'

'Jake! It's Jake!' snapped Fang.

'Jake then. He's going to teach here.'

'Where?'

'They haven't decided yet but the authorities have just got to get permission from Landu. He could be here for months!'

Fang's immediate thought was of a long hot summer in futile street patrol.

'Who told you this, Qiao?' he asked, lounging disconsolately on the bed and peeling an apple with his sticky, hairy knife.

'Interpreter Li of course! He's been sent over to Landu today with a letter. He should be back with the reply by Wednesday.'

'They'll never allow it. And even if they do he'll be teaching the brats in middle school. *We* won't get to him – at least, I won't . . .'

'Don't be so stupid. Of course he can't teach the brats. He can't speak Chinese, remember? No, he'll be doing some sort of graduate course, for intermediates.'

Fang suspected Qiao had inside knowledge but he was careful to avoid sounding too interested.

'Which graduates, then? Which intermediates?'

'Us of course! We just have to tickle the bellies of our bosses and we'll get a place. During office hours, too!'

'Well it's all very fine for you. Your buddies down at Foreign Trade will let you go without any trouble . . .'

'Don't be so sour, Little Fang! I don't know yet if they're going to take me. It's likely of course and they're bound to be interested in my language skills. But your standard's even higher than mine.'

'What use is that', said Fang gracelessly, 'if I get stuck behind a ping-pong-bat machine for the next two decades?'

'Don't be thick! You know perfectly well graduates get on quicker – it's the system, it makes sense.' He paused and then enquired in a voice suddenly softer, 'Grandfather hasn't done anything else, has he?'

'No!' barked Fang. 'He hasn't as it happens. But then he doesn't really need to, does he? The die is cast and there's enough bitterness in Yanzhou to keep me down for ever.'

Fang instinctively thought of the dispute between their parents. But they had vowed never to discuss what little they knew about that. 'Fu's used up all our "back door" with her marriage anyway.' That was true: as far as the family had any pull with officialdom in the city, Fu had used it for her marriage at twenty (three years too young) to Hong aged thirty (three years too old and not from Yanzhou). She had tugged at the strings relentlessly, certain she would get her way. Events seemed to have justified the effort but Fang had always suspected the real pressure to release the marriage certificate had come from Hong's side.

The story behind their union was rare enough to have needed a big shot's help – and big shots didn't shoot from Yanzhou. Two years ago a retired general and veteran of the blessed Long March came to the sanatorium where he happened to be assigned Fu as his nurse. The old man took a fancy to her and she wisely allowed herself to be photographed sitting on his knee after a ward rave-up. The evidence of this intimacy was touched up at a smart Peking photographic studio and, a fortnight after his departure, sent to Fu as a memento of the smelly old warrior.

Early the next spring he was back and their 'affair' continued, Fu being too pleased with the presents to complain about his other, palsied attentions which were inspired by the Chairman's belief that liaisons with young virgins enhanced longevity.

But when the general was collected by his nephew at the end of the month she allowed her head to be turned: Hong Wei was captivated and the old man fervently encouraged the suit, seeing it as a way to get his nymph to Peking.

Thus the marriage permit had hit no obstructions. Fang liked to think of it flying high through the corridors on a carpet of medals from the struggle for Liberation and the Korean War. But the general had died before the residence permit could get the same easy passage; his wind had continued to blow posthumously but without the same force. Hence the present delay.

The BBC's reception was outstandingly good that afternoon and they caught most of an interesting drama set around a faulty photocopier in a London office. Fang's spirits revived and he even allowed himself to show some enthusiasm about Jake's possible class.

He headed home in a better mood and, although he could not resist a long detour to the Dong Lan side of the city – just in case – he was not cast far down by its failure. He was sure to meet Jake soon. It had to happen and when it did life would begin to shape up.

six

When Fu came in from work the following evening she dropped a folded sheet of paper on to the table.

'Letter from Hong, Mother. It came to the san,' she said as she breezed through to the bedroom. Carefully drying her hands, Mother sat down on the stool and opened up the thin paper. She put on her glasses and leaned back slightly. After a few seconds she looked up and smiled at the single overhead bulb as though trying to charm it into more enthusiastic illumination of Hong's writing.

'Dear Mother-in-law . . .' she started reading aloud. But the bulb went out along with Fu's tinny pop music. She cursed through the wall but Mother just sighed and stared at the bulb again. Powercuts: she really believed she could stare them out too.

'It'll be off for hours, Mother,' said Fang, slamming his textbook shut. He had spent a useful forty minutes on the gerund, the sort of linguistic frill he hoped would raise his stock in Jake's blue eyes. (Certainly Qiao had no idea of the gerund − 'Like semi-colons I suppose?' he'd said at the last English Corner!) A square of orange heat provided a little light from the stove door. Mother still sat motionless.

'Grandfather?'

'Yes, boy?' came gruffly through the other wall.

'You all right?'

No reply, just the clink of those metal balls he rotated for hours in the palm of his hand, clockwise, anticlockwise. 'Healthy Balls', he called them − another of his secrets. With Healthy Balls and chickens he apparently had no need for young virgins.

The bulb flared and then dimmed again, reluctantly emitting a weak yellow light as if to show them that it could handle electric shocks without getting too excited. Fang suggested he read the letter to Mother.

'Dear Mother-in-law,' he began. 'This is a formal letter of

thanks for having me to stay. It must have been very incon-
venient for you' (Fang would have appreciated a plural 'you')
'and I am very grateful. There have been developments in
Peking during my absence: Fu's permit really is nearly through
now and I should be able to send it down in a few weeks.'
(Great! Even the bulb perked up suddenly.) 'I am bringing in
more furniture. Our home will be beautiful for your first visit.
The other news is that I am changing work units again – to
work for a Hong Kong business' (Hong Kong! Bloody Fu's
done it again!) 'as official driver for their office in Peking.'
(What a relief! I don't think I could have coped if she had
landed Hong Kong just like that.) 'I start work for them next
week. No more American dumpling for me!' (Mother didn't
get the joke.) 'I will be using my old car without the taxi sign'
(I bet he sticks it back up after his shift and doubles his . . .)
'but I can stick it back after my shift and double my salary.'
(Does he realise who he's writing to? But judging from
Mother's grin he seems to have hit precisely the right note.
Bandit!) 'I hope there may be a clerical opening in the office
suitable for Fu's talents' (dabbing her nails with French var-
nish) 'but until then she can work at a PLA sanatorium here.
A colleague of my late great uncle is seeing to it. How happy
Great Uncle would have been to see her there!' (Hah, a
misjudgement! Mother is frowning at this reference.) 'I hope I
can reassure you, if you still need reassurance, that Fu is
leaving one fine home for another where her husband is
waiting and' (getting richer and richer no doubt) 'getting richer
and richer! Your respectfully affectionate Son-in-law, Hong
Wei.' (With a bit of money even a worm can become a dragon.)

Fang looked up.

'She's done very well, hasn't she,' said Mother, voice low
and intense, eyes skewering Fang. 'Hong is a fine young man,
a modern man with the brightest of futures. I'm glad her
period of uncertainty will be over soon.'

Fang had hardly expected this sort of attack, so gently
devastating. The good news in the letter had surprised him
too – as had Hong's conceit. It did seem that everything was
fitting into place for pouting Elder Sister. She'd damn nearly
got Hong Kong too! Lying next door, leafing through those
big-city magazines, she surely didn't deserve it. Her frustration

was so coarse, so inferior to his. Her sordid, materialistic ambitions – quite similar to Qiao's in fact – had no right to be achieved before his had even been identified. And yet they had been!

Her struggle was a short story which began with the general's hoary hand on her knee and ended with this letter. The Yanzhou Syndrome had been escaped. 'Green with envious', Fang gave himself up to the new English phrase.

Mother was still crouched under the bolshy bulb, marking books now. Fu minced in to make some tea so Fang had to go through to see Grandfather, cross-legged, smoking on the bed. His Healthy Balls were back in their box. At least there would be no praise of Hong and Fu here.

'What is it?'

'Nothing, Grandfather.'

'Yes it is.'

'Well . . .'

'I can tell you're angry, boy.'

'Not angry . . . Just nervous, depressed . . .'

'Nervous, depressed – it's all the same, boy. It's really anger, that's what it is. What are you angry about?'

'Oh, my job assignment, you know, what am I going to get and all that . . . and, well, pretty well everything is bothering me at the moment.'

He had never confided in Grandfather but he saw no harm in it now. The old man seemed flattered and unusually communicative: 'I know how you feel. Believe me, I know anger. For me it's calmer now – but not much. Problem is for you, boy, you can't stick the thought of Yanzhou for the rest of your days, eh? I'm right, aren't I?'

Fang was surprised by the accuracy of this simple diagnosis and the calming effect it had on him to hear someone else deliver it. He nodded.

'Now, I lived in a hole like this all my youth too – and bloody depressing it was. I was no scholar, mind – none of that evening study you get up to – but I still felt it. And d'you know what I did, boy?'

Fang suspected he would have heard already if it was anything of note. Grandfather was preparing to smoke the last of a herd of Flying Horses, squeezing it between thumb and forefinger: the loosely packed tobacco fell on to his ankle. 'Nothing, boy! Absolutely nothing!'

He lit the cigarette with a flourish and an inch of empty paper flared up.

'Why, you ask? The time wasn't right, see. And I realised the time wasn't right. So I just turned to the sword. That's where my life's energy went.'

Fang had never heard this one.

'Now I don't believe you can imagine that sort of sacrifice,' he said, speculating accurately. 'Perhaps you call it giving up, a defeat – but I call it sacrifice. There were forces at work in the country then, unbelievable forces. Cruelty you would not even be able to read about nowadays. The dogs, the bloody dogs had it best then.'

Fang nodded knowingly, and then regretted it.

'Why?' growled the old quizzer.

'Why what?'

'Why did the dogs have it best? You were nodding.'

'Oh, I – er, don't know, Grandfather.'

'Listen, boy – because there was always a man's torso to gnaw at somewhere out there. Dog's life was best. Nothing else was life – people did "time" but not life! There was not much of that. You cannot understand. Don't try. But you *must* listen, boy.'

Was he talking about what the Japanese dwarfs did to the Chinese or what the Chinese did to each other? Perhaps that wasn't the point. What was the point in this bizarre confession?

'From '49 till the Cultural, as many as 26 million enemies of Communism were liquidated. You went to sleep one night with ten people in your dormitory and woke up to find that three had just vanished. But you didn't ask any questions – that would have been madness. You just accepted it. What sort of a government can find itself 26 million enemies, among its own people, eh? I ask you that! But if you didn't get a club in the head – and for some reason I didn't – then there was only one way to carry on! Inside yourself! Sacrifice the rest and turn inside! Internalise – that was the word. Strengthen the soul, try to perfect it, protect it. The only way! And how? The sword! Cut! Thrust! Lunge! I really gave my life to it . . . and now the blade's yours, boy. My life, your life, the Way . . .'

Fang had never been too interested in the philosophical background of the sword dance. It was no longer relevant; it had nothing to do with reform and openness, English idioms or even the Four Modernisations (agriculture, industry, science and – what was it? – technology). He did find some satisfaction in the graceful steps and body actions themselves but, actually, he was just doing the sword for Grandfather. And, in fact, he was doing Father's flail to keep Mother happy. Filial piety – perhaps he took it too far! If he was perfectly honest, only the chunky dumb-bells were for him – for his own muscles, for his own development.

Fang rubbed his bruised shin. Grandfather spat. So he didn't have a great war. But things had hardly improved after 1966 either. A small landlord in the immediate vicinity of Shanghai, he had caught the first spasm of Red Guard activity and then an even more conclusive second wave when they discovered Grandmother had sometimes cooked for a 'rightist' employee of the Hongkong and Shanghai Banking Corporation. Especially conclusive for Grandmother that had been. It was not the sort of story which improved with telling and Grandfather did not mention it now.

He must have had to 'internalise' during the Cultural, with the sword as his only prop. But Fang had always been slightly doubtful of Grandfather's devotion to the philosophical side of it. The Taoist belief in the yielding, passive approach to life might indeed have helped thousands through China's twentieth century (rigid oaks may fall but supple reeds will brave the storm, as they said) but the violence in Grandfather's love of cut and thrust and lunge did not quite square with the Taoist ideal of *wu wei* or non-action.

'But now!' Grandfather switched brands, lighting a Kingfisher with the butt of his Flying Horse. Now he was speaking to the present and the future. 'We Chinese have always had to spot the main chance. If it's not there then there's no point in going for it. But if it is, we must! And that's where your life comes in, eh?'

'What?'

'You listening?'

'Yes. I just . . .' He was listening – so hard that he had been tripped up again.

'Because there's a bat's squeak – more than a bat's squeak – of a chance for you lot and you're bloody well right to refuse to think about staying here and bloody well right to envy your stuck-up sister and her Chauffeur Ponce – because they are going to be in the right place. Not that they deserve it, but you, boy – whatever you're after, and I hope to God it's money – I think perhaps you do!'

Fang was astonished.

'You look at me like that. I know what you're thinking. But I'm not such a dead head! I've still got some ideas for anyone who wants to hear them. And some anger! I may have bottled it up when I was young but sixty-five years later it spills out a bit – vintage anger, boy. I don't like being cooped up in Yanzhou any more than you do. Difference is, I've got no choice now. But catching a snake in a bamboo doesn't stop it wriggling: I kill chickens, I kick up a stink, I wander – my way of showing them my sword's still up and quivering,' he said. 'Remember one thing, boy, if you remember nothing else: the most miserable thing in the world is the death of the heart . . .' Grandfather suddenly reached over to take him by the shoulders for a brief – and immediately embarrassing – moment. '. . . and I'm a long way from that! Now go to your Mother,' he growled. Such eyes deserved younger sockets! 'Oh, and nip out and get me some more Horses,' he added. 'I can't abide these pissy little Kingfishers.' The small frame bucked into another great hawk and Fang had to turn away.

Only later, as he lay in bed, did Fang realise that Qiao's Interpreter Li would by now have returned from Landu. Sweat suddenly warmed the backs of his hairless thighs and he began worrying with new alarm. Could he possibly expect to see the Two Great Unlikelihoods come true? One, that permission would have been granted for Jake to teach in Yanzhou; two, that Fang would get a desk in that classroom. Everything he knew about life pointed to frustration – anger – on both these questions, but he still hoped. The power of hope – Grandfather's, his – astonished him. He gave himself up to his dream.

The following morning it was snowing so hard that Fang didn't do the sword. Grandfather winced some disapproval but agreed it was impossible to dance in a blizzard. Fang dressed quickly and drank tea in silence with Mother at table. The wind chucked snow at the windows. He looked into the yard. The hen was motionless at the back of its run, giving up four days early.

He was preparing himself for a ride down to the city when there was a rap on the door and Qiao blew in wearing a mantle of snow, flakes clinging to the long black hairs on his upper lip. He was smiling even more than usual.

'Morning all! Good morning, Madam Fang!' He had called her Aunty before.

'Hello, Little Qiao. A nice surprise.' He rarely came up these days.

'What's the news?' asked Fang.

'Good news! The best! They said yes!'

'Yes to Jake?'

'Yes to Jake!'

'He can teach?'

'He can teach!'

'Fantastic!'

'Teach what?' asked Mother. 'Who – what – is Jake?'

But the boys were dancing around the table.

'What is going on? Will one of you explain?'

As Fang chuckled into his tea Qiao told her; then he stood up and announced he had to get back.

'Back?'

'Back to work, Fang. You know, work!'

'Of course, you've started already, haven't you? How did you manage to get away then?'

'No problem. And I just had to tell you the news!'

'It's brilliant! But when do we know about the class?'

'They're working it out over the next week, asking companies whether they want to put people forward and so on.'

'And you?'

'Well, I'm already in. The boss is very keen.'

'Ah . . . that is good news.'

'And I've told Interpreter Li about you.'

'Have you, Qiao? That's good . . . See you later then.' Fang opened the door.

'You must drop in and see me at the office.'

'Thanks. I'll do that. See you. Goodbye.'

He slammed the door against the wind. But all his delight over Qiao's news had already blown out. Fang was on to the second Unlikelihood and mulling bitterly over his friend's inordinate good fortune which, on top of keeping him ahead at every turn, seemed to make him Jovial Arbiter of Everyone Else's Fate too.

seven

It sometimes seemed to Fang that Yanzhou's only hope was in the timely arrival of outsiders. Left alone the city would have destroyed itself long ago, so many were the private conceits and the wranglings, and so fierce the heat generated by interests conflicting, faces being saved, and corners being fought. Like a great puffball unable to contain its boisterous spores, Yanzhou would have exploded.

The present mayor was a good example of the outsider theory. He had been imposed by the wise mandarins of Landu who secured his transfer from some city on the Korean border. So he had arrived, a symbol of the powers beyond Yanzhou, a reminder. The little bigwigs raved about the injustice, of course, but Landu's eyes soon turned away and their tiny politicking could begin again.

And Fang sometimes thought of it as pans of sweet potatoes, simmering on hobs all over the province. When they look like boiling over, add a splash of cold water and, *in extremis*, pluck out a spud and gobble him up.

This had happened with the sand factory on Baihao Hill Road. One of the many business concerns of the PLA, it had been left for several years under the executive control of a civilian, Manager Xi. But he was a byword for laziness and operated the plant in such a slothful way that 'a job at the sand factory' had become local slang for skiving.

Eventually, however, Xi had been tripped up by a PLA investigation of the factory, part of a general review of their assets in the province. The reporting major had interrupted a game of poker and, although a runner had been scrambled to alert workers along the inspection route, Xi had failed to convince his guest that anything was being produced at all. He was sacked that night.

The story, which was passed on by rumour rather than the less garrulous columns of *Yanzhou Daily*, had delighted the public – especially those people, like Fang, who lived so close.

There were hilarious scenes as the hated sand lorries were prevented from getting out on to the Baihao Hill Road for as much as half an hour at a time. Young people took turns to lie in the path of these lumpy mastodons while cyclists streamed past tinkling their bells and jeering at the drivers. Fang himself had done a stint on the driveway. The police had chuckled too and tolerated the chaos for a few heady days – until a woman put up a poster demanding compensation from the PLA for her son, killed by a lorry a year ago. The authorities weren't about to let that start.

The sand factory was Yanzhou's most public commercial failure ever. Although many, many businesses had failed just as conclusively, these had been muffled booms compared to the crash of the sand factory, the first business to have really copped it from the new spirit of reform and efficiency. 'Managerial accountability' was the fine phrase on everyone's lips and the people loved it for the chunks it had snapped out of Xi and his poker gang. There were many other drawn-looking cadres in Yanzhou after that.

Immediately, the PLA had tried to sell the factory which, it was now revealed, had always been supposed to produce cement as well. But then the next news was that they were bringing in a sappy new outsider, a young PLA man, to run it. The old hoarding was replaced by a bright new one (PEOPLE'S CEMENT in Chinese and English) and the PLA flag flew from a high pole stuck up in the courtyard.

Public interest subsided accordingly since nothing bores like efficiency and soon, as the lorries' workload mounted, cyclists were slamming on their brakes more than ever before.

For Little Fang, though, the saga came to have a special importance. Three months after Manager Xi's dismissal, and a week after Qiao had brought up the good news about Jake, Fang heard his own job assignment: People's Cement. Report for duty next Monday, 12 December.

So this was how he was going to serve the Motherland. Well, it was nice to know . . . but he had very mixed feelings about the decision. It was incredible to him, still, that people had to be told what they were fit to do and it hurt to hear the decision which bore directly on him, on Little Fang. Little Fang the Cement Man?

'But I don't understand why you feel so hard done by, Son. It's the same for everybody. It's the way, the system.' And in that maddening way of hers she looked quickly up at the wall, up to Tolerance which hung there next to the clock.

'You know perfectly well how the system works, Mother. Best jobs come through the "back door" and the rest of us end up a list of names on a junior official's desk or, more likely, as chips in the next game of office poker.'

'Don't talk like that, Son. It's bad talk.'

What relief, though, to be a chip and not a parasitic tick – or the son of a parasitic tick. There was a certain indignity in being associated with the sand factory but Fang knew this would pass. More important, the new manager was still unknown, an outsider. He could only be an improvement on Xi. He might even be good. After all, the PLA's sense of pride was so highly developed – its most highly developed feature in fact – that they could not tolerate another failure.

Accepting that Foreign Trade was the best option, followed by the Bank of China, Fang put the rest on a level, the dead-dull level. At least it was too early to label People's Cement. So that was something. But what about the biggest question: would there be English-speaking opportunities?

He had no idea why he had been given this place or, rather, why this place had been given him. No precise job description had accompanied his summons. The two other graduates assigned with him, dull Wong and the greedy Ling, were not known cement enthusiasts.

Fang wasn't sure what to think – but one thing was certain: he would never again be able to pelt the Pigeon past the sand factory without a care. Like it or not, their fates were now intimately connected.

eight

'He's gone to the Education Department.'

'What, already?'

Scrubbed and excited, Fang had swung by Qiao's block on his way to the first class so they could arrive together: Frank Fang and Charlie Qiao, the heavyweights from the English Corner. He was most disappointed to hear from the mother that he had gone – and especially that he had gone *there*.

Fang felt snubbed, and then foolish to be feeling snubbed. It was not that they had actually planned to go together but just that it had seemed fitting. Clearly Qiao was keen to maintain his position as He Who Met Jake First and, no less important, He Who Has the Ear of Interpreter Li.

Fang clattered back into the morning's tinkling traffic, aware again of that old inferiority opposite Qiao: the fear that Qiao was allowing him the lead at English Corner because he was confident enough to pull away in every other field whenever the need arose.

But hang on! Can you, just occasionally, feel some satisfaction? Why does Mistress Ambition always slip ahead of your sense of achievement? Why does she always dart on a few steps and stop to wiggle her lizard hips at you again? What are you doing now, Fang, if not pedalling towards day one of Yanzhou's first-ever English-language graduate class? Are you not now on a collision course with the American? He can't dodge you today!

A bean-curd salesman, whose wares quivered in a large tray on his back wheel, swung in front of him. Fang swerved away – into the path of a youth with a ton of cabbage on his tricycle-truck. The boy had to brake hard, which in turn caused a series of shuntings and entanglements behind them. Cabbages fell into the gutter.

And how about a vote of thanks for Manager Sun, Fang thought as he accelerated out of the mess. Although a soldier by training, the new sand chief was not anti-progress and he had decided they should not miss the chance of a place in the class. Ling was irredeemably lazy anywhere off the basketball court but, just when Fang thought his own selection for the course was settled, dull Wong had launched a challenge, wooing Sun with a wad of immaculately written English. The unlikeliest people were studying these days!

Luckily Fang had seen the sheets on the manager's desk and had had no hesitation in revealing the true extent of Wong's ability: the dolt had written one sentence over and over again, up and down seventeen sides of thin-lined foolscap: 'Even if I am unsuccessfully 100 times I must not give up because it is only then that I truly fail.'

Fang had enlightened Sun who then laughingly declared that a man with that sort of diligence was just the one to set to work on the backlog of fifteen years' neglected invoices — 'which leaves you, Little Fang, as our only other choice for the course. But why should *you* have the place?'

Damn his meritocracy! Fang replied with instant passion about the export opportunities for Yanzhou cement in the West and concluded with the first ten lines of 'Snake' by Mr D. H. Lawrence, which he repeated to double the fine impression he was making. 'Right, good, good — yes, you can stop there. You've talked your way on to the course. Don't waste it, Little Fang.'

The classroom was half full when he arrived. There were no surprises. He could have predicted who would win secondment. Most were former classmates from college and they sat in the same old groups. Those girls who had got into hotels occupied the middle row: Pretty Pei had brought her limp copy of *Hotel English*. (Fang sincerely hoped this wouldn't be required: 'Welcome you to our establishment, please may I make your bed and accompany you through all-our-cart menu?')

Miss Pei was a good-looking girl — a bit of a Fu face in fact — and she had managed to land a place on Reception at the Dong Lan. Next to her sat Miss Chang, now on the desk at the Blue Mountain Guest House — downmarket but she had creditably long legs. A couple of other hotel girls giggled at the far end of the row.

Those poor devils sent into teaching were clustered up at the front. No problem about secondment for them! They only worked a six-hour week as junior staff and the leaders were desperate to train them up as English teachers to fill the quota demanded by Landu.

Mother had told Fang that Lin Hu, a serious youth now sitting by the window, had astonished staff at No. 2 Middle School by reporting discipline problems during his oral English lessons. The headmaster had made it clear that the fault must lie with him because no one else had ever had such difficulties and the poor fellow was now under surveillance himself in all classes. At least his embattled look, described so accurately by Mother, was eased now by the prospect of someone else having to defend the podium.

Fang felt that the class of '88 had not done too badly overall. Admittedly there was one very bright girl who had ended up in the department store's Musical Instruments section, but the rest had got quite reasonable assignments, mostly in offices in the factories where it was becoming a symbol of reform to have at least one English-speaker on the staff. Fei was here from Tyres; next to him, Lan (Water Pumps); Ban had got Flax; Leather had sent two – Deng and Tang; Zhei from Animal By-Products. Even Liu Wei, Jake's shy herald, had persuaded Arts and Crafts to send him along. It was curious to be thinking of them all in light-industrial terms now rather than nose-picking, fouling at football or indiscreet mastur- bation.

Fang was surprised to see an envoy from Heavenly Tinned Foods – not Podgy but a brawny girl called Lo. She had once chopped him down on the volley-ball court, confirming Fang's suspicion that she was brutal and ambitious.

He took a seat next to Little Xin, whom he had lavishly pitied ever since hearing that he had got Sporting Goods. Known without affection as the 'ping-pong-bat factory', this place was run by an old-fashioned bully who intimated his loathing of all graduates by giving them six months making nothing but bats every hour of every day. Fang knew that Xin was now enduring this trial which he had once feared would be his own fate.

'How did you get out?' he asked, clapping Xin on the back.

'I said I was enjoying the bat bench so much the boss got suspicious,' he replied. 'I was too convincing – he decided to move me.'

'You lucky devil.'

'Shrewd judgement more like. Tell them you want to go one way and they'll do their best to send you the other. It's called the small-town philosophy of career frustration. I'm surprised you haven't come across it yet, Little Fang.'

'Oh, I have, I have.' He was rather taken aback by Xin's urbanity, which he had never noticed before.

'The annoying thing is that I really was enjoying the bat bench. It's the glue, you see. Lovely stuff! They're all hooked on it down there. I was having the best time of my life!'

'You got high?' Fang suggested, uneasy with the word's mysterious meaning.

'All the time! The bat bench is the best place in Yanzhou. They're strung out so far it's amazing they ever make a bat at all. Somehow they just manage to avoid the sack.'

'Well, there's nothing like the concentration of the addict who is fearing for his supply,' said Fang, deftly adapting something he had once heard from his pretentious sister. 'You must miss it,' he added, trying to run on into empathy.

'I was out before it became that serious, but I still love the stuff. I go back to help with the overtime – when I can get a stool, that is. You know what they say? "You never really leave the bat bench."'

Fang felt Envy, his old foe, swivel its foil and prick him a pang in the usual spot: now it was envy of Little Xin who seemed to have found his own means of survival in the unlikeliest place in town!

He looked up to save the next desk (for Charlie) from a middle-aged man whom he'd never seen before. The fellow meekly moved away, self-conscious among the young English-lovers. It was rare to find Mother's generation speaking English. At school they had been allowed only Russian until that too was suddenly criminal – replaced by a decade of Mao-speak. But this was December 1988 and now three other older students had taken up seats. The classroom was nearly full.

There was a lull in the chatter and they all turned to face

the door. The delegation had arrived, led by a Government Man who gave a surreptitious 'rise' sign as they entered. Fang felt violently excited but had laid plans for controlling himself: the first measure was to stare rigidly at the floor between his feet.

The thrill of the wrapped gift! Could it survive revelation? Fang accepted that his expectations about Jake had long since broken the bounds of possibility. Yet he refused to confine them: they were his shield against boredom and hope's best ally. He revelled in the fantasy.

He crushed a butt of green chalk with his foot and forced his eyes shut again. This was the gift of a lifetime – wrapped in weeks of rumour and ribboned in tantalising sightings by almost everyone he knew. To unwrap Jake was to risk the biggest disappointment ever.

He swayed and, unable to keep his eyes shut, watched his finger follow the Hong Kong skyline on the cover of his new exercise book. Sexy skyline! He screwed his eyes shut again.

Fantasy galloped and kicked and bucked and snorted. Around him the murmurs grew as the delegation processed towards the front. Within him there was anarchic shouting, great-throated cries in his shut-eyed darkness: He's beautiful! He is kind! Tall and beautiful! He will like me! I will love him! He will love me! We are coming together at last! Jake! Chrissie! America! Together at last! Beautiful! Together! America! BEAUTIFUL!

This last word was a shriek which quite split his inner ear and must have pierced further because now Xin jabbed him sharply in the ribs. Fang looked up. Everybody – including the being he had never seen – was staring at him. Including Jake! Jake unwrapped!

But the pump had started the blood-thump around his face and Fang was forced to engage the hostile stares of the four officials who comprised the course's launch party. Qiao stood at their side slowly shaking his head.

'Well!' The leading Government Man, in full black wool Mao suit and blue cap – dodo! – began to address the class, keeping the smarting Fang pinned by his glare. 'It is my pleasure to introduce to you today a young American called . . .' He looked closely at the paper in his hand. '. . . Ja Ke – Ja Ke Ell Yot.'

General sniggering at this ludicrous pronunciation forced the official to dispense his bountiful disapproval equally among this batch of graduate upstarts, and Fang had the chance to dip his eyes away.

'We have invited Ja – him to teach one three-month term at the Yanzhou Graduate Training Centre for Specialist Skills.'

Fang stared at Jake. He was beautiful, certainly: his eyes were like the sea, his hair the colour of straw and – ah, his nose – his nose was a magnificent mountain. Even the bloody pimple in the cleft of his chin strangely added to the beauty. And he was so tall: a good head – what a good head! – taller than the babbling official, and he bore an enchanting expression of amused incomprehension. Clearly his Chinese was negligible.

'Mister – he graduated from . . .' Now most irritated, the official turned for help from Interpreter Li who declared Jake's credentials to be a Teach English Overseas Diploma – plus honours – from the Wilmington Central Night School, Delaware, USA.

The Government Man resumed: 'He is therefore an experienced teacher. We welcome him in the hope that he can raise the pitiable level of our graduates' English.'

There was general clapping and Jake nodded charmingly several times. Official whispering then gave way to the extended throat clearance of another member of the delegation who began speaking in dull Radio Moscow tones.

Fang was trying to use sporadic eye contact with Jake to fuse a look of apology for his outburst to an honest offer of the deepest possible friendship. Only when the failure of this scheme suggested that his eyes were incapable of projecting such complex emotions did he appreciate what was being said by the twisted old bureaucrat on the podium.

'. . . You may of course offer your help if you see him in difficulties with his bicycle. It would be most regrettable if his inexperience were to involve him in a road traffic accident. But I repeat: you must not consort with this foreigner outside class in any other way. He is here to work, not to socialise. Offers of hospitality are forbidden. You are well aware of the dangers of Spiritual Pollution. By all means capitalise on this opportunity which the People's Government has provided, but do not put yourselves at risk . . .' He looked peevishly at Jake who gave a broad, uncomprehending smile and yet another bow. '. . . and you must be wary even within these walls.'

The previous speaker tried to launch another burst of applause but by the third clap he realised the graduates were not going to join in and he stopped. A rat-like human being who identified himself as the institute's director now jutted his face forward to give some details about the course which he entitled Business English. Qiao grinned and then simpered as his appointment to Class Monitor rank was announced.

Stepping forward, squaring up to his responsibilities so nobly, Qiao brought out a piece of paper to be passed round so that each student could insert relevant details into his carefully ruled columns. Finally the speechifying was crowned with a few words of execrable Chinese from Jake, who said he was delighted to be their mouse (and effectively confirmed that the course would have to be conducted in English throughout). Although the classmates wanted to hear his mother tongue not theirs, he was fiercely applauded.

Fang's own displeasure was refined by Jake's complicit nods at the sleek Interpreter Li and Qiao: they must have composed this nice little speech together in the centrally heated comfort of the Education Department. Perhaps they even had a 'working breakfast'. He joined in the applause and then began to fill out the form which Xin had passed across. The Name List of English Classmates, Qiao had written in English at the top of the page. Then, from left to right, the columns were headed as follows: Number, Chinese Appellation, Transliterated Appellation, Aged, Sexual Distinction.

Xin was still sniggering at his entry, 'Outstanding kisser and a naturally gifted fondler', which Fang had seen him write in and then rub out of the Sexual Distinction column, Fang filled out the offensive sheet, and passed it on. But then his fury was further rarefied: as the party marched out, Qiao turned to announce that this was merely the opening ceremony; the course itself would not begin for another ten days, Jake having a tight schedule of receptions and meetings and 'a small

Christmas celebration' to attend. Qiao contrived to give Fang a prissy little smile and scurried out after the VIPs.

Everyone was disappointed to hear about the delay but the frustration was hardly extraordinary. As they all gathered up their various textbooks, Fang was generous enough to consider offering them an introduction to the gerund but he was still aware of having drawn enough attention to himself already. And the classmates were not letting him forget.

'What on earth was going through your mind when you shouted that?' asked Liu Wei.

'That's just it – I thought I was talking to myself.'

'Easy mistake!' said Xin, drug addict and sex maniac.

'You know when you are eating glazed crab-apples?' Fang continued. 'Well, do you ever wonder whether anyone else can hear the crunching noise going on inside your head?'

They sniggered. No one was going to understand. Fang left, reflecting that at least they weren't accusing him of being in love with Jake.

On the road he adopted his usual ploy of pedalling out the frustration, going faster and faster towards the city centre. And, as usual, the exertion did seem to help – if not to make frustration disappear, then at least to channel it off into some less accessible pool of his troublesome psyche. (Fang could easily reach 35 mph with this frenzied pedalling and had learned to keep the Flying Pigeon well serviced as a result.)

Originally supposing that he would go straight back up to work, he now decided he would not be missed because everyone there thought the course was starting today. So he veered left past Podgy's office and slipped in through the back entrance of the Yanzhou Roast Duck Restaurant just down the street.

The first birds of the day were almost done and already emitting their sweet-smelling advertisement. Yes, Ling and Wong could go on processing the production figures without him for a while longer.

Fang greeted his friend, a former neighbour who had lately risen to No. 3 Duck Roaster. It was a useful position and Fang's hopes of using it were never disappointed. Old Fen just happened to be whipping out a 'trial duck' which he swiftly dismembered as they talked.

'And how's that grandad of yours?' Old Fen was one of the few people who got on with him.

'Much the same. Quieter maybe.' He thought of their conversation the previous week. 'More the philosopher, less the action man these days.'

He gratefully accepted a plateful of crisp duck skin and fat, glistening and hot.

'Thought we'd better try one out, eh?' Old Fen winked and Fang gorged. 'And you? How are things with the young scholar?'

Fang prepared the obligatory cheerful lies on this one as he added spring onions and rich red-bean sauce to the skin, wrapping it all in a steaming pancake which he peeled from the top of the day's column.

'Fine, Old Fen, I'm fine.'

'Working?' he asked, with the smile of a senior who suspects that the young are never really going to get down to anything.

'Yes, up at the sand factory – I mean People's Cement. Started there last month.'

'And that's why you're down here during office hours, eh?' Fang's mouth was full. 'I thought there was new management up there. My daughter tells me sand lorries are on the move as never before.'

'Yes, it's true. But I've been down for an English class.'

'Haven't you had enough of all that yet?'

Fang rather thought he had. Sauce spurted into his lap from the bottom of his third (fourth?) pancake.

'There's a foreigner teaching a graduate course and the factories have sent in people to improve their speaking ability. You know, import–export and all that.'

'Foreigner?'

'Yes, an American. Jake.'

'Well, why didn't you say? The American's due here today. Guest of the Government. Table for six. Three duck. Arriving any minute.'

Fang craned his gullet into an unnaturally speedy swallow. 'I'd better be off,' he choked.

'Why so soon?'

'Well, there was a bit of an incident in the classroom today.'

'What sort of incident?'

'I shouted something out but I thought I was shouting to myself.'

'What *do* you mean? You really are the old man's grandson!'

Yes, I am pretty weird, I suppose. But again Fang saw no point in elaborating further. It had been incomprehensible incontinence on his part and repeated telling just made it worse.

'Sit a while longer anyway. They won't come in here, that's for sure. Tell me about your sister. Still as beautiful as ever? They say she's finally going to leave us.'

And so Fang brought the kindly old duck-roaster up to date with Fu and Mother and everyone on the alley. Fen's family had been one of the first to be moved out into a modern block. He claimed it wasn't the same, which Fang thought obvious enough: it could only be better.

When a waiter came in to say the foreigner and his cortège were arriving, Fang settled himself obliquely behind a hatch to observe the procession anew. It wound round the central table and hovered about the chairs. How surprising they hadn't taken a private room. Perhaps foreigners don't like that sort of thing. But what must Jake be making of the absurd amount of pre-prandial fuss? What an advantage not to be able to understand a word of the pompous belly-aching! Jake took his seat between the political commissar – Spiritual Pollution expert – and Interpreter Li. Place of honour!

Jake immediately reached for his glass of beer and drank. The hosts looked at each other in surprise and then raised their own glasses; but as they began to drink Jake put his glass down and they therefore had to do the same; then the Government Man who had opened the classroom ceremony stood up to propose a toast and they emptied their glasses in solemn unison – all except Jake who was obviously no longer thirsty; they gently insisted he down the warm beer with which the rodent had refilled his glass.

'Drink it all, please drink it all,' they gurgled and Jake had to oblige. Then the Director nipped the top off another bottle with his prominent incisors and filled Jake's glass to the brim again.

Qiao shot a couple of wary glances at his superiors and then chose his moment for another toast in Chinese: 'On behalf of the classmates I would like to thank and thank again the Yanzhou Municipal Government for arranging the course and thank Ja Ke Ell Yot for making such a long and glorious voyage to speed our improvement and thereby aid China's modernisation programme.'

He quickly translated for Jake, who nodded foolishly and suppressed a belch; then with sudden aplomb, Class Monitor cried, 'Down the hatch!', a phrase Fang had taught him at the last English Corner.

The Chinese finished in three or four seconds, leaving Jake stranded mid-glass, pretending to drink but really snorting for air. When eventually he surfaced and tried to lower his glass to the table, it was refuelled in mid-air. Jake protested and then had to raise a hand to cover his mouth once more.

Buoyed up by the success of his toast, Qiao was now being desperately charming; Fang could hear nothing against the percussion of duck preparation behind him, but it seemed that Qiao was trying to speak English from the expectant way he kept looking at Jake and laughing enough for all of them for all time. Rice wine was called for and Fang's bile boiled.

He quickly thanked Old Fen and remounted his bicycle in an even worse temper. Now he felt sick too and his stomach argued as he strained up the hill. He thought he could just afford to miss another half an hour's work, so he passed the factory's gates and covered the short distance home. But any hope of quiet duck digestion there was thwarted by the great commotion he heard from the end of the alley and saw as he entered their yard.

Mother was dragging Grandfather towards the door and they were both screaming like lunatics.

'Why? Why on earth?'

'Everybody does it! The boy does it! The neighbours do it! Why shouldn't I?'

'The young people did it once – but not now!'

'I'm younger than you think, girl! I can make a point too you know!'

'It'll kill you, this wandering!'

'Better than the death I'm living in here!'

'Don't talk like that, Father! Bad talk!'

Fang stole behind the frantic old man and managed to

release his right claw from the front-door frame; together they eased him inside where he gave himself up to a hawking bout of such ferocity that they had to shut the door and return to the yard to make each other heard.

It seemed that Mother had been coming back from the morning's teaching when she had seen Grandfather throw himself in front of one of the sand lorries as it swung out of People's Cement. Fortunately for him, both the driver and the lorry were in good enough repair to stop – a rare enough coincidence even under the new regime – and Mother had personally pulled him out from beneath the front bumper. Grandfather had clearly decided, a fortnight too late, to add his tiny weight to the protest.

Fang could hardly restrain his admiration and even felt flattered by the old axeman's support. But the matter could hardly end here. The driver would have reported the incident already and Mother said the gatekeeper who had come rushing out would probably be able to identify Grandfather; she was sure the instant crowd of onlookers would have helped with that.

He was shouting in his bedroom, reminding them of one of his favourite proverbs: If a family has an old person in it, that family truly possesses a jewel. It was only a matter of time before Fang himself was involved in this affair. He decided that he could not afford to be absent any longer and, with duck-fat belly and leaden heart, he freewheeled back down to People's Cement.

nine

Fang was determined to confront Qiao but could not catch him at home or office over the next few days; he even missed English Corner. Every time Fang was told he was out he fought to suppress the obvious conclusion that Qiao was 'in' where it counted.

He thought he would kill time with a revival of his desultory love affair. Miss Ping's complete ignorance of English, which had always been her chief (her only?) deficiency, now added to her ever more disturbing physical charms. Since the mere thought of a gerund or English idiom was giving Fang bronchial spasms, Miss Ping would serve to keep his mind off the frustration. But Fang was not about to get too involved. He had to be free to rush into the Jake-breach whenever the moment came.

Thus he reasoned as the week began and he was not surprised when on Monday evening his renewed attentions were welcomed by the adoring Ping: that was right and proper. But her unspoken call for some response from him was problematic. While he had really been unable to muster any passion back in the summer, he was now struggling to master it. But this was his task. The more she tempted him to unleash that bull, the tighter he would knot himself. Master it he must.

On the surface, the week seemed to be passing without much danger. They spent some time in Moon Park, where they were photographed against three metres of a chipboard Great Wall; they went to the cinema (Fang's responses to her nuzzlings here were interrupted by the aisle attendant, angry about the popping of sunflower seeds in which Fang was simultaneously engaged); she led him around the department store, fondly pointing to her favourite glass vases and plastic blooms in the Interior Decor section. In short, they did everything a young couple could do, stepping out together in Yanzhou.

Several people saw them and it was especially distressing to

Fang that Xin had witnessed the cinema episode. Fu spotted them in the park. But there was still not enough evidence (Fang congratulated himself on this) to call it a 'hitch' and his true feelings remained hidden from everyone, including Miss Ping. Yes, they reached Friday without a hitch.

However, in tying down Passion, Fang had failed to keep Guilt covered and that monster now began to stir. Although he had no practical idea how to proceed with the relationship, Fang felt some development, some escalation, was expected of him – by Mother, by his more perceptive friends and, above all, by the wretched Miss Ping. The English phrase nicely expressed this girl problem: you give them some inches and they want a mile – the Golden Mile, the dash from virginity. But that was simply out of the question now, in his present mercurial condition; he had too much on. Master it.

As he agonised, Miss Ping forced the issue by suddenly shedding her shyness (mere coyness, in fact), evidently deciding that this was the best way to get above illegal cinema snacks in Fang's pecking order. And she was shapely. The friendship she offered threatened to become carnal at any time. By Saturday Fang was beginning to fear that the cow was actually about to charge the bull.

He rationalised desperately: sex was merely the fragrant atrium from which he would be propelled into the prison of marriage, soon shackled to a mewling Little Fang of his own and locked in Yanzhou for ever more. There was no sex without strings – without chains – and that threatened his ambition. Ambition you had to keep pure and keen and at all costs free.

On Sunday afternoon he managed to uncouple himself, although her physical resistance to his departure almost undid all the week's intense effort. For now it was her musky perfume as she said goodbye which set a manikin in fluffy pixie boots darting about on his lower belly, leaving him with a most uncomfortable ache.

He held her off with the prospect of one of Qiao's long-promised tickets for the flax-mill dance party on 17 January. A free agent once more, he hurried down to English Corner that afternoon. To his relief Qiao was at home at last.

'Long time no see,' said Fang nonchalantly in English as the door opened. He was pleased to see Qiao grappling with the meaning of the slick new phrase, a process only just too fast to be called laborious.

'I have so much things to tell you actually, Frank.'

'Yes, I should think you have. Mutual confidence is the pillar of friendship as the Chinese like to say . . .'

'Yes, yes, I know. I've been – out of touch – but actually there's been so many activities and installations to organise.'

'Oh yes?'

'Happy Christmas, Frank! Today we have held Happy Christmas Party – for Jake.'

Fang's cool tone suddenly evaporated. 'Was it fun?' he spat.

'Very fun actually since you ask. Interpreter Li asked me to learn English Hymn "Good King Wenceslas" especially. Do you know it?'

'No. Who else was there?'

'Well, there was me and Interpreter Li . . .'

'Who *else*, Qiao?'

'Keep your hairs on! Just some Government Men, perhaps you don't know them. Just to stop Ja Ke – Jake – missing his home on his important day.'

'I see. Nice. And what about these "installations"?'

'Well, Jake is actually moving his house from the Dong Lan Hotel.'

'Actually?' 'Actually' was Qiao's new English word. Pathetic.

'Really. The Government is renting him to a small apartment in the official reception building on Bright Future Street and we are organising. Furniture and – how do you say? – creature comforts. And his clothes too. We have helped him to buy clothes.' Qiao grinned; Fang's lips began to purse but he pulled them back into line.

'I see,' he said.

'I was wanting to ask you to help us so you could become familiar with Jake . . .'

'Meet him, do you mean?'

'Well, you have meeted – met – him already, haven't you? That is the problem actually. Hard to explain in English. When I suggested you to Interpreter Li and some other officials they remembered your shoutings in the class . . .'

Black mark.

'. . . and Interpreter Li said you could not be relied upon with the foreigner.'

'And what did Jake say?'

'Oh, he just laugh after at lunch – we had lunch actually after the ceremony. He has never spoken about it again but then he doesn't speak about much things at all. Shy.'

Fang was a little heartened by this last comment: clearly Qiao and Jake were not getting on like flaming houses.

'Where is he now, Charlie?'

'In apartment flat. I think he is preparing for first class.'

'Don't you know?'

'I paid visit nearly one hour ago before,' Qiao crashed on through the mockery, 'and there was no answering. I looked through the hole-key and saw him on the desk.'

'On the desk?'

'Under . . . I mean at!'

'Was he ignoring you?'

'Please?'

'Pretending not to hear you, Charlie?'

'Oh no, he didn't hear. They have very, very good concentration, Westerners, you see. It's very dangerous to disturb them when they're like this.'

Fang was feeling better and better, pleased too that Qiao was still speaking in the ingenuous, respectful manner he always used when addressing him in English (hard to be otherwise with that syntax, of course). But wanting now to probe a bit deeper, Fang suggested they speak Mandarin.

'There is something I must tell you, as a friend, Qiao.'

'What's that?'

'About the way you've got yourself involved with Jake and Interpreter Li and all the Government Men.'

'Yes? What about it?'

'Well, let's just say it's not going down very well with the rest of us.' (Actually, Fang had been dismayed by how little anyone else had noticed the grotesque fawning.)

'Oh yes? And just who exactly are you talking about, Little Fang?'

'I'm not going to get into a list of names.'

'And why not? I'd like to know who!'

'It's such a general feeling, Qiao, so widespread. People always get suspicious when someone starts spending a lot of time with those Party guys. You must know that?'

'What do you mean?'

'These new friends of yours – they won't do you any good. "An official for one lifetime has seven rebirths as a beggar", remember?'

'Listen Fang, I don't know what you're trying to say but I think you should be able to understand that since I have risen to the position of Class Monitor I must take the responsibilities it brings . . .'

'Ah yes – Class Monitor. That *was* a lucky break.'

Qiao was beginning to shake: a regrettable loss of cool, but provided he didn't turn violent it could still prove useful.

'Right, I'll make you clear about one thing, Fang, since you seem to be so screwed up: I've got my reasons for all this.'

'And what might they be?'

'Never you mind. That's all I'm going to say. Just don't think I'm touting for a few cheap pluses from the bureaucrats.'

'Well, I'm afraid that's just what I – and everyone else – imagine because that's precisely what you are after! What else could it be, Honourable Class Monitor?'

'Don't push me, Fang. I've nothing more to say.'

But Fang had already seen what Grandfather might have called a bat's squeak of a chance . . .

'I know what it's all about, Qiao. You just want to keep all your back-door hinges oiled, don't you? It's swung open for you nicely so far at your old man's bidding, but now you feel, quite commendably, that you've got to make your own going. And you're well placed, I grant you that: Foreign Trade, girlfriend's family big in Animal By-Products, a fairish degree, a certain facility with English—'

'Watch it, Little Fang, before I smash you—'

'Wait – we can get on to that in a minute but I haven't finished talking yet. You've seen a new way to advance yourself: perform well as trusted sidekick to Interpreter Li and you will move up into the smiling front line of the Grand Yanzhou Reception Committee for Foreign Business Friends. Little Qiao welcomes you to Yanzhou!'

Fang leapt into a sort of war dance, whooping triumphantly and sitting down again only when Qiao seemed to have curbed his most passionate anger.

'Have you quite finished?'

'Yes, and I'm quite right too, aren't I?'

'Shut up, Fang. Let me speak now. I'm so sick of this that I'm going to tell you something to clear the picture. Perhaps I owe it to you. But don't tell anyone else!'

Fang settled deeper into his chair.

'You're wrong about my motives. Three months ago I got some interesting information through certain channels from Landu. The Trade Bureau there has just done a cultural exchange deal with America. We hire some of their teachers for a year and they give us scholarships to study in the US.'

'Scholarships! How many?' It was Fang's turn to shake.

'Three for the first year.'

'Is this what Jake's arrival is all about?'

'No, no, Little Fang. Jake's come as an individual teacher. And he is from Delaware. Next year's teachers and the scholarships have been offered by another state.'

'But they're bound to go to Landu people.'

'They can't! Part of the deal is that only one can go to Landu – the other two have to go to other places in the province.'

'Eighty million people to choose from!'

'But how many English-speakers? Eh?' Qiao grinned. 'Half of them can't even read or write their own language!'

'And so you're entering, are you?' coaxed Fang.

'Have entered actually, but don't tell anyone!'

Fang thought he would soon need to spit. 'When was the closing date for entries then?' he murmured, moving towards the window and praying that he was not talking history already.

'Tuesday, this Tuesday coming.'

Fang's relief was throttled immediately. He gripped his throat, flung up the window and shot a jet of mucus into the yard seven floors below. Two days! The postal service would never do that. How could he possibly enter on time?

'Congratulations,' he managed, turning round to face Qiao again. 'This certainly is a bit of news!'

'Top secret!'

'Of course. You must stand a pretty good chance, don't you?'

'Well, I think so. You're about the only person under the age limit round here who could have posed me a threat and . . .' He looked suddenly confused.

'And?'

'And, well, I knew you wouldn't be interested – otherwise of course I would have told you weeks ago.'

'Is that why you didn't?' Fang was holding the upper hand in Mandarin for once. He remained cool: his future depended on it.

'I thought you might . . . you know, laugh at me for entering! You can be quite superior about your English. Besides, I hardly thought it was your sort of thing. You've never seriously mentioned anything about wanting to go abroad – and you've got your mother to look after, and now you're into sand . . .' Qiao seemed to be gaining confidence in this explanation. 'No, Fang, I suppose I've always realised your love of English was academic – a love of the language itself – and, thanks in part to you, I have come to realise how beautiful it is. I will always be grateful.' He might almost have added that he would send him a postcard from Disneyland.

Fang wasn't quite sure what he was hearing. Could Qiao really be speaking the truth or was he turning black into white? Was such dewy-eyed complacency possible? Could it never have occurred to him not only that Fang would chop off limbs and gouge out organs in order to get abroad but that also, on his English ability, he stood by far the better chance of getting a scholarship?

Fang had never publicised his dream even at English Corner but could he have covered it up so effectively that Qiao believed he had no interest at all in this opportunity? Qiao was brighter than that. Wasn't he?

But this thinking was a waste of precious time: Fang steeled himself to the task of getting the rules of application out of the hallucinating Qiao without alerting him to a rival challenge.

'So, I suppose you had to write an essay or something . . .'

'Yes, that's all – and a couple of references.'

'How did you hear about it? I'm amazed you didn't tell me, you dark old horse you!'

'Father has friends in Landu. One of them passed it on.'

'Who checked your essay?'

'Interpreter Li looked it over, actually.'

'So he knows about the scholarship too?'

'Yes.'

'And did he write one of your references?'

'Yes.'

At least Qiao still had the decency to look a little sheepish now about this.

'And the other? The Mayor I suppose!'

When Qiao nodded again Fang had to look away to recompose himself. These connections ran everywhere, a sort of provincial grid of massive power. With this backing, Qiao's challenge had to be good, if not unbeatable, no matter what sort of a mess he had made of the application essay.

'So,' Fang continued, 'you packed that little lot up and sent it to . . .' A delicate inflexion was enough to lead Qiao off the prickly subject of his personal relations with the Mayor.

'To the Landu Provincial People's Government – a Mr Chen Ge in the Trade Bureau.'

'Not the Chen Ge who was in government here for a time?'

'I believe so – but I don't know him at all.' Qiao smiled with relief.

'Well, you seem nicely set up.' Qiao had to be stupid, not scheming. He had hopped into Fang's trap with both puds. But was he just playing the possum?

'Good luck! When do you hear?'

'I should think they'll decide by the end of April or May – to give them time to get through the formalities before the start of the academic year.'

'Which university is it, Qiao?'

'Somewhere near Shi Cargo. Jake's heard of it.'

'So he knows about all this too, does he?'

'Oh yes, I've told Jake. But he's nothing to do with the scheme. I just told him as a friend.'

'I see. You really are getting on in the international community, aren't you?' said Fang. 'That's great. Happy, happy Christmas!'

Qiao hit the switch and, for the first time ever, Fang delighted in the BBC's persistent failure to provide them with a decent service – even on this festival day. The radiogram's rasping and retching, interspersed with some spits from Radio Moscow, gave him the excuse he needed to leave.

Their friendship was still intact and Fang's plans were already laid. Now he needed every minute before Tuesday to carry them out.

ten

My humbly applying for your scholarship is a step along in my ambition to internationally promote the fortunes of the Motherland. If I was to get selection it would be not only as recognition of my diligent grammatical study hours but, infinitly more important for me, an opportunity for the gathering of more and more information about the West in order to speed up the glorious Four Modernisations. In a word, it would be a mean to an end.

Fang looked up at his reflection in Fu's dressing-table mirror and ran a hand back through the razed spikes. The English syntax was flowing nicely but what should he put next? He wanted to be able to address specifics but he didn't have any.

It was an impressive start anyway. The opening sentence had a gerund and 'the Motherland' – a persuasive combination; he was happy too with the complex second sentence which he had closed just as it threatened to slither out of control; in contrast, the 'mean to an end' part was creditably succinct. It supplied the higher concept which he wanted to lodge in the bureaucratic mind.

He felt quite confident Qiao had not withheld any details in his confession that afternoon. Quite confident. If the Trade Bureau in Landu was behind it, then the application should have this sort of commercial bent. But, then again, the PLA owned theatres and restaurants in Peking, didn't they? You could never be sure who was behind that. These were his two biggest problems: Qiao and China.

I am not sharing my contemporarys' belief that the West is a paradise. I am not dreaming to indulge in excesses which are available freely there. But, without overblowing my trumpet, I must say to you that I have also escaped the predjudice of the recent Chinese history.

Although our Chairman Mao was a great leader, he make mistakes as we all now know. The cutting off of China from the rest of the world was grevious diservice. I know he had his reasons but the damage he done by isolating the Motherland during the early vital era of man's greatest ever technological revolution has been incalculatable. It was sad that when our great leader was old and his brain not so fresh the West was exploring the new bright world of micro-chipping. A sad coincidence indeed.

But as we Chinese say, 'one generation opens the road upon which another generation travels'. Our generation must not be weepy. We must make up for lost time by marching out into that white heat and bring back all we can. The gathering of information has been the key in the success of our Japanese rivalls: they have managed to perfect the ideas they plucked from the Western plum tree for free. They call it 'selling the West to the West'.

Although it is hard for us we must be humble enough to learn from the Japanese how to learn from the West and then, in time, all peoples will have to acknowledge the supremmacy of the Middle Kingdom.

At the end of the second rewrite Fang glanced at his watch. It was past midnight! He was cold. It was a treat to have lost track of time. A new sensation. He, a citizen of Yanzhou, had started running and then jumping a little along the potholed runway and then he had bumped up into the air. Yes, Yanzhou time had actually carried him awhile; together they had flown.

But it was the essay which had really lifted him. A fulsome extension of his occasional patriotic thoughts, the final version contrived to heap all blame on to Mao, announcing the author's huge dissatisfaction within the currently permitted framework of criticism.

He hoped to cast suspicion on his rivals' motives by frankly discussing the 'occidental paradise' view and then rejecting it himself. Nor would he be inveigled into admitting his passion, his dream, if he were called for interview. No, he had been impressed by how easily the appropriate words had found their place.

Earlier that evening he had visited his former middle-school teacher, a timid man who had once let slip a slight admiration for his precocious English skills. Fang had felt he might produce a reference – nothing flashy, but good enough. The teacher had agreed and Fang was to collect it tomorrow.

As he waited now for his coursing adrenalin to permit sleep, he felt pleased with the progress. But there was a way to go yet.

The first two hours of the working week were pleasantly spent, leafing through the company's enormous, pre-Liberation English–Chinese, Chinese–English dictionary. To his delight, Fang had been sidelined from invoicing for some translation work. This had yet to materialise but, if challenged, Fang claimed he was warming up for the English cement manuals which Manager Sun had said he would want him to explain.

Moussaka, mousaka: he doubted whether that would ever come in handy but, just as he was thinking about shutting the book, Fang hit lucky with fellatio. The dictionary was like that, always springing enough surprises to keep you interested. Another word he carefully transcribed into his pocketbook was twerp which joined the morning's crop of floccinaucinihilipilification, floosie, cynic, cleavage and logodaedaly.

Then, as the office clock approached eleven, Fang said he had business in town and – to employ another of the morning's new words – he mizzled off. Fortunately his immediate boss had already left for a banquet-meeting and no one demurred at Fang's departure.

Within five minutes he had parked the Pigeon outside the department store and run up the staircase to the offices on the top floor. Relieved to discover that Old Liu was in, he asked for his name to be announced.

Fang had already outlined the scholarship scheme to Mother (although he had skimped on the sketchy details and so guided her clue-groping that she clearly thought he was trying to get on to some fertiliser course at Landu Agricultural College). He had then had to endure the perennial speculation as to when Son was going to follow Daughter's example and settle down. But Mother was not so blimpish as to refuse to consider his need for a second reference, and Old Liu had been her suggestion.

Fang sipped his tea and stared at a high-relief felt picture of a heron winging over some purple mountains with a fringe of dust along its neck.

How odd to meet Old Liu again! Once an admirer of

Mother's, he had not been mentioned at home for years. Fang had been quick to see the sense in her suggestion because Old Liu now had quite a reputation as manager of this huge store and, even by Qiao's mighty standards of traction, he had some pull in Yanzhou. Fang only hoped he would show that benevolence which he felt had been one of the strongest forces in his childhood. He hoped too that shrewd 'uncle' would not press him too much on details because he was eager to keep the scholarship bid secret against the horrid possibility of failing to get it – and against the more alarming contingency of his not even managing to apply for it.

He had just finished his tea when Old Liu emerged and tugged him into his office with exclamations of welcome.

'And how's your mother?' he asked almost immediately. His expression suggested the question was still important.

'Very well, busy, healthy. She sends her respectful best wishes, Old Liu.'

'Good, that's good.' He interlocked his fingers and after pondering them a while he looked up. 'And what can I do for you, Little Fang?'

The handsome Liu, wearing a Western-style suit still unusual for men of his high rank, listened to the details. He tipped back in the chair, passed his hands through his silver hair and flicked his nose: Fang remembered each of these traits and found them strangely encouraging.

Five years ago Old Liu's visits to the alley had suddenly ceased. Grandfather had been the only one to dare mention him to Mother since and even he soon found it was not advisable. Liu, on the other hand, had been less discreet and by his open grief he had confirmed the rumour that she had refused his offer of marriage. Mother had become famous as 'the woman who turned down Manager Liu' and had thus aroused jealousy long before the wool success.

Fang soon finished talking – he covered everything except the American angle – and then had to face a long silence and a surprisingly gormless stare from Liu. Had Mother misjudged him hideously? Eventually Liu pulled a sheet of paper from his desk drawer, formed a few characters across the middle and, under his carefully written signature, placed the imprint of his personal chop. He pushed the paper towards Fang who read this sentence: The past is as clear as a mirror and the future as dark as lacquer but you have the power to turn the future gold for the son of Little Fang.

Fang looked up. Old Liu was grinning so he grinned too.

'But who do I give it to?'

'Haven't I written his name? Silly me! Give it back here.' He added two more characters to the top left-hand corner.

'Chen Ge!' Fang exclaimed. 'So you know him?'

'Know him! We were together during the Cultural – with your father too. He admired him as much as I did – and owed him a geat deal.'

Never had Mao's lunacy, his ten-year power-binge, seemed sweeter. It was divine intervention, that's what it was. But had Mother known about this three-way friendship all along? The Statue of Liberty sprang up on the horizon and Qiao was out of sight.

'Er, perhaps I shouldn't be seeing this . . .'

'Of course you shouldn't. Give it back at once.' Old Liu smiled and sealed the paper in one of his store's rough brown envelopes. 'But I thought you'd be interested to know.'

'It's . . . it's wonderful. I can't thank you enough . . . Uncle. May I call you that?'

'I don't really think it is appropriate.' He led the suddenly smarting Fang to the door. 'But you can tell me one thing . . .'

'What, Old Liu?'

'It's America, this scholarship, isn't it?'

'Well – yes, it is actually but I don't want—'

'Relax, Little Fang. I understand. I'm a friend, remember? I just wanted to know for myself. You see, Chen Ge used to talk for hours about the USA. He had nearly got there himself on some medical exchange deal but 1966 stopped that. I'd heard he'd been trying to start something like this over the past few years but I'd no idea he'd managed it. Good luck! It's a very rare sort of opportunity for a provincial Chinese – but I suspect you're a pretty rare sort of provincial Chinese, eh?' Liu chucked him affectionately which was pleasantly embarrassing (a secretary saw) and Fang thrust the priceless 'reference' deep into his coat.

The air froze on his cheeks as he pedalled through the snow

to No. 2 Middle School where he bumped into Mother in the bicycle shed; she was leaving after the morning's classes.

'Well, Son?'

'He did it! He did it in style!' Fang tried to embrace her but she held him off with a quick smile and went away. He found his former English teacher eating melon seeds in the staffroom, a large cupboard, and just for form's sake collected his second reference – hardly necessary now! But, driving himself back up to People's Cement, he realised that if the next step were to fail, all would have been in vain.

Podgy Peng's special relationship with a corrupt assistant at the Yanzhou Friendship Store had recently become most important to his classmates and bounced him back to prominence. For as they graduated from the naïve meritocracy of schooling to a world in which gifts of a material kind counted for more, access to such things as imported cigarettes and thick bars of chocolate in blue wrappers marked Cadbury's became essential. Through this assistant, Podgy could provide the access.

Officially the store was used only by government men and their business visitors for they alone could get their hands on the Foreign Exchange Certificates required to buy the goods. Recently, however, Podgy had persuaded his ally to extend the store's 'friendship' to a few of the classmates and, accepting the decline of the Heavenly Tinned gatehouse, he had stepped into the vanguard of Yanzhou's spiv culture. The Friendship Store was his new power base.

And there Fang had gone for a carton of Marlboro. The only problem had been the enormous expense, made greater still by Podgy's squeeze: a bar of what he called 'CDM'. (Ever slothful, the fat man delighted in his witty abbreviation: 'The only English I ever want to know!' he said. He had already guzzled so much Cadbury's Dairy Milk that his figure was becoming absurd. Bicycling was barely possible and at times he was too clogged to speak.)

Back at the office, Fang was obliged to deal with some invoices which the vile Wong had channelled on to his desk during the morning, but he soon got a chance to slip down to the compound's garage. He was apprehensive about this visit

– into the beastly den – and he feared an especially foul reception in the driver's mess where he would have to face the disembodied heads which had been scowling down at him from cabs for years.

But the timing was fortunate. There was just one man, legs and all, in the filthy canteen.

'Hello, comrade.'

The comrade grunted.

'I'm from accounts,' said Fang, trying cheerfully to establish their brotherhood. But the comrade (perhaps he would prefer 'mister') seemed more interested in his cigarette. 'I've come to find out about lorries to Landu.'

'Haven't you got a fucking timetable up there?' The comrade could speak.

'I couldn't find one.'

'Bloody typical.'

Silence.

'So, er, would there be one down here?'

'Could be.'

'Could be, er, where?'

'Right behind you.'

'Thanks, mister.'

The driver crushed his butt between his fingers and with a slow head action lifted some dilute phlegm into the ashtray before walking out into the lorry-hall, muttering as he went. Fang turned to look at the timetable and soon discovered that there was a load of cement or sand or something going out to Landu that evening.

His informant had joined a group of fellow-drivers clustered around a roaring engine. Fang went over and tapped him on the shoulder. He snarled something inaudible but just as he was turning back to the spark plugs, Fang let the top of his Marlboro carton peek out from under a lapel. With a yank of his head he beckoned the driver away.

They walked to the rear of the articulated vehicle, Fang discreetly wrenching one packet free from his supply.

'I've discovered there's a lorry to Landu this evening,' he said when they were out of sight. 'Number seventy-three.'

'Oh yeah?' The driver's eyes were fixed on Fang's chest where his heart beat furiously against the carton.

'I need to know who's driving that lorry.'

The comrade's insolent silence had to be broken so Fang gave up a packet. 'I've got to get something delivered,' he said with mounting desperation.

'Oh yeah?' He was looking again at Fang's heart.

'It's vital. Life or death.'

'Well then, son, you'd better keep 'em coming – the whole fucking carton, please. I'm your number seventy-three!'

Fang boggled. His luck had finally run out. The entire American campus did a back-flip in his head.

'How do I know you're telling the truth?' he said miserably.

The driver produced a filthy worksheet from his pocket and with an ugly thumb, which looked as if it had been caught in some machinery for several minutes earlier in his career, he indicated that he was indeed number seventy-three. Gratefully he gathered the Marlboro to him. 'For a carton of these smokes I'd bloody hop to Landu,' he said.

Fang explained the details of the errand. The driver did now show some attention and even volunteered the information that the relevant office was not far off his route through the huge city of Landu. But would this manky fellow honour his word and make the drop?

'What's your name, comrade?'

'Yang.'

'And when do you get back, Mr Yang?'

'Late tomorrow night. Come down here Wednesday morning if you want to check up on me – comrade!' He patted the bulge in his overalls and chuckled horribly. 'But there's one more condition,' he said.

Fang suddenly felt violent. Can't these greedy bandits ever get enough? What sort of a society is it that forces you to entrust your entire ambition to the likes of Yang?

'What?'

'Just keep that bloody grandad of yours locked up at five fifteen. I nearly did for him last time!'

Fang yelped with relief and clapped Yang rather too hard on the back. Even if 'brotherhood' could hardly be said to have been established, there was at least some hope of safe delivery. They parted.

Fang left work early, saying he was ill (he was in fact

suffering from nerve-induced diarrhoea) and went straight
home. There he played seven successive games of Chinese
chequers with Grandfather and only when he was sure Yang
would now be out on the open road did he lie back on the
under-heated bed and let out an exhausted fart.

eleven

Qiao nodded a greeting at the door-lady. Fang tried one too.

'Who's he?' she said, tensing in her box, pen poised over the little book of comings and goings which comprised her day's work – her life's work.

'He's with me.' Fang bristled under Class Monitor's protective wing, wanting to snap it off and pluck it. The suggestion that being 'with Qiao' somehow sanctioned him undermined Fang further. He was shaking like a bamboo switch anyway.

So the old hag's stout refusal to accept Qiao's bluffness provided a quick pleasure to temper the familiar outrage at having to register details wherever one went.

'I don't care who he's with, Little Qiao. Name? Work unit? Reason for visit?'

'Poor old sow,' said Qiao as they bounded up the stairs afterwards. 'It's the high point of her career having Jake living here. She's now in the front line, valiantly exposing herself to spiritual pollution in order to protect the people of Yanzhou. She sees herself as Jake's gaoler – she's told me that!'

'And how's she going to get polluted?'

'AIDS, capitalism, rape, robbery – that's the order of risk which she faces every day. Makes the sand factory look pretty tame, eh?'

'Doesn't AIDS come *after* rape?'

'She thinks she'll get it from touching the same door handle as Jake.'

The AIDS angle had never occurred to Fang before, but his jokey tone hardly faltered.

'So *we're* bound to die,' he quipped.

'Oh yes. Interpreter Li and I are servants of the state, doing our duty, just like her. But anyone actually wanting to visit Jake must be mad or suicidal. I'm surprised she didn't try to talk you out of it – she normally does.' So Qiao had been shipping in other visitors before his old Frank, had he?

Their steel-capped heels clicked down the corridor to Jake's door. Qiao knocked. A chair scraped backwards within and then, three heavy seconds later, the door opened. Jake 'at home'.

He smiled almost immediately and ushered them in with great ceremony, perhaps affecting the Chinese way; it really was extensive, verging on mockery.

'Delighted to see you, Keeow, and – er . . . ?'

'Fang. This is Little Fang.' So, battle was joined: in Qiao's voice-box the prefix 'Little', a widely used sign of familiarity, could mutate into something more indicative of withering scorn.

'You were sitting next to Keeow in class today, weren't you?' It was most interesting to hear what Jake's voice-box had done to Qiao's name.

'Come on, Little Fang – weren't you?' said Keeow, as if he were speaking to a retarded Korean.

'Yes, I were, I did,' mumbled Fang, his stomach vaulting with nerves. Let's hope this was the extent of his part in Jake's memory.

'Well, come on, sit down!'

Jake moved on Qiao, playfully pushing him back into one of the pair of chairs which were separated by a small white-wood table. Fang despised their easy manner with each other and Qiao's smarmy good humour in particular. He perched on the second chair and wished he had not persuaded Qiao to bring him along.

'Tea?'

They automatically waved their hands in frantic obstruction of this idea but Jake insisted. Fang was impressed that he had already picked up on this aspect of hospitality but, just as he was thinking he might cite it to the door-lady as evidence that the American could be tamed, Jake stopped his parrying with the teapot and put it down. He had not poured a drop.

'Okay, so no tea!' he said. A barbarian still! Of course they wanted tea. Fang felt relief, however, at being spared the risk of infection from a dirty mug. He must be vigilant – but he must *say* something.

'Well, what did you think of my first lesson? Do you reckon most people understood me?'

'Good! It was so very good. Talk more faster if you like,

next time,' Qiao gurgled. Fang decided it was not the moment to score cheap points on comparative adjectives. He would just endure Qiao's bilge-water.

'I hope you're right. But remember you are probably the best speaker. I'm not sure everyone else is with me.'

'Mmm . . .' Qiao nodded: point taken. 'Maybe right. I hadn't thought about it from another angle of view. But please remember, Jake, all of the students know they are very lucky to have this opportunity of a lifetime. They are eager to benefit from it with devoted study.'

Fang was sure Jake wasn't impressed by this sort of government-brochure pap and he decided to risk a little speech.

'Everyone enjoyed your class,' he said, determinedly interrupting Qiao, 'but I'm afraid half of them understood very little indeed.' Qiao started in horror.

'It's not just that we are slow getting used to your accent but also very few of us have the fluency you might taking for granted.' Fang concentrated fiercely on his BBC enunciation and it seemed to be working on Jake who said he appreciated the point. It had been made quite clear that morning during a chaotic dictation about the difficulties of using chopsticks.

'Did you write that yourself?' Fang asked quickly, hoping to keep Little Keeow right out of the conversation.

'Yes, I did actually.' Jake seemed flattered. 'True story too. Dropped it right down my shirt!'

'The fish head?' said Qiao. Yes, well done – of course we're talking about the fish head.

'But it didn't really slip through to the floor,' Jake went on, 'and the waitress didn't really skid on it.'

This piece of narrative licence had provided some histrionics on and off the podium as Jake demonstrated the riot of his first meal in the Motherland. It had made for the most action-packed dictation ever. Even those who managed to preserve only the odd conjunction or definite article on their pages seemed to have followed the story judging from the shrieks of laughter. (Fang had also caught some subversive tittering from the hotel girls: 'Red-faced hideosity! Big-nosed devil!')

'I was so concerned about the different standards that I spoke to Li about splitting the class.'

'Oh yes. What is the results?' said Qiao.

'He telephoned just before you came,' (So Jake's got one of those, has he?) 'and told me the Director said it's no go.'

'Please? No go?'

'Not possible.'

Relieved that it was Qiao who had once again exposed his ignorance, Fang made a mental note of this curious use of the verb to go.

'That is characteristic of the management,' said Fang. 'I am also sure he told you, "The weaker students must work harder to catch up and the stronger ones must aid them in their struggle."'

'Well, yes – that's exactly what he did say, Fang.' His name sounded very fine on American lips. 'So I thought next lesson I would pair off each of the good students with the bad – I don't mean bad – with the weaker ones.'

This disastrous idea had to be stopped. Fang was not about to be shackled to someone like Spotty Zhang for the next few months. He had had enough three-legged racing with Qiao. Now he wanted to pull ahead on his own.

'I'm afraid this would not work at all, Jake.' Another shiver from Qiao. 'You must excuse me but I fear this will waste our invaluable time with you.' Qiao now looked appalled – especially since he never could remember the meaning of invaluable. 'We will labour to raise the weaker classmates' level in our own time but with you we must – how do you say? – keep up the pace.'

'That's very interesting, Fang. You speak well too – a rival for you, Keeow! I must admit I would prefer to go along faster. What do you think, Class Monitor?' But Qiao's leadership qualities appeared to have left him: he could only manage a nod, so choked did he seem by Fang's impertinence.

'Many of us were also very relieved', continued Fang, 'that you did not mention any pacifically – ha, sorry, *specifically* – Business English. The graduates really feel we can benefit much more from your general approach – idioms, proverbs and even maybe some slang.'

'I'm glad to hear you say that too, Fang. You know my heart sank when I heard the Director mention Business English in that opening speech. It was the first I'd heard of the idea.

Although I'm an American, I'm not interested in business. I guess he just said it to make the course sound better to the other officials — but you won't be getting much Business English out of me!'

Fang looked across at the beleaguered Qiao and realised that he could now afford to retire. Victory had been complete.

'I must go now, Jake. Duty calls — isn't that what you say?'

He rose and let Jake usher him to the door. Qiao remained slumped. The tongue is like a sharp knife: it kills without drawing blood.

'Perhaps, Jake, we could do some work on gerunds next class. They're particular favourites of mine.'

Jake suddenly looked rather unsettled himself. 'Sure,' he said.

'Are you interested to learn Chinese, Jake?' Fang leaned casually against the door frame and he spoke softly to exclude Qiao.

'I am, yes.'

'Well, we must fixing up some lessons. I teach you, one at one?'

'Great — great idea, Fang, thanks!'

'First lesson is pronouncing the name of our Honourable Class Monitor.'

'You mean Keeow?'

'No, like "chow".'

'Really? The Italian farewell?' Jake turned to seek confirmation of this from Qiao, squirming with hot fury in his seat. But when he turned back to shake Fang's hand, his face held a new enlightenment.

'Wait a minute,' he suddenly shouted. 'It was you — at the opening ceremony the other day, wasn't it! I'm beginning to tell you guys apart! "Beautiful!"'

Qiao turned his brimming malice into laughter and it gushed. Fang hurried off, his triumph utterly poisoned. It was only when he saw the door-lady that he realised he had touched the American as well.

twelve

At home that night Fang tried to forget the visit to Bright Future Street and think instead of new ways to win favour and beat Qiao to the nirvana of Jake-friendship.

He was enjoying the calm and watery pork and cabbage stew, when Mother made her first full enquiry about the foreigner whose lair she knew Fang to have visited. Fu left at once, in protest at the conversation.

'On his desk, Son? What did he have on his desk?' (Her questions were very much possession-oriented.)

'I hardly had time to see.' But she knew her boy would have taken the opportunity, however brief, to cast a careful eye over the American habitat and Fang surprised himself with the extent of his nosiness and how easily he pulled the items out of his memory.

On the desk there was a folding photograph frame, a wonder blonde on one side (VOA's Chrissie could hardly be better) and a family group (with a dog!) on the other; a neat cassette-player and travelling speakers, Sony; tapes (probably the very latest Clayderman); some old books and pills (for AIDS?); clever letters which seemed to be envelopes as well and bore desirable stamps – one of which had already been plundered in transit, probably by those collector bandits at Peking central sorting-office; three glossy Christmas cards (such bright colours); and, stuck to the wall, a picture of a naked lady wantonly reclining (Jake had referred to her mysteriously as Renoir).

'Clothes?'

'No, Mother, absolutely none!'

'Ja Ke! What sort of clothes does Ja Ke have?'

'He didn't show me into his bedroom, Mother.' But Fang admitted to an interesting glimpse of backpack propped against the bed with variegated T-shirts (again such colours!) and some real jeans spilling out of its side.

'And what was he wearing?'

This was a good question. Having been caught out badly by the climate Jake had had to buy fast as the skies dumped days and nights of heavy snow on to Yanzhou. The result was the most grotesque winter line Fang had ever seen – as though Jake were trying to outdo the lowest sandman or the wildest pig-farmer.

Qiao had been party to many of these shopping trips, which had taken place in the pre-course days, but he was refusing to accept any blame and Fang was anyway unwilling to accord him much influence.

The first wodge of yuan (in Foreign Exchange Certificates, needless to say) had apparently gone on a black wool Mao jacket, a transaction responsible for the destruction of a full-length mirror and a shelf unit of ladies' pants which had given way under the pressure of Jake-watchers. Whatever the association, these jackets could look very smart when buttoned to the neck but, because the sleeves of this one failed to cover several inches of Jake's forearms, the overall effect was ridiculous.

Qiao said it had been the opposite problem with the coat which Fang had seen massed behind Jake's living-room door. The shop assistant had dug out an army greatcoat with turn-up cuffs and broad lapels, a design discontinued many years ago. This was no ordinary example but the very same coat which had attracted so much attention in the display window on the line's launch: then it had graced the one-and-a-half-lifesize wax Lei Feng, the government propaganda department's 'model' PLA soldier' whose beatific smile had provoked Fang's first-ever shudder of anti-establishment anger when he had seen it from Father's shoulders as a toddler. 'Learn from Comrade Lei Feng,' they chanted through kindergarten. It was Lei Feng's turn for a lesson, his turn to shudder, now that an heir had been found for his coat!

Qiao said Jake could hardly walk in the cocoon of sun-bleached padded khaki and that when the busy little assistant yanked down the cuffs – with two explosions of dust – only the Jake-feet and, of course, the nose were visible. Qiao had pleaded with him not to buy but Jake had refused to listen and his delight in the monstrous coat almost matched that of the assistant who had given up all hope of ever shifting it.

(With this sort of first-rate action going on in the department store, Fang had been counting shoppers and patrolling freezing streets!)

Mother was also fascinated to hear details of the dreadful pair of trousers Jake wore often. These too were Yanzhou-made and Qiao had again attended the purchase. Dissuasion – on the grounds that corduroy was 'peasant cloth' – had failed again and there had been the usual problem of size: in order to get them long enough in the leg, Jake had had to buy trousers of such gargantuan girth that Qiao had thought he was seeing confirmation of the current rumour that peasants were now so rich they were clothing the hind-quarters of their cows to boost milk production.

Once again Jake had been thrilled, and once again he had brought the house down. Crowds parted as he left the shop and then converged to catch verdicts from those instant cel-ebrities, the assistants who had served him. He was certainly aware of his box-office pull and if he did not actually play to the audience, he clearly enjoyed the adulation. Fang remem-bered Jake telling the class how he had inadvertently disrupted an entire kindergarten by walking past the window. The children and their awe-struck teachers had rushed out to follow him down the street.

But Jake stepped over from understated charm into shame-less provocation when he bought a bright pink artificial silk necktie 'to stop the Mao collar rubbing my capitalist neck'. Qiao had managed to persuade him that such an effeminate accessory – on top of the austere jacket and baggy corduroys – might offend his fans. Today at least Fang had seen no sign of the scarf and his long neck was now pink and sore rather than pink and silky.

'And his feet?'

'Boots, Mother, great big boots!'

Her excitement bubbled and burbled through the evening and interrupted Fang's scrutiny of CCTV's English service news bulletin which was now reaching Yanzhou twice a week. The world abroad was choking in the usual tear gas: Korean students hurled; Irish terrorists exploded; American activists demonstrated; American politicians adultered; Russians moaned; their ethnic groups revolted; Japanese tycoons re-

signed; and through First and Third Worlds alike disease
rampaged.

Mother wittered on, quite unconcerned with the Chinese
interpretation of the chaos. She was smoking by the time the
newscasters had returned to the Middle Kingdom (only her
fourth cigarette since the end of the Cultural) and Fang was
sure something substantial was snagging on her wise old
Chinese patience at last. But what?

Domestic news opened with squeals of delight about record
pig-iron statistics; then came footage about a new hair restorer
which was luring lucrative 'lotion tours' from Japan; and a
blizzard near Harbin had destroyed power lines and blocked
the main road. The newscaster added that seven children and
a teacher had died when a school's roof had collapsed in the
storm. He was into the sixth minute of an interview with a
train-driver who had been given a Second-Class Model Worker
Award for caving in the skull of a suspected bandit when Fang
turned the television off.

'What are you worried about, Mother?'

'Tell him, girl. Tell him and shut up. She's gone foreigner-
crazy, like you. HHHHhhhhhhhhrrrrrr-ccccccrrrr.' (Grandfather's spitting had been gathering force lately, ever since a
Public Security Bureau man had come round with an official
caution for his sand lorry demonstration.)

'I'll tell you. You see, Son, I've had an idea – a business
idea. But I'll need your help.'

'What do you want me to do?'

'Well, you know advertising is still under tight control and
the small business has no chance of a permit. I was thinking
we might make some use of this American friend of yours.'

'Beware all foreigners: they are silver-coated bullets . . .'

'Sssshh, Father, please!'

'How can I help, Mother?' Fang was surprised how instantly
protective he sounded.

'By getting him into a pair of my woolly socks! How high
are these great big boots of his?'

'Not high, just long, Mother. But how do you know he
needs any socks?'

Even as he spoke, Fang realised Jake would have no hesitation in adding these to his maverick wardrobe, especially if

they were multi-coloured which they probably would be. Worn over the bottoms of his corduroy trousers, they were bound to appeal to his sense of discreet flamboyance. And as an advertising campaign it was quite brilliant. How things have changed since Lei Feng's window-display days! Adorning Jake, Mother's wools would soon be catching every eye in Yanzhou. His Western cachet was enough to win over the young and she might even tap the middle-aged market. (When Fang had bumped into Old Liu the other day he had said there had already been a run on Mao jackets, sleeves shorter the better, and corduroy.)

'I'll ask, Mother, but I don't know how Jake'll take it.' He had to damp her enthusiasm somehow: she was smoking again. 'You and your business ideas!'

'She's a different person down there at market, I can tell you,' growled Grandfather.

'And how would you know about Sunday market, eh, Father?'

'You forget, girl, I used to get out a bit – before the bolts slid across . . .'

'And you'll get out again, if only you learn to behave.'

This was standard talk and it did not hold Fang for long. He went to bed and, under the covers with dictionary and torch, searched unsuccessfully for 'Molotov cocktail' many of which CCTV had said were being served up in Seoul. Could you get them in Peking?

thirteen

The next week's lessons disappointed Fang. Despite Jake's early pledge to keep things rolling along fast, he seemed either too conscientious to leave behind the hotel girls or too cautious to abandon the standard English textbooks provided by the institute. With their tales of esteemed Foreign Friends like Edgar Snow and Norman Bethune, tying Mao's boots and massaging his chest, these hardly stimulated. Anyway Fang had memorised them all at middle school.

Qiao, on the other hand, saw it as a valuable opportunity to 'polish' his skills (as well he might). The rest of the class seemed fully stretched and enraptured; Jake had pitched it right for the masses.

Fang resolved, therefore, to intensify his own extra-curricular campaign. Mother approved. Mother beseeched. She was now questioning Fang daily about Jake-contact and had unexpectedly provided invaluable practical help at the government reception block that Saturday afternoon. For there she had indulged the bored door-lady in an hour and a half's womanly chat while Fang was upstairs with Jake.

The next time he went to see Jake, Mother stuffed his coat with balls of wool — for she had discovered the door-lady's price — and Fang let them plop out into her box as she pretended to be taking his details. As the practice became established it worked out at about one medium-sized ball per half an hour's uninterrupted chat.

Now that Fang had unlimited access (though the wool was provided on condition the advertising campaign was under way in ten days), he had to consider how many visits Jake would tolerate. Daily? Twice daily? It was hard to gauge. He realised that Chinese blanket-style hospitality and attention ran the risk of stifling the American and that he might do better to find other approaches. At the other end of the scale there was the possibility that Jake enjoyed being alone from time to time – which Fang rejected immediately as wasteful and negative.

Plain speaking had worked with Jake before and Fang resolved to retain it against the government brochure-speak which Qiao and the others who dared visit were still using. And he was encouraged in this tactic by something Jake happened to pass on about Qiao: 'When we were on the road the other day he said I was a skilful cyclist! It was nice of him to say so but I've been cycling since I was five – longer than you guys for sure. Qiao was just being polite but I had to tell him we Americans are through with cycling by the time you start. He looked kind of pissed off.'

'He probably did not understand you, Jake,' Fang had cooed, noting that he must never ever risk a mention of bicycles himself.

Although it accorded with the spirit of his campaign, Fang could see that inviting Jake to have a bath with him was dangerous. It would certainly be the most earthy invitation he had had in Yanzhou yet and Jake naked was an alarming – but fascinating – prospect. How would he who had moved so easily through official roast duck banquets and other civic junketing cope with Yanzhou Public Wash-House No. 3?

Fang slept on the question for three nights running. He concluded – as he always knew he would – that he should issue the invitation and that Jake would certainly accept. Presumably, he reasoned, an American who chooses to set himself up in the middle of the Great Northern Waste expects a little adventure. Chinese hygiene might possibly come into that category. Certainly hygiene was an American hobby-horse: the stars of VOA's educational soap operas were forever going to the bathroom.

The decision was put beyond doubt by the door-lady, whose attitude to Jake had altered greatly: from that of gaoler/quarantine officer it was heading fast towards the maternal. Nowadays she applauded his every faltering step in the Chinese language, praised him fulsomely and chucked him under the chin without fear – the rash on his neck was certainly not AIDS. If she was still fierce with visitors it was now because she feared 'Ja Ke America' might be overdoing it.

One evening mid-week, as Fang disgorged his wares, she

confided in him her fear that Jake was not keeping himself clean. Her informants were claiming that he was never seen in the basin-room: since the showers did not operate in the winter, this was the building's only source of running water – freezing but plentiful; nor was he using many hot water thermoses: the floor-girls were always on the alert but they rarely scrambled at Jake's request. In short, he could not be washing.

Presenting his favourite wash-house to Jake and seeing it through his eyes, Fang suddenly found himself criticising it as never before. For now the building seemed as drab and dirty as any in this drab and dirty city. And he was embarrassed to note on one side a wooden construction which appeared to be propping it all up. Steam rose from another wall fracture. The Red Star over the entrance looked as though it had long since beamed all its perfect light down upon an ungrateful earth and the paint was peeling off the points.

They paid at the booth – at least Fang paid. He grandly waved aside Jake's fumbling offer of the required cents and, with a nod at the desk-man, he led the way inside.

At the changing-room entrance, he held aside the plastic tassels for Jake and watched amazement resurrect the drowsy occupants of a hundred day-beds; one by one they sat up as the foreign presence was felt like a breeze against their warm flesh; and they stared.

'Where's the opium?' Jake muttered what Fang supposed to be some sort of joke to ease the tension. He looked very nervous. Was he up to it?

The attendant found them a two-man alcove and shuffled off. Above their heads a string ran the length of the room, sagging with bath flannels. Fang reached up to pluck one, coloured dirty brown and beginning to crispen. Jake looked up doubtfully but the attendant returned with a much newer flannel from his special supply, and some tea.

Fang stripped to the waist and stuffed his clothes into a locker between their couches. Jake followed suit, revealing a surprisingly plump white belly. Too many steamed buns. Jake caught Fang's glance and sucked his stomach in, slapping it as he did so.

'Yes, getting a bit of a veranda over my toy-box already.'
Fang smiled indulgently but he was not making much of Jake's
nervy chatter. They tugged off their shoes and trousers, slipped
into the plastic sandals provided and were about to go through
when a fellow-bather stopped by their alcove stark naked. He
hawked, and spat on the floor. 'Ja Ke,' he said with a quick
smile and disappeared.

'Who was that, Jake?'

'No idea. More and more of them are doing it nowadays.
Perhaps I should keep my shades on.' That would really help.

As they set off for the bathroom happiness welled up inside
Fang and instinctively he put an arm round Jake's shoulder.
But Jake shook him off and hung back a couple of yards. 'Go
on, I'll follow,' he said testily, holding his de luxe flannel
demurely over his genitals. Fang was surprised by Jake's
sudden rudeness, and by his shyness. I thought Westerners
had great big ones. You should be proud of it.

The bathroom was dim, the sun sending only a few crepuscu-
lar rays through the blue-tinted glass of the angled ceiling.
Electric light beamed dully from each corner of the space
which was taken up by a pair of steaming plunge pools sunk
into the ground. The lying-out area around the edges was now
fully occupied by supine males, who trawled lazy limbs in
the water. The atmosphere was not exactly infernal, just
menacingly submarine. It was Little Fang's favourite place in
Yanzhou.

He lost Jake for a moment and then spotted him hanging
back near the doorway, still protecting his Western Pride,
staring at the pairs of males who rubbed and scraped each
other's bodies with their rented flannels.

'The dead skin,' coaxed Fang. 'It comes off easily like that
– after a soak.' He steered Jake towards the first of the tubs,
emptier of bathers than the other but brimming with scalding
water. Jake kicked off his sandals and, muttering something
about lobsters now, dangled a trembling foot into the bath.

He leapt back, screaming. The audience, five or six in the
immediate steam cloud and any number watching from the
blue shadows, whooped in delighted reply.

An introduction thus effected, they closed in, besieging Fang
with questions and, to his horror, prodding the American

buttocks. Jake was swatting them away and hopping round and round on the tiles, revealing a batch of red blotches on his back. (He must have had moxibustion treatment for flu at the hospital – a secret initiative of Qiao's?)

His buttocks were bright pink and, what with that dishevelled yellow hair, red cheeks, collar rash, hairy chest, bulging white belly and, yes, a satisfactorily large penis, Jake looked like nothing ever spotted before in this neck of the ocean. Fang could not resist staring with the rest of them as they beckoned him back to the edge, but when he slipped on a splotch of phlegm and crashed on to the tiles Fang marshalled three thrilled volunteers to carry Jake to the water. He himself had entered already (with a brief, experienced gasp) and now he tilted his head back to look at Jake upside-down. But from that angle he was all unhappy face and penis.

'Ja Ke! Ja Ke!' The others were now chanting encouragement and advising him which part of his fascinating body to lead with. He inched down with stentorian groans which became breathy squeals as the water covered his ribs; then he whinnied and then, finally, there was peace.

They lay there, quite still. Across the eye-level slick of body oils, which supported bits of dead skin and other human debris, they exchanged smiles, one wan, one proud. A great moment, perhaps Fang's proudest ever: a moment quite wrecked by the terrifying new thought that the fair Western skin would be marked for life by the scalding water.

Fang leapt out immediately. Jake followed (he needed no coaxing), his body a uniform scarlet and his mouth an ugly grimace. Angry certainly, but perhaps not seriously injured.

'Now we rub each other,' said Fang encouragingly. But Jake snapped out an absolute refusal – which meant that Fang had no one to rub off his own dead skin. He wondered if Jake had thought about this.

Men were splayed against the wall, their partners driving the flannels up and down backs, buttocks and thighs. Fang waved away several other offers to do Ja Ke and the bathers shrank back into the steam as the pair moved through to the shower-room. Now, surely, they must have these in America.

Soaping was a more individual activity though it could

usefully be combined – Fang noticed Jake noticing – with urinating into the open drain at the foot of the wall. Jake disguised his horror so poorly that Fang refrained from pissing as he soaped, although he had done it every week of his life and enjoyed it greatly. Face to the wall, Jake shampooed furiously and after a quick rinse he jammed his huge feet into a pair of plastics by the door to walk off without so much as a glance in Fang's direction. His host soon followed, reflecting that it had been the speediest bath since the Great Water Shortage of 1979, and found Jake swathed in towels, sipping cold tea in their alcove.

'Did you enjoying yourself?'

'I certainly did, Fang. Thanks for bringing me here.' Inscrutable Westerner.

'I thought perhaps you weren't enjoying it . . .'

'I did, Fang, I really did . . . Just scalded my, you know . . .'

'Your you know?'

'My dick, Fang, scalded my dick!'

Of course! That was it – his dick! Fang nodded frantically. How stupid he had been. Not a problem for us Chinese but Westerners are much more sensitive; they must be, with all the girlfriends (Chrissie, Renoir) they have to have before they marry. Dick! He might even be so good as to pass that on to Qiao. A synonym!

Jake was lying on his back – being very brave – when a slight figure smoking a cheroot appeared between their beds.

'I am doctor, amateur doctor,' he said in English.

Jake looked up.

'I give foreign friend massage?'

Fang could not exactly shoo him away because he was middle-aged and even in his nudity he looked distinguished. Besides, Jake's bath-tub gloom seemed to be lifting.

'How about doing my back?' he said and rolled over.

The amateur beamed and yanked away Jake's grey towels, throwing them at Fang, whose astonishment had pinned him to the other couch. Then the doctor made an agile upwards leap and settled himself carefully astraddle Jake's bottom. He worked energetically, straining his wiry frame into effortful massage of the broad, rather spotty shoulders. Fang was concerned that he could not monitor Jake's expression, his face being buried in the pillow, but the repeated grunts suggested continuing consent.

The doctor added to his own evident enjoyment by reminding himself of parts of the anatomy in English. As he yelped out each term he looked across for confirmation from Fang, whose gaze kept returning to the doctor's diminutive dick, flicking about as he rode the American.

'Soldiers!'

'Shoulders,' corrected Fang.

'Neck spinal colon!' A pair of loud clicks and a whimper from Jake.

'Ear lob?' He wrenched it hard.

'What the hell did he do that for?' Jake reared up from the bed and Fang caught a flash of flushed fury.

'Lobe,' said Fang, jumping to his feet. 'Perhaps he has had enough now . . .' But the doctor forced Jake back down and regained control of his bucking body. The massage proceeded.

When he eventually dismounted (with a loud thwack on Jake's 'bottucks?') he announced that he would be happy to do the other side: it was quite all right, he had the time, no, no problem. Jake remained mysteriously acquiescent and, with sudden fresh alarm, Fang thought of Grandfather's claim (once made with regard to the Peking Half-Man) that the vocal cords could be stunned with the right sort of punch. But Jake had already been flipped and amateur doctor was back in the saddle, yanking and clicking every joint in the arms, hands and fingers, as brisk as a butcher. (Fang was relieved to see now that Jake's dick was not the charred root he had feared: no redder than the rest of him actually.)

When he was not grunting, Jake retained a smile and objected only to an assault on his leg, saying he had once had water on the knee after a football accident. At last the doctor jumped off and settled himself on Fang's bed to light another cheroot. He looked well satisfied and his upper body shone with sweat.

'A real massage! Thanks, doc, you certainly know your—' he broke off to explore a track of blood blisters across his shoulders. The doctor apologised to Fang for his vigour, explaining that he had drunk a great deal at a midday banquet. Had Fang wished to translate this there would not have been

time, for the doctor suddenly moved on Jake, intent on another
paramedical programme – a body-scan apparently arranged
along the lines of water-divining.

He braced his outstretched fingers together in a V-formation
and sent them on hover patrol over the American landscape.
Above the stomach, they shook violently and the doctor in-
haled sharply. But then they calmed down and, to Fang's great
relief, passed over Jake's nether regions without hitting the
slightest thermal. There was a little turbulence over the left
knee but the fingers reached Jake's toes without further
tremors. As Fang translated the findings, amateur doctor
sought approval from Jake's eyes.

'He thinks you have the beginning of some serious stomach
disease but he is satisfied it will hold off for some years. And
he discovered some bad things around left knee.'

Jake frowned at this and Fang was aware of offence being
taken.

'Does he think he is some kind of wizard divining the state
of my health?'

'Maybe it is a form of *feng-shui*, Jake. I don't know.'

'*Feng-shui?*'

'Work out things on the principles of wind and water . . .'

'Are you trying to be funny, Fang?'

'Me? No!'

'Well, you can tell Doctor Spock here that I think he's a
fraud. There's nothing wrong with my gut and he knew about
the damn knee anyway.'

The doctor's face darkened at this peevish tone and he
gathered his pack of cheroots and lighter.

'Huh! I never even heared you!' he said and marched off.

fourteen

The sword was above his head again, Fang poised to unfurl its first, complicated descent of the morning, when Grandfather's hawk's eye pierced through the kitchen window and deep into his concentration.

Adapting himself to the conditions, Fang went into the dance with great, and largely phoney, enthusiasm. He lunged at the woodshed door, rose on his toes, turned and then, with something much more like conviction, he stabbed at the kitchen window.

Fang held this groiny pose for several difficult seconds and then, as if liberated by some glint of congratulation in the hawk's eye, set off again across the yard, alternately prancing and posing, until he had reached the moon-gate.

But this physical exertion was as nothing compared to the fierce mental struggle: for Fang's mind, which had to appear quite mesmerised by the spirit of the Blade, was actually only allowing him Jake-thoughts. Grandfather must suspect nothing.

As well as the *psychomachia*, he had to control the weapon so as to avoid fresh leg wounds if at all possible. It was a hell of a way to start the day.

He fell into the next sequence of steps, which took him back to the woodshed and set the chicken wittering. He posed, pranced, poised, stabbed, quivered, held himself in, let himself go – but most of all he wondered: wondered at the chances of the only person in Yanzhou who really sweated over Jake, who got absolutely involved, who marginalised everything else (even Fu! – she no longer featured in this English-speaking world of his), who pinned all his hopes on Jake, who (and this was most frightening) could hardly imagine life after Jake – he wondered at the chances of that person being him, Little Fang.

It was a sweet pain and it hurt. But how much more painful to deny it! To be chosen for the hardest course, that was his prickly fate and he would do it the honour of sticking to it no matter how many barbs it stuck in him. Nothing else for it; he despised the mediocrity of all other lots.

He downed the sword and collected Father's flail; his audience snapped away in disgust. Then, as the swingles whirled, Fang's thoughts did another awkward jive, taking him not to Father as usually happened now, but to Qiao.

Did he feel fate's prickles too? They had never been able to discuss Jake like adults so it was hard to know. But observing them together, Fang had concluded that there could be no real friendship between Jake and Qiao. They merely used each other: Jake used Qiao to communicate with the Government and Qiao used Jake as grammar guru, someone to salvage the syntax and feed his greed for prestige.

No, Qiao was driven by the scholarship, not by Jake. But some troublesome facts remained: Qiao was always involved in the pompous trips to factories which the Government arranged for Jake; it had indeed been Qiao who escorted Jake to the hospital for the flu treatment and, according to sources close to the acupuncturist, was still doing so as Jake was treated for some back problem; furthermore, he knew from the door-lady how much time Qiao was spending in Jake's room ('That Class Monitor! He brings such gifts – beer, biscuits, eggs. They must have grand fun up there!').

But unlike his unctuous rival, Fang was not interested in externals. He wanted something deeper and, in achieving such a relationship with such a diffident and unpredictable foreigner, he must expect some difficulties. Take the side effects for example: beginning to see Yanzhou through round eyes, he grew more alienated from his fellows – and the more stifling, the uglier, grew Yanzhou. But perhaps this was also his fate: to be goaded further and further into the wilderness with Jake alone at his side.

His mind obligingly provided another theatre of envy – Qiao's scholarship bid. For although Fang had screwed some confirmation of the 'drop' out of Lorryman Yang and although he was pretty complacent about his own application essay, he was always awed by thoughts of Qiao's 'back door'.

Fang swung the flail faster and faster and his thoughts spun him dangerously close to gloom. Then when he allowed the batons to slow – always the trickiest part of the exercise – he received a sharp blow across the back of the head. Why was life so predictable?

And of course bloody Grandfather just happened to be shuffling out to fetch wood at that moment. He said nothing, which infuriated Fang more than if he had cackled the cackle he was certainly suppressing. Fang hawked, spat and pumped his dumb-bells at the mangy old buzzard.

fifteen

He was very irritated to find Qiao when he called on Jake immediately after work on Monday evening. Did he ever do any of that foreign trade?

The door-lady had been difficult too because Fang had given her just one small ball – the last Mother had allowed him. (Still he balked at carrying out the scheme. Could he really ask Jake to be her walking advertising hoarding?)

He was also alarmed by their sudden silence – for so it seemed – as he entered Jake's flat. Had Qiao been outlining another jolly little excursion? And did he know about the bath?

Nowadays their few conversations were extremely tactical, neither wishing to give anything away; even English Corner had been suspended after ugly scenes. And in Jake's presence the thrust and parry became even more tense. Needling was too light by half; it had to be lunge and stab.

'Oh, have I interrupted you?' Fang managed to accompany this with a distorted smile which twisted further as he noticed the bag of apples Qiao had clearly just presented.

'Oh no, Little Fang,' said Qiao. 'We were just reviewing lesson.'

'Yes, Qiao was asking me to explain irony and sarcasm. Sit down, Fang. Tea?'

'No thanks.' Fang sank into the second easy chair. 'And which part of lesson was that, Qiao, Little Qiao?'

'No part exactly – I just make general enquiry.' Bloody show-off.

'And I was making a real mess of the explanation.' Jake's head was back in his dictionary, allowing Fang and Qiao vicious mutual survey over the bag of apples.

'Perhaps, Qiao,' Fang whispered, 'you should not – as English-speakers say – try to run before you can walk.' But far from looking floored or even flummoxed, Qiao just looked blank. With ignorance such a trusty ally, he hardly needed irony!

Jake looked up. 'Here, I think I've got it. Irony is the tough one. A sarcastic comment is simply a hurtful comment – which might be hurtful because it is ironic. Okay? And irony is when you make your point by using – the dictionary says – "words of directly the opposite meaning". If I turned to Qiao, say, and said, "You really are the hottest little English-speaker I ever taught" . . .'

Qiao reddened.

'Well, a bad example,' said Jake with an embarrassed laugh. 'Or if I said, "China is just light years ahead of the Japs in micro-technology" or, er, "President Bush is the most . . ."' Jake was flowing like that Reagan at a news conference and he wasn't helping Qiao whose brow was still knitted in stupid incomprehension.

'In story today we were reading about the steely determination of Norman Bethune in Chinese wintertime,' said Qiao effortfully, 'That "steely" – it's like irony, yes?'

Fang had to admit there was a sort of quirky inspiration at work here but so long as it kept him thrashing about in verbal cul-de-sacs like this there was no danger. He favoured Qiao with a fond regard, sympathetic and magnanimous. Then, to his further satisfaction, Qiao made to leave.

'What about those tickets to the flax-mill dance party, Qiao?' he asked in Mandarin. Class Monitor looked immediately shifty and hastened to the door without replying.

'You've got me a couple, haven't you?' Fang persisted. 'Miss Ping's been talking about nothing else.' Still no reply.

Seeing him out Jake said in his twangy tones, 'So we meet here before the great disco, eh, Qiao?'

'Tomorrow, six o'clock.' Qiao vanished. And well he might! That was his game: phase me out and invite Jake instead. Why didn't I think of it myself?

'Are you coming to this thing?' Jake asked as he sat down again.

'Yes!' said Fang. He would just have to visit the Podge and go back door.

'I'm nervous as hell. Qiao says disco is only part of it. The ol' fandango isn't one of my strengths – I can't even waltz!'

'Oh, that will not matter,' Fang replied with absolute certainty. 'Everyone will be so pleasing to see you try.'

'I'll be all right after a few firewaters I guess.'

'There is no firewater at Yanzhou dance parties. Just tea and fizzy pop.'

Jake looked amazed. 'So what's the point?'

'We Chinese like to dance because it promotes good relations between workers.' For once Fang was in accord with brochure-speak; what other point could there be to all that shuffling around?

'But none of us works at the flax mill.'

'No problem, Jake. There are methods to get in.' The American shook his head and changed the cassette; more alien music filled the room.

'Please will you tell me about dance parties in your homeland?'

After a few minutes of fascinating revelations, Jake said he wanted to go to the bathroom. Fang leapt up: had he had second thoughts about mutual rubbing? But Jake was just speaking American again.

Fang remained standing as Jake excused himself with John – another one of his lavatory expressions – and took the opportunity to lean over the desk. He opened a large, hardbacked notebook at a page covered in close handwriting. Jake's diary! He seized on a paragraph:

This place is like therapy. I feel so calm. Haven't even seen a plane for weeks! Everyone so friendly and, I sometimes think, so genuinely happy. I'm amazed by their good humor. They seem resigned to their situation – and so dignified! But they are blocked by government at every turn – number of kids, job, where they live, where they travel. But then I suppose it's better now than ever before. The Political Thought of Chairman Jake!

The swing-door sounded down the corridor and Fang snapped the book shut; he went over to stand reflectively by the window. As he came in Jake replaced some spare sheets of newspaper on a pile under his washstand.

'I'm getting better at it, there's no doubt.'

'Pardon?'

'The squat. I don't have to prop myself up like I did.' This subject fascinated Jake, even featuring in a dictation, one of the 'My Early Experiences in the People's Republic' series. 'Soon I'll be able to read in there too.'

'I thought . . .'

'Oh no! These papers are way out of date and anyway *China Daily*'s not fit for reading anywhere, even there.'

'Where do you get them?' This maligned edition of the Government's English-language organ was one of the first Fang had ever seen (all the others he had ever seen were on the pile under the washstand).

'I can't stop Interpreter Li giving them to me. I don't want to either – *China Daily* is indispensable!'

Such bold irreverence was thrilling. Jake had mentioned 'free press' once before. It seemed to be another American hobby-horse and one that Jake was perhaps keener to ride than hygiene.

'What is your opinion of the Chinese people?' Fang asked abruptly.

'High, Fang, pretty high.' He looked surprised by the question.

'Why, Jake?'

'Well – lots of reasons really: they're kind, friendly, a great sense of humour and . . .'

'And?'

'. . . and they seem so brave and patient.'

'What do you mean, please?'

'I hope I can make myself clear. I've learned a hell of a lot here in Yanzhou. Of course, I knew nothing about China before and I came straight up here after flying into Peking. But I had this idea – not exactly original in the States – that China had something which we, the West, miss out on. All that inscrutability bit, that's what we wonder about – your spiritual side. We know you're not just willow-patterned plates and Chinese whispers and *tai chi* – but we don't know what else you are. And with you being a fifth – a quarter even – of the world's population, we really need to know.'

Big nose.

'The Communism thing isn't too much a part of it, we reckon. For us Communism is Russia – or, these days, nutty

North Korea and Cuba. Here we look for something more deep-rooted, evidence of that "oldest civilisation on Earth", for Confucius-he-say, ancestor worship, street life, one-hundred-year-old eggs . . .'

'And you find?'

'Well, it's hard to say – but if I tell you about a guy called RJ it might help me explain. He was the one to really get me thinking about this. Full name, Reginald Johnston, from Scotland. He recently got what we call "fifteen minutes of fame" in the West because his life was acted out in *The Last Emperor*, a film about your Pu Yi, you know who I mean? – he was his tutor in the Forbidden City in Peking. The film was all very pretty but not much else – except that it alerted me to RJ. The very next week I found a copy of a book he wrote in a secondhand store.'

Fang's eyes sheened and narrowed further. He couldn't see how his original question had been hijacked by some old tutor from a state he had never even heard of. But Jake was going on.

'Apart from being a fine anthropologist, RJ could really write. Very haughty of course – a true Brit – but very much pro-Chinese too. You should hear him on missionaries! Hah!'

'Hah!' Missionaries? Look them up later.

'He said the way they trafficked God was just as bad, morally, as the British trade in opium and cocaine. So as you can imagine he put himself out of the running for the governorship of Hong Kong.'

'Ah yes, Jake!' But Fang could not have been less interested. History! History was history and it had no role in his scheme of things. Why was Jake banging on about it? Fang was, moreover, eager to get back and check on the geography of this Scotland which seemed to have shot across the Atlantic.

Jake rummaged in a drawer.

'Here you go – this is the book, published 1910. I can lend it to you.'

'Why?' He couldn't help asking. Jake stroked the ancient volume.

'Because it will show you what I mean. Come on, Fang! The point is that RJ saw China, your Motherland, when Mao was in diapers. You won't get another chance like it – to discover what a well-educated scholar thought about the future as this twentieth century got going, before Mao got his hands on China and damn near put the whole thing beyond doubt. As Mao was growing up, RJ was growing alarmed – about reform. Not just Communism but anything endangering Chinese tradition. There is fear and warning here, Fang.'

He brandished his precious book.

'So take a look. RJ was right . . . that's what I've learned, not that China has so much for the West to learn but that China *had* so much – that's the discovery. RJ was ignored, as he knew he would be, and the reformers had their way. You don't starve, and I suppose that's something even in the twentieth century, but you have to put up with a hell of a lot else – and that's why I admire you . . .'

'Why do you say Mr RJ knew he would be ignored?'

'It's just my feeling. We know very little about him because he was a very private man and ordered all his papers to be destroyed when he died. But he spent his last days on a tiny little Scottish island which he dedicated to Confucius and old China – as though the young reformers could not be entrusted with their own heritage.'

'You think the future is bright for us now?'

'Who'd make predictions about your political system? But I'm worried about the modernisation programme: you're on course to make the same mistakes we made in the West thirty years ago. Take housing: you all long to live in high-rises instead of traditional lanes. We know what they do to people but you don't want to listen. And cars – which are making places like Mexico City and good ol' London uninhabitable: you have planned this industry as the great Chinese growth area. But first will come motorbikes. Ever been to Taipei? Of course not. I haven't either actually but they say it's hell there because every little guy who would have a bicycle in the PRC has a screaming moped. And fridges – Chinese refrigerators are death to the atmosphere and you're all crazy about them. Of course it's just development and progress on the Western model but it's small-minded. We haven't done so well. Can't you see we've tried it and are paying the price. You don't have to. You can skip the messy parts. But you do need a government which can show some imagination, some originality. At least Mao had that. Now you want someone to be original enough to listen to RJ and Confucius and identify the true Chinese strengths – celebrate them, don't deny them! Tell me something, Fang, would you like to go the US?'

Fang squirmed. What did Jake know?

'Oh no.'

'Don't believe you!'

'Well, perhaps for a little while . . . but don't inform!'

'I won't, Fang.'

'I want to go to the States more than anything – anything. I am living with this idea every day and every night.'

Jake was shaking his head again as he led Fang to the door. 'That's quite an indictment of the Motherland, isn't it?'

'Indictment?'

'Quite an accusation, an insult, Fang, to say that you want to be somewhere else all the time.'

'Yes,' he said. 'Yes, I suppose it is.'

CCTV's English-service news that evening enthralled him by nipping across the sea from the gore and gassy tears of Northern Ireland to a feature in Scotland. A young man from Edinburgh was making his name by eating cockroaches and allowing rats free access up his kilt in front of admiring audiences. For the first time ever, Fang welcomed CCTV's curious sense of news: they gave 'Ratman' several minutes' coverage, and even provided a map of the British Isles to identify his homeland – and Mr RJ's – at the top.

Later Fang pulled the book out from under his bed. With some difficulty he made out the title on its spine: *Lion and Dragon in Northern China*. He flicked through its pages and then began to read one of several passages which had been marked by Jake:

One of the gravest dangers overhanging China at the present day is the threatened triumph of mere theory over the results of accumulated experience. Multitudes of the ardent young reformers of to-day – not unlike some of the early dreamers of the French Revolution – are aiming at the destruction of all the doctrines that have guided the political and social life of their country for three thousand years, and hope to build up a strong and progressive China on a foundation of abstract principles. With the hot-headed enthusiasm of youth . . .

Fang was cold but a little interested too.

. . . they speak lightly of the impending overthrow, not only of the decaying forces of Buddhism and Taoism, but also of the great politico-social structure of Confucianism, heedless of the possibility that these may drag with them to destruction all that is good and sound in Chinese thought.

Confucianism (or rather the principles and doctrines which Confucianism connotes, for the system dates from an age long anterior to that of Confucius) cannot be annihilated without perhaps irreparable injury to the body-social and body-politic of China . . .

Enough of that. Fang flicked on:

'How is it that you Government officials, as soon as you have learned the language and studied the customs of the country, become either mad or hopelessly pro-Chinese?' This is a question which in one form or another is frequently asked by unofficial European residents in China. It may be that there is something in the nature of Chinese studies that makes men mad, and indeed I have heard this soberly maintained by persons who themselves are careful to avoid all risk of contagion.

Steely Mr RJ, eh Qiao?

But it never seems to occur to such questioners that there may be some solid reasons for the apparently pro-Chinese tendencies (they are generally only apparent) of their official friends: reasons based on the fact that the latter have discovered – perhaps much to their own astonishment – how much there is truly admirable and worthy of preservation not only in Chinese art and literature and even religion, but also in the social organisation of the Chinese people. If there is one statement about China that can be made with perfect assurance it is this: that if in the long process of reform she learns to despise and throw aside all the supports she has leaned upon for thousands of years, if she exchanges for

Western substitutes all her ideals, her philosophy of life, her ethics, her social system, she may indeed become rich, progressive, powerful in peace and war, perhaps a terror to the nations . . .

Hardly!

. . . but she will have left behind her very much that was essential to her happiness and even to her self-respect, she will be a stranger to herself. And what will be the outward aspect of the China of those days? Great industrial cities there may be; harbours thronged with ocean-liners and with great battleships flying the Dragon flag; miles of factories, barracks, arsenals and shipping-yards; railway trains, motor-cars and airships coming and going incessantly from province to province; warehouses, banks and stock-exchanges full of myriads of buyers and sellers, each straining every nerve to excel his neighbour in the race for wealth.

And where, in this picture of China's possible future, are the thousands of ancestral temples where to-day the members of every family meet to do homage to their honoured dead and to renew the bonds of kinship with one another? They are to be seen no more. In their place stand thousands of village police-stations.

Fang dropped the book and burrowed under the quilt. After a minute his hand wound out and over to the dressing-table where it retrieved the list of new words he had compiled as he read. He pondered them again by the light of his pocket torch in the quilt cocoon: ardent, abstract, heedless, variance, contagion, arsenals, myriads, kinship. And missionary.

He would have to ask Jake about 'stock-exchanges' and Grandfather might have some ideas about these ancestral temples which Mr RJ found so important. But he had followed the main idea – and it astonished him.

Perhaps Mr RJ, studying history at the world-famous Oxford University when Mao Zedong was a peasant sprog kicking around in Hunan province, had been right. Perhaps something *had* gone from China and, as Fang tried to sleep that night, he realised with a series of sweaty shocks, that he would never know what that something was.

sixteen

Down at the office Fang had decided it would be wise to appear a little more dedicated to People's Cement. It was not that he was getting any trouble from above (Manager Sun was too busy purging the upper ranks to have time to worry about the graduate intake – and anyway he rightly saw Fang as crucial to his plan for catching up with the West); but these days there was a bit of gyp to be taken from the other low-grade cement clerks.

It was only too clear to Little Fang what was happening: they had been embittered by the task of sorting out the chaotic records of the old regime. Their spleens swelling with boredom and spite, these limited people were beginning to vent them on him. Why? Because he had avoided any part in their lumbering labours, thanks to the long-winded translation of some manuals which had accompanied three new cement mixers from Manchester, England. He had now been working on them for a fortnight (and shielding his file from Wong who occasionally dared challenge its minute progress).

Defeated in his bid to join the course, Wong could only be holding back from outright hostility because he doubted he had the reserves of confidence to cope with an aggressive backlash from Fang. But this doubt diminished daily and, to add to Fang's worries, even the phlegmatic Ling was growing surly.

So in order to forestall any explosion of bitterness – to dam this lake of bile – Fang joined these two colleagues in digging out a new batch of invoice backlog one morning. He rather feared they might pass some scornful comment on this occasion, his first visit to the storeroom, but they said nothing, and appeared to accept his pompous pledge to help them out in office hours from now on and to do most of his vital translation work at home.

Over the past weeks Ling had apparently insisted on their taking only the most accessible boxes and folders from the dust-filled shelves but they had now to reach for the more distant reams, at the back and at the top of the large metal construction. To show willing Fang volunteered for this and, using the shelves as steps, he scrabbled up and managed to recover a large box file marked 1972. But as he turned to descend, a spasm of activity from some rodent resident of the shelf so startled him that he dropped the file and lost his footing, having to cling to the framework to avoid falling on Wong and Ling.

Littered with invoices disgorged from the box file, these two were now bombarded by another volley from the rocking shelf-unit – 1975, 1978, 1976 and 1969. Only 1975, a quiet year in cement (if not in the Fang family fortunes), contained itself despite hitting Wong full in his upturned face; the others readily spilled their contents, which joined those of 1972 on the concrete floor.

Fang dropped lightly down and was about to apologise when a girl looked in to say that Sun wanted to see him about the translation. Ling and Wong had already sunk to their knees to begin picking up the hundreds of forms.

'I've, er, got to go, boys. See you . . . later.'

Ling kept his silence but not that prickly Little Wong.

'Thanks so much for all your help,' he sneered.

These whippersnappers start learning English and before you know it they're on to sarcasm. Fang vowed 'to take him down some pegs some time' as he hurried off to talk English cement mixers with the boss.

That evening he met Miss Ping outside the cinema as arranged and they bicycled to the Young People's Palace of Play where the dance party was to be held. Fang was pleased with the way she was turned out and wished he could tell her as much: Miss Ping wore a tight turquoise turtleneck; the skirt was tight too and her stockings, far from petering out mid-calf like so many did, might even have been suspended from the thigh. Only her shoes disappointed – the usual clod-hopping black pigskins which he would have to watch out for if it came to a samba.

As they approached the Palace they saw crowds of people on the main staircase, probably trying for last-minute tickets.

This pleased Fang. The coloured light bulbs outside and the purple glow within excited him. Jake's description of American club ways had altered his view of dance parties and he was quite looking forward to this one.

With accelerating heart, he tried to whisper something faintly romantic in Miss Ping's ear as she locked her bicycle to his. But she stood up suddenly and scrunched his nose flatter with the back of her head – and then annoyed him further by apologising too much.

Nevertheless, as they began climbing the Palace steps, he offered silent thanks to Podgy Peng for managing to provide their tickets at the final hour. Unusually there had been nothing improper about the deal: Ma Peng had got them for her son who was, like them all, under pressure to find a girl. Podgy, however, claimed to have one already and she was 'not the sort to want to spin round and round with a bunch of over-excited flaxxies'. So, taking an almost painless commission, Podgy had sold them on to Little Fang.

Suddenly Miss Ping tugged his arm. 'Look at that boy!' she said. They both stared at a teenager in baseball boots and Baihao haircut who was entertaining his ticketless friends by walking on imaginary ice-cubes on the stairs.

'Breakdancer!' she gasped. (Like Fu, she studied 'style' magazines. In fact they were her chief interest in life and Fang had got a surprisingly testy reply when he'd once asked what she planned to do with the trends she spotted: 'What do you do with your damn English?')

But now Fang himself found some thrill in seeing a new trend in operation on the staircase. He felt suddenly jealous of the sinuous youth and, patting his own head, even wished he had been less severe with the spikes. This was an occasion where they would not have been out of place; they might have been just the thing. He really felt something in common with the breakdancer, some shared stuff which he had never yet dared to strut.

But his regret died as he handed their tickets to a worker at the door and surveyed the dance party proper. This was no place for spikes. Short, flat and greasy – that seemed to be the current flaxxie style. About 150 young people, bussed in from their dormitories next to the mill, sat quietly on orange plastic chairs around the edge of the dance floor. A glass globe on the ceiling rotated lugubriously, casting purple light now on to the drab men, now on to the drab girls at the other side. There was no music.

Seeing a non-flax acquaintance sipping pop at the bar, Fang led Miss Ping over and bought her a sweet pink drink which she sucked through a straw.

'So when does it start?' he asked.

'It's their fault,' the young man replied grumpily. 'They're holding the whole thing up.' He indicated a group of technical types in the corner.

'It's a camera and special lights,' said Miss Ping with delight (film being another one of her subjects). As they took seats by the window Fang looked outside, suddenly mournful. The middle-school students had now abandoned all reserve: everyone was breakdancing on the steps of the Palace of Play. Extraordinary, quite extraordinary.

He turned back to his own generation, his flaxen-faced, inhibited peers. At least there was music now: the well-known beat of Descendants of the Dragon was setting the odd foot tapping – and both of Miss Ping's pigskins.

As the cameramen wheeled their equipment into the open, Fang overheard a worker say they were making a film about the Yanzhou area.

'What on earth for?' another asked.

'They want to encourage more young people to come and live up here.'

'So they make it look like one long dance party?' said his neighbour.

'Come on, if they want to get more people here, they'll just send them.' One man tried to suggest that this was no longer the case but everyone told him to shut up.

The flax-mill manager, a vigorous and popular man who was said to have the only private car in Yanzhou, then blew into the microphone. But before he could speak there was a sudden gasp and all eyes fixed on the door. Jake was arriving – with Qiao on the tips of his toes behind him trying to whisper something in his ear, and Qiao's girl, Bo, following. They were shown to some seats as the Manager paddled down the excited chatter.

'Welcome to you all,' he began, speaking Mandarin. 'And especially to our resident American, Ja Ke! We are delighted to have you here and we hope you can publicise our flax mill when you return to your country . . .'

No one was grinning more than the cameramen for they could not believe their luck: day one in the sticks and they had already found a Foreign Friend to top the feature. They panned over the seats and locked on to Jake, who was wearing his pink tie and some dark-green trousers which Fang had not seen before.

'. . . So let the dancing begin!' The Manager gave them a hip swivel and stepped down from the stage.

First up was a waltz and within seconds the floor was full of flaxxies, spinning, weaving, spooling about. But after just a minute the Manager called a halt. Not one girl was dancing. 'This is supposed to be a *modern* dance party,' he shouted and strode across the floor towards the female camp, breaking up coupled men as he went.

Fang watched scornfully as the hags twittered on about their shyness and inexperience. But as the music restarted he was suddenly aware of a very different sort of twittering in his right ear – Miss Ping on full sense assault: her perfume teased his nose and her nails grazed the back of his hand as she spoke into his ear and – steady on, floosie! – touched his lobe with her lips. 'Dance, Little Fang! Let's dance!' she whispered.

He was just getting up, ransacking his mind for details of the American 'smooch-grope', when the Manager ordered the disc jockey to stop the music again and leapt back up to the microphone.

'Friends, I can see we are going to have to start right at the beginning with you tonight. Now, please, choose a partner – no, not like that! Man and woman, man and woman, man and woman – and space out across the floor side by side facing me.'

Everyone formed up into neat ranks. Fang and Miss Ping were at one end of the back row, Jake, Qiao and Bo at the other.

'Right, now, with me, in time to the music, a one, two, three . . .'

Tremendous shunting caused a dispute mid-floor and gave Fang the cover he needed to make his one-two-threes in a sideways direction until he was in a position to do some whispering of his own.

'Well, Little Qiao, what a nice surprise! Glad you could make it.' He was pleased to see Qiao redden and lose his step. Fang also dared to shoot an insolent look at Bo and then waltzed back to the other end of the line.

The Manager soon abandoned general tuition to devote himself to improving the rhythm of a young technician with neat buttocks. But his aim had been achieved: flax-men and flax-women were now paired off and the floor was full. The standard was definitely improving and the sneering break-dancers who had been clinging to the window-sills during the awkward opening moments had disappeared (probably dropped off, laughing).

Fang actually began to enjoy himself and relaxed his hold on Miss Ping in such a clever way that her body was able to make its presence really felt. Cleavage! He suddenly remembered the English word and wondered if she had one lurking in her turtleneck. This was pretty nice. His hand moved 'another inch across her back and she smiled. Wicked.

The Descendants of the Dragon tape went on and on. The thrill of romance had such a grip on Fang – and he had such a grip on his delightful companion – that he was only mildly irritated to see Qiao skilfully accomplish some pretentious waltz cornering with his Bo. Tonight she didn't look any sexier than Miss Ping.

But when he caught sight of poor Jake surrounded by inarticulate flaxxies he had to act. Fang knew the sort of 'conversation' they would be having – establishing names, guessing ages, peddling vacuous flattery – and judging from the pained expression of this exotic wallflower they were trying out some English as well. He steered Miss Ping over to the group.

'Jake, I would like to introduce you to my . . . good friend Miss Ping.'

The workers fell back when they heard his English and Jake stood up. Miss Ping nodded at Jake's elaborate bow and leaned hard against Fang's shoulder, her fingers still locked in his leading hand.

'How are you enjoying dance party, Jake?' he asked, feeling his girl tug him gently. Insatiable.

'It's good. I'm just kind of short of partners, that's all.'

Fang glanced at Miss Ping, who immediately looked down, wincing or scowling. No, that wouldn't work. But how odd to see Jake unwanted. He seemed suddenly pathetic.

A flax-man then spoke up: 'My friend here is very eager to dance with your foreigner. Can you ask him?'

'Jake, they want you to dance with . . .' But Fang found himself introducing Jake to an enormous weaver with a sleepy eye. 'Didn't you hear your manager?!' said Fang reprovingly. 'No men with men!'

The flaxxies insisted: 'He's gone already. Anyway he wouldn't mind – he was just trying to get the girls going.'

'Jake, will you dance with this . . . person?' But Qiao suddenly spun into the group with Bo.

'Here you are, Jake. Bo will waltzing with you!' Jake's expression lightened at the sight of her flushed and pretty face and he led her on to the floor. The weaver meanwhile, pale at the shock of rejection, had staggered backwards, swearing obscenely. As they tried to calm him he wrenched two metal legs off a chair and began stamping on another. The original mediator begged Fang to retrieve Jake so he skidded across to the couple.

'You must come and dance with him,' he said. 'You've made him lose face before all his workmates. He is very insulting – insulted.'

The weaver had used these intervening seconds to bite off the top of a bottle of cherryade and destroy two more chairs. He was searching wildly with his one busy eye for further theatres of war when Jake swept over and, just in time, took him in his arms.

To the cheering of the flax-mill workforce, they waltzed away the insult until the weaver, like a great mastiff, slumped contented against Jake and was led back to his corner by three very grateful colleagues.

There was now just half an hour to go before the buses headed back home. The disc jockey, who turned out to be the flax mill's political officer, had allowed Descendants to play unchanged all evening but he now relented and inserted Jack Son, ostentatiously blocking his ears as he did so. Waltzers rushed back to their seats, leaving only a few flaxxies trying to catch the thrilling beat under the disco globe.

Everyone's attention – and the cameras – focused on Jake. This must be his scene. There would be no stopping him now. Like a nervous parent, Fang turned away from Miss Ping to watch and, sure enough, Jake rose to his occasion. He walked to the centre of the floor (the flax-men there scrambled out of his way) and began to wave his limbs about, rather heavily in fact. Miss Ping tittered derisively. He would soon get into his rhythm. But Miss Ping tittered again and came behind Fang to stroke his neck. Perhaps that bloody amateur doctor had wrecked Jake with the massage. He was still looking most ungainly and embarrassed – not a natural mover at all.

Fang watched Miss Ping who now ventured a couple of yards on to the floor to catch the beat. Now, *she* had it! And there must be a cleavage in there, a small one at least – her breasts were clearly outlined as she danced. Her hips too looked good. It suddenly occurred to Fang that she was dancing for him, at him. Erotic. She beckoned and Fang felt he might almost be about to go and take her in his arms when he saw the shameless Qiao and the huge weaver boogie out to the middle of the floor to join Jake. The three of them stabbed the air in time to Mr Jack Son's whimpers. Was this what Jake had meant by 'groping'? He looked rather like the Statue of Liberty; Qiao looked pathetic, disgusting; and the weaver – oh, the weaver wrecked everything by punching a hole in the revolving globe.

This was confirmation – as if it were needed – of the destructive influence of Western culture and the console commissar gratefully extinguished Jack Son, replaced Descendants and announced the last dance.

Furious with Qiao about his disco initiative, Fang now decided this final waltz would be his. He left Miss Ping disconsolate and whisked Jake on to the floor. But the pair of them could not get going at all and Fang realised how much he had relied on his girl to lead him. They kicked shins, knocked knees and even crashed into the film crew's lights.

'Back home they'll be amazed at this. I'm not exactly known for my dancing!' breathed Jake.

Fang could not afford to lose concentration by replying; he was determined to do better than the weaver at least and, so far, this was in some doubt.

'And dancing with another guy – I can't get over that!'

They wheeled into a loudspeaker and restarted.

'Tonight is the second time . . . I have danced with a girl,' Fang declared, spinning Jake inexpertly but fast across the floor. 'Other time was graduation party. Sorry, my fault! One, two, three . . . But I think I begin to like dancing with girls more . . .' He was just fearing this might offend Jake when another painful collision distracted them.

Then suddenly Fang remembered Mother's last words that evening. The ten days were up: the advertising campaign had to be mentioned now.

'Jake, I wondering . . .'

'Yes, Fang, what?'

'Well, I wondering whether at the moment you have enough socks.'

Jake suddenly stiffened in his arms and pushed him away. The cameras whirred.

'Enough what?'

'Socks.'

'I'm fine thanks, Fang. I appreciate your concern but I think we'd better stop now. See you round.'

He turned abruptly and went back to Qiao and Bo. Fang stared as they left together immediately. He returned to Miss Ping, his head spinning.

'What's wrong?' she asked. 'You're white, Little Fang!'

'I think we should leave.'

'Yes, but are you really all right?'

'Yes, fine, I'm fine . . . It's just that I think I've offended Jake.'

'Oh, forget him for a minute, will you? You're obsessed with that Ja Ke.'

She growled with irritation and, grabbing the very ear she had nibbled earlier, led him out of the Palace ballroom. Fang was too stunned to fight this indignity although it was being recorded by the diligent camera crew. They would surely lose this footage in the cutting-room: who would want to see a row with a foreigner and a woman berating her man? Hardly good propaganda for Yanzhou was it? They could edit out their black marks; Fang could not. Never.

He cursed Mother and her stupid scheme. And himself for agreeing to it. A month of eradicating the 'beautiful' stigma just thrown away! This was another, and so much worse. Black Fang. Once Jake told Qiao, he would be ruined. And he would hardly blame Qiao: the stakes had risen so high that Qiao would be mad not to take the chance to finish him off.

He should have known there would be trouble when he tried to talk business with Jake: the naïve Chinese blundering into the American domain and outraging him with such a low proposition. He deserved whatever he got. Mother must be made to realise. They were all ruined!

He gave Miss Ping a bicycle escort through the silent streets to her block. At the foot of the stairs she mellowed and, holding his lapels, breakdanced gently against him. Fang had been aware earlier in the evening that tonight she expected – deserved – more than the one stark kiss he had managed one night last summer, but he was now so distraught he forgot even that. And although she turned away with a grunt and clomped up the stairs, it was only ten minutes later, as he pushed his bicycle into their yard, that he realised the omission. The day which had begun with an avalanche of cement invoices was ending in cataclysm: he had managed to lose Jake and Miss Ping.

seventeen

Fang darted for the packed lift and crammed inside as the doors shut. He was concertinaed between a couple of hotel receptionists on one side, which was quite pleasant, and Spotty Zhang on the other, which was not. The lift juddered upwards. From this wary crouch he looked up at the peaceful, bland faces of two of the middle-aged classmates; Xin had managed to spread himself against Pretty Pei; the gutless Lin Hu was folded into his angst-ridden self in one corner; Volley-Ball Lo was stocky, self-contained and silent in another.

And there at the back, stalks of yellow hair grazed the ceiling. The students chattered their ill-formed English and grinned at Teacher Jake whose expression, the morning after, was one of tolerance just snatched away from straight bad temper. Then, over the grinding activity of the shaft, Fang heard Qiao's voice apparently issuing from within Jake's arm-pit.

'What have you prepared for our today's lesson?'

'A little bit of this and that.' Jake grimaced. Yes, he looked really bad today.

The lift stopped at the fourth floor even though the button panel and past performances proved that it could reach the two remaining storeys. The lift-girl often chose to express her hatred of the graduates in this way.

'There are too many students,' she said with feeling. 'It is dangerous. Get out here.'

They debouched on to the landing and walked the rest of the way up to their dusty classroom where a dozen students were already waiting.

There was silence as Jake mounted the podium. With an ugly smile, he pulled a single sheet from his bag: 'Dictation!'

Hands scuffled rat-like through every satchel, fossicking for fresh paper and pens. Nervous sights and natterings. Dictation!

'Not too difficulty, Teacher Jake!'

'Easier than the last one, please, Ja Ke!'

He still looked as if there was a pile of buffalo dung under his nose and although Fang now offered up an expression even more apologetic than the one he had arranged during the fateful opening ceremony, Jake was refusing to meet his eye. He began.

'There is no title.'

Fang scribbled across his empty page and then quickly crossed out these four words. Qiao sniggered on his right.

'America – capital A – is often regarded by foreigners as paradise on earth colon.' He repeated the sentence against a ripple of panic from the reception desk.

'You – small y – can have the best of everything dash bigger comma glossier and tastier dash so long as you have the money full stop.'

Fang's mind turned to blondes, dressed today in puce and pink, and swinging sassily through that white university campus.

'The film industry concentrates on wholesome middle hyphen class america to foster this image of plenty and to export the good old – inverted comma – american dream – capital A and D, inverted comma – worldwide – yes, that's one word – full stop.'

Fang was lost – but not alone. Jake had never spoken like this before. There was something feverish about his delivery. Last night's fury with Fang was clearly spilling over into his work. At the desk to his left, Xin had written only 'material', 'parra dice' and 'glossy'. The level of protest was rising. And now Qiao seemed to be snaring Fang with a reproachful look. See what you have done to Jake!

He drawled on: 'The heroes are tough hyphen talking self hyphen seekers who get what they want and the girl dash . . .'

'Slower, please!'

'Again, Teacher Jake!'

'. . . because comma in america comma determination and ability must always win through in the end stop new paragraph.' He looked up. 'I'll go back over the last bit. I know this is not easy for you to understand but you must try.'

And he was off again: 'If comma however comma america is judged more realistically it is seen to be a very different place full stop. The democracy it holds so high is really very corrupt full stop. Behind all the free hyphen speaking open society' (Fang wrote furiously) 'there is a dark system of crime comma bribery and racism . . .' He paused. Only Frank and Charlie were still in the running – and Miss Lo. '. . . which supplies a gross national product – capital G, capital N, capital P – of twenty thousand murders a year full stop. Hard drugs and aids – all capitals – are the hot new exports of today's america.'

Jake's agitated voice was now competing with the electronic rendering of the Red Flag which jarred across from the clock-tower on every hour; the bicycle bells on Liberation Street sang a frantic chorus to his tirade.

'Meanwhile the great american public comma two-thirds of which will be illiterate by the year 2000 – write it in figures – is stupefied and controlled by the instant gratifications of crack – no, forget that – of fast hyphen food and television which will comma within the next generation comma have produced the most dangerously ignorant and irresponsible population of materialists on earth full stop the end.'

Jake reread the whole piece. Fang tried to make something of the scrawl in front of him. At first it had seemed like a few frames of the American Dream. But then a different tone came in – and that word 'democracy'. So all was not well in Jake's motherland but what exactly were the problems? They didn't seem to be the usual sort. What's wrong with television? And that 'fast hyphen food'? Why do so many Americans kill each other?

'. . . dangerously ignorant and irresponsible population of materialists on earth full stop – the end,' Jake finished the reread. They had the usual two minutes for checking and then they swapped scripts to go through the whole passage all over again. Dictations reminded Fang of politics in middle school: by the end of the lesson you knew it off by heart – but did you understand it? And did you believe it?

(During the break Fang noticed his neighbour Xin trying to force a pack of crystallised apples on Pretty Pei. He had seen this happen before and had noted the beautiful colour she turned as she refused the gift.)

The second half of the period was spent with conditionals and idioms. Lin Hu, the young teacher whose discipline problems were growing, further irritated Jake by insisting on the phrase 'steady as a cucumber'. Lin had already passed this form on to his flock and was clearly alarmed at having to lose face — what little remained — on his own podium that afternoon.

Finally Jake dished out a comprehension exercise for homework and, as the bell sounded, he stalked off before anyone could present the usual lists of linguistic enquiries which lay extensive in every pocketbook.

'He seemed a bit bolshy today, eh, Qiao?' said Fang, resigned to discovering the full extent of Jake's umbrage.

'Yes, he is.'

'I can't think why . . . Can you?'

'He just got some bad news before class — from the Government. Something about his visa expiring sooner than he thought. That's all.'

'So he's got to leave?'

'Of course he's got to leave — eventually. He's not here for good, Little Fang, remember that. But it won't affect the length of the course — it just means he doesn't have so much time for travelling around China afterwards. They take their travelling very seriously, Westerners, you know.'

Qiao explained this peculiarity as they walked down to the fourth floor where they just missed the lift.

'So Jake's not angry about anything else?' They continued down the stairs.

'No. Why should he be?'

'Nothing about last night? The dance party?'

'Well he did seem to clam up right at the end. Did you tread on his toes or something?'

So Qiao did not know! There was still some hope.

Fang left him at the bicycle shed and raced to Jake's block. The swiftest horse, as all Chinese know, cannot recapture a word once uttered but Fang whiz-clattered through the streets in the wild hope that Jake might not be lost. He smiled winningly at Madam Cerberus, dropping a spherical gift into her lair, and was well clear by the time she realised it was a cabbage. The door was ajar. Fang knocked and entered.

'Ah, hello,' Jake said with hollow civility, tensing in his easy chair. 'I've just got back. I have this letter I must get off . . .'

'I'm very, very sorry I come here so soon after the lesson,' said Fang miserably. 'I know how tiring it is for you teaching us stupid lot of persons – but I wanted to return Mr RJ's book.' Jake took it. 'So, so interesting – thank you. And . . .'

'And?'

'I wanted to explaining about last night.'

'Don't bother.'

'It was just . . . just a terrifically stupid idea of Mother's.'

'Your mother?' Jake was incredulous.

'Yes, she thought you might be interested to trying—'

But Jake barked through his bleating: 'Look, Fang, it's no big deal – it happens all the time back home. I guess I just over-reacted because I wasn't expecting it out here too.'

'I know. I should not of suggested it to a foreigner . . .'

'Perhaps I should have seen it coming from day one – that outburst of yours – but I've never been very good at picking up those sort of vibes.' Fang rocked in the other easy chair. The pain! 'You're a great guy and I really appreciate all the trouble you've taken over me . . . but I'm, er, I'm really not interested in you in that way.'

'Which way, Jake?'

'Sexually, Fang, sexually!'

'Please? Sexually?'

Jake shouted: 'I just don't happen to like having sex with other men!'

Fang's mind hurtled through the short silence.

'Socks!' he yelped, 'Jake, I asked you if you having enough *socks*!'

They stared at each other over the little table. Fang suddenly remembered that brief triumphant moment in the bath together. This was even better: several seconds of perfect clarity, truth even, beauty, American and Chinese at one. Fang was exultant and soaring and, at the same time, knotted and convulsed: relief had such effects. He was as tight as a cannonball, bowling through the ether. And from here, from Heaven, he surveyed their friendship in all its stages of development: the initial frustration, the first meeting, the joy of Jake 'at home', scrutiny of his possessions, his magnificent naked-ness in the wash-house, the last waltz. Suddenly it seemed as if sex was expected – as with Miss Ping – as the next logical step in their gradually mounting intimacy. What an awesome thought! Homosexy! The Party had only just legalised a word for the concept. But no, sex they would not manage – Fang had only just started to face his 'normal' stirrings (though they seemed pretty bizarre). He and Jake would have to get closer and closer in other ways. Plutonic. Fang hurtled on through the stars.

Jake was laughing now and Fang joined him, quite helplessly: 'Socks! Sex!' they cried. 'Socksy sex! Sexy socks!' Eventually they were aware, through Fang's sniggers and Jake's hollers, of knocking at the door. It was Qiao. He had brought a young colleague from Foreign Trade, a renowned hack, to meet his 'revenerable English Teacher'. Jake greeted them – and the hack's business card – with a gratifying lack of enthusiasm and slumped back in his chair in preparation for more of what Fang had heard him call 'baby-talk'.

'Welcome you to Yanzhou. Please my English level is very, very bad,' said the hack. Jake suggested they both sit down – speaking in his bizarre Mandarin – and the newcomer burst out again: 'Oh, you speak Chinese? You speak very beautiful Chinese. You are very clever and handsome and . . .' Hack, hack, hack, hackety hack.

Jake had begun to shake his head and, unable even to look at the flatterer's face, he leafed through some book which he clearly wanted to be reading.

'Do you have short cut to learn English tongue?'

'No.'

'We have come to play with you,' the young man persisted. Jake looked up wildly.

'Not again!' he said and caught Fang's eye. They fell about laughing for another good minute.

As Fang got up he arranged a withering sideways look for Qiao, who was plainly subjecting Jake to this intrusion in order to win favour in some new area of the Foreign Trade Bureau. Perhaps his latest ploy was to get a Party card. Shameless! Fang whinnied with amusement and left, delighted to have been laughing at both ends of Qiao's interruption.

Leaving the building he noticed the door-lady still a little way off, bicycling back to the office from the butcher (a small hunk of meat dangled in a loop of string from her handlebars).

Quite suddenly a white sedan sharked out of a side road. Its front wing clipped her wheel and she crashed to the ground. Three men leapt out and rushed to the front of the car where she was picking herself up from the slush. They knelt down to examine the damage, running their fingers along two small scratches in the white paint. Behind them the door-lady had struggled back to her feet.

As Fang pedalled over to see if she was seriously hurt she drew a great draught of air into her lungs – they were not impaired – and launched into screaming abuse.

'Fucking government hooligans! People-bashers! Brown-noses!'

The men turned, surprised, to face her; they solemnly lit new cigarettes and got back into the car. Fang picked the meat out of the gutter for her as the sedan swept off.

'Fucking government hooligans!' She snatched it from Fang and hurled it after them. This diverted the attention of the spectators and, as they swarmed off to see if the slushy hunk of pig bum had any culinary future, the door-lady pushed her bike off to the shed, limping on her left leg. The back wheel was buckled and there was blood on one of her new two-tone woollen leggings. Fang felt terrible about the cabbage trick now and resolved to reward her spirit with some large balls of wool next time – even if he had to buy them off Mother.

eighteen

He felt quite transformed on attending the next class and, feeling so good, he marvelled that he could ever have felt so bad.

Jake seemed to be in high spirits too, bantering with the reception desk as he came in (he managed to amuse Pretty Pei who actually laughed with him, not at him, for once). He even endured some pre-lesson chat with Spotty Zhang who had – Jake had told Fang – the worst breath in the class.

The lesson featured one of Jake's favourite exercises – the write-back. The last topic covered in this manner (by which they had to write back in their own words something uttered by Jake) had been cryonics, the Californian practice of freezing your brain cells just before you die so they may be thawed out again for more life in the future. The gulf with the West could not be wider, Fang had thought: Mother wants a fridge for her eggs; Jake a freezer for his head.

But today's topic was closer to home: how to get aboard a Peking bus.

'Listen carefully, dear students,' said Jake. 'This may come in useful if you ever get down to the big city.'

Fang looked around at the beaming classmates, perhaps half of whom had ever made the journey. He himself had not but nor did he need Jake's mocking tone. Get on with it, Big Nose.

'On my way up to Yanzhou I discovered in Peking that there are two ways of getting on board a bus. Since one nicely demonstrates the active mood and the other the passive mood, I thought they might be of some help for your English studies. Which mood affects you depends entirely on your position in the line. Now, at a busy stop – in Tiananmen Square for example – this is not an orderly line of bodies but a battle of elbows.

'If you happen to be near the front you will be put on to the bus – passively – by the comrades heaving up behind you.

No effort is required. You just relax and get shot up into the fellow-passengers already jammed inside. I remember one moment of horror in the Square, at the stop closest to the portrait of your Chairman Mao: I was going along on my hired bicycle' (here Jake thrust out his arms and wiggled his hips, always the actor!) 'when I got caught up as a bus swung into the pavement to stop. The doors opened and I felt myself and my bike being forced off the ground and up into the bus. I only just managed to get out of that one – with a buckled back wheel.

'Then, second, there is the active mood which you must use if you happen to be at the back of the line. Now it is up to you to apply the pressure, steadily, relentlessly and very, very hard. As you get near the door and the guys above you begin to topple back, you have to take hold of the hand rails inside and thrust yourself up with a great *whoosh*' (more histrionics accompanied this word) 'of effort – into whatever spine, buttock or thigh happens to be above you. And then – you're on!'

What a lot of fuss about nothing!

'But don't relax yet. Unless you want to be spat out at the very next stop, you've got to use the time now to move right into the body of this beast. Wriggle on through. As a foreigner I got prodded and laughed at. I think they thought I should be in a taxi. One time I tried to give up my seat for an old lady but as I got up to let her in, a Little Emperor, about five years old, squeezed in behind me and took the seat himself. The lady just smiled and let him stay.'

Silence. No one knew what to make of this rubbish.

'Now write down the gist of what I've just said – yes, in your own words – and next week maybe I'll tell you how to get off a Peking bus.'

Fang was still irritated about having his capital explained by a foreigner and he was pleased to think how easily Brother-in-law would rip Jake off if he ever got him in the back of his cab. Mr RJ and Jake – they both seemed to know China better than Fang ever would.

But he was not so peeved as to miss escorting Jake to his block after class, something he often did these days. (Now that the sex thing had been cleared up they could be 'just good friends'.)

Other students tagged along for a while but made their effusive farewells one by one and vanished into gloomy light-industrial compounds: Nails, Telephones, Heavenly Tins, Tyres.

It was a sunny morning and since Fang had nothing more urgent than the invoice backlog from 1971 to deal with at his office, he suggested they push their bicycles and enjoy the air. He was relating the door-lady's experience when Jake asked him about several thousand cabbages which lay in their path.

'The Government subsidises sale so our people can buy enough through the winter.'

'But back home all these would be trucked away the very first night. Doesn't anyone steal?'

'A few bandits do stealing but most of the people come during the day and they pay.' Odd question.

Though they had stopped only briefly at cabbage corner, a crowd was already forming. A man with Spotty Zhang breath sidled up and murmured a tentative 'Ja Ke.' Jake nodded tolerantly and they moved off.

But soon it was Jake's turn to stare – at a huge dragon which lounged in the road, gently trembling. Leaning his bicycle against the wall, Jake approached but it suddenly sprang to life and squirmed off at speed.

'Rehearsing for Spring Festival,' yawned Fang. 'The creature is unmothballed every year. Only they change the legs – junior-middle-school legs. They are allowed off from politics class to practise. I was Honourable Ninth Segment in 1979.'

'Do you know, Fang,' said Jake, 'I think you're becoming a bit of a cynic. Congratulations!'

He was ready for this one.

'From Greek derivation: one who doubts human sincerity, yes? Well, we are all cynicous about Spring Festival. It is supposed to be such great fun but it really makes us feel sick. CCTV television said once that murders by hand gun in New York increase by 100 per cent over Christmas when all the families come together. We do not have the guns but many of us are wishing we have. Once you're too old for dragon work there is only dumplings and beer left to enjoy at Spring Festival. And of course people camerate the dragon.'

'Beg your pardon?'

'You know! Say cheese! Click! The great moment of the year – dumplings and beer and camerating a geriatric old dragon!'

'So when is it, Fang? I can hardly wait!'

'Two weeks from Monday. But it goes on for five days – to give you a chance to see all your friends and relations. Ha!'

'Does your family get together?'

'The aunts are in Shanghai – but they visited earlier this year. There is just one aunt in Yanzhou, dull woman. Not married! It will be a quiet Spring Festival for us. But Mother may bring in some friends.'

'What about Grandfather?'

'Grandfather?' How did Jake know about him? 'Ah yes, Grandfather! He is at his very worst over Spring Festival.'

'Fu?' And who told you about her? This was the problem with a high-profile black-mark family behind you . . . 'Oh, her? She's gone to Peking.'

She had got the good news about her residence permit last week and had declared immediately that she would be off well before Spring Festival. She said she had waited long enough; Husband would be fabulously busy over the holiday period; she would be needed (if only to count the cash); the capital called. Surly to the last, Fu had insisted on travelling to Baihao alone to catch the 340. She had waved when the minibus passed their alley but as Mother – unnecessarily tearful – turned for home, Fang had seen a cyclist felled by a bag of pears hurled from the departing vehicle.

Now, as they were sauntering along, Fang suddenly decided to invite Jake to see in the Year of the Snake with them, in their home. He would have to do it all formally of course, after discussion with Mother. But she was most unlikely to object: hemlines raised slightly and under-trousers began to come off after Spring Festival and it was now or never if she was going to get anywhere with the Jake-sock. They had to meet.

And Grandfather? He grimaced every time the American

was mentioned but Fang had not decided whether it was in amazement or horror; more likely the old warrior just couldn't fit the concept of Jake into his mind. 'What? A tapir-face! Living here? In Yanzhou! Never!'

They stopped at a bicycle-pump station and another crowd formed as Jake inflated his Forever's tyres.

'I got even with one of them yesterday,' he said as they went on.

'Yes? How?'

'At the hospital – I did some staring myself for once!'

'Staring of what?'

'Staring at, Fang, not staring of!' Fang stopped to scribble in his pocketbook. Wretched little particles! 'After my needle session Qiao took me down to the operating theatre,' Jake continued. 'His cousin is chief nurse and so he can drop in any time. First up was a circumcision – this guy just spread-eagled on the slab. They stuck him with a dozen needles – that was all the anaesthetic he got! – and then they went in with the scalpel. It was kind of neat to watch.'

You weren't so cool when yours was on display.

'Did the needles work – as a anaesthetic?' The manikin was breakdancing across Fang's abdomen again.

'Seemed to, but we couldn't see his face because he was wearing a surgical mask and cap. I thought he took it really well. Qiao tells me quite a few young men have it done to be sure of getting it right for their one kid. No one wants to risk a systems breakdown.'

'I believe that is correct.' Fang's manikin flipped a somer-sault: yet another reason to delay miserable marriage.

'Back home we get that sort of thing over with much earlier – like cycling I guess.'

'The patient, he must have been surprising to see you, Jake.'

'"Surprised" – sort out your moods, Fang! Actually, I don't think he was because we had to wear masks too.'

A policeman stopped a pair of youths, clearly peasants, on a single wobbling bicycle near by and swiftly administered the fine. Serves them right for coming into our city. Fang had seen more and more of these young primitives hanging around lately, and heard rumours that the brighter ones were trying to better themselves through learning English. Why couldn't they just stay in the fields where they belonged?

'Have you ever seen the picture display outside the hospital, Fang? I couldn't read the blurb of course but it seemed to be showing off their operating skill.'

'Yes, that would be likely,' said Fang. 'Doctors in our China are extremely skilful.'

'But what a way to do it! There was one batch of pictures which really threw me.'

'Throw up?'

'Damn nearly. The first snap showed the smashed ankle of some poor worker – close up.'

'Ah yes, that would have been an industrial accident.'

'Next picture along there were tweezers coming in from all sides picking out the bits of bone. Number three – the ankle full of needles with a scalpel at work, blood everywhere, and then – hey presto! – the final frame showed the repaired foot, marching off. Back to the factory no doubt.'

'Yes. Well?' What was Jake's problem here?

'Just seems an odd thing to have outside the hospital.'

'Maybe.' But it made sense – as everything did – and if Jake was really interested in the Chinese Way he better get this into his straw-topped noddle.

They had reached the government reception block and, as usual, Fang was wondering whether to loiter in the hope of further conversation or to leave – because Jake might want to read some RJ or to write one of his interminable letters. But happily his decision-making was postponed by the door-lady who now bustled out into the sunshine and handed Jake an envelope.

'Thank you, old friend,' he said in sort-of Chinese and bowed.

'No need to thank me, Ja Ke America.' She squeezed his arm and smiled proudly. Jake ripped the envelope and the thin paper within. Piecing it together he read aloud:

You are a magnificent member of a great profession. The reason why a teacher is great is that he is engineer of the people's souls and the leader of life. He lights others up and destroys himself like a candle.

'I get this sort of thing most days now,' said Jake.

'Don't worry please. The exam is not far from now. It is normal. You will get very many more.'

'There's weeks till the exam, Fang – well, a month at least. And it's not just letters. I get presents too.'

'They have started already?' Fang had got so caught up in his pursuit of Jake that he'd forgotten to take such basic precautions.

'Sweet potatoes yesterday. A wind-up hen laying tin eggs on Monday. I even got some sugared apples from Miss Pei.'

(Well, that was something at least: if she was passing on Xin's presents then she might be resisting his monthly assaults on her honour. The rebuff should knock his drugged, ping-pong-glue pride! A fine girl that.)

'You coming up, Fang? I want to show you something.' Another milestone! The first time Jake had actually issued an invitation. This wouldn't happen for Qiao!

Once they were in his living-room Jake handed him a piece of stiff, yellowed newspaper.

'I was about to use this yesterday when the headline caught my eye. Just thought you might be interested. It's way out of date but still . . .'

The date on the *China Daily* cutting was 11 April 1988 and the headline ran SIT-IN DEMONSTRATION AT TIANANMEN SQUARE. Fang read on:

Eighteen university students and a teacher staged a sit-in on Tiananmen Square in the heart of Beijing yesterday, demanding more money for education and improved living standards for intellectuals.

The demonstrators, fom Beijing University, Qinghua University and Beijing's Teachers' University left the square at about 3 p.m.

Their demands did not go beyond proposals already put forward by NPC deputies and members of the CPPCC at the sessions of the Seventh National People's Congress and the Chinese People's Political Consultative Conference which closed here yesterday . . .

Meanwhile, in Hefei, Anhui Province, students at the Chinese University of Science and Technology, the cradle of student demonstrations in December 1986, have said that they are satisfied with the present method of choosing NPC deputies.

They said that the competitive election system, which allows 20–50 per cent more candidates than positions to stand for election, is a sign of democracy.

Students who took part in the 1986 demonstrations were objecting to the procedure for electing deputies to the local people's congress. Wan Ruihua, a participant in the demonstration at the time, said on Saturday: 'We can learn something from capitalist countries, but this doesn't mean everything is good in those countries.'

Some students are inclined to make comparisons between China and Western countries in an over-simplistic way, a student's union official said: 'This is because they did not fully understand the complexities of Chinese society and were ignorant of the actual conditions in capitalist countries.'

To overcome this trend, the university arranged for students to work in rural counties during the subsequent winter vacation to learn about society at large.

One student discovered, during his two months in a rural area, that the primary concern of most Chinese people was to invigorate China's economy.

(Xinhua)

Fang looked up. He felt he had been able to make this particular discovery long ago, even in Yanzhou. He couldn't imagine anyone still needing to be enlightened by a spell in 'rural counties'. The very idea of it was chillingly familar.

Everything had changed since the Cultural of course: if you got sent down these days you might discover the art of intensive quail-farming or earthwormery; and of course you could make money too, become a 'ten-thousander' even.

He could think of nothing to say to Jake, who was searching his face for some reaction.

'I was just surprised they printed it all,' said Jake. 'Of course it's riddled with propaganda but it shows the authorities have made some progress. Even just printing the word democracy! They are slowly realising there is no alternative. With you lot growing up, your leaders have got to grow up too.'

Fang remained silent. He felt somewhat foolish to remember nothing about these student demonstrations in 1986. Had they marched and waved banners and screamed like those furious foreigners CCTV so loved to show? He looked down again at the cutting to hide his uneasiness and then examined the other side. Under 'Opinion' a China Daily Commentator had written an article headlined 'Burgeoning Democracy'. This bit of paper was almost a year old: what was going on in Peking now? Fang replaced the cutting and hurriedly excused himself.

Jake's China-watching might be his way of getting back at the Jake-watchers but it could come to no good and Fang had little time for it. Jake should spread the words, idioms and proverbs: they were the proper concerns for English students, not this democracy thing. The corridor echoed with Jake's surprised farewell.

They didn't speak over the 'weekend'. (Fang liked that term though it hardly described those two days which actually provided very little relief from the usual shifts and schedules; on Saturday he had to go into the office and now, with English Corner postponed indefinitely, there was nothing to make Sunday any brighter either.)

He swung by Jake's of course – two or three times on Saturday – but he seemed to be under siege from middle-school students doing some project on western etiquette (any excuse to get time with him!). There were so many adolescents in the hallway where the door-lady had allowed the display to take place that Fang could not even make eye contact with Jake who was busily going through knife-and-fork motions and offering his seat to imaginary old ladies and – a particular favourite – blowing his monstrous snout into a piece of cloth. Needless to say he was enjoying all the attention and Fang had soon slipped away – having made sure Qiao wasn't in the crowd.

He called in on Sunday too – twice – but the door-lady absolutely refused to let anyone up, having prescribed several hours of complete rest for Jake. Fang failed to move her with promises of many, many sheep's worth – any colour you want – and moped off to kill the afternoon with a double bill at the cinema. At least, he sat through two showings of a *kung fu* classic called *Mirage*.

nineteen

Jake seemed quite refuelled by Monday morning and on belligerent form. He had managed to berate the lift-girl with such effective Chinglish that she had taken them all the way to the top. By the time he mounted the podium he looked very spirited indeed.

'Right, folks, today we will have a debate,' he announced. 'Who knows what that is?'

No one did.

'Well, I'll tell you. You take a topic, an issue, and one person puts one side of the case and another the other side. Then there are speeches, as we say, "from the floor". Finally there is a vote.'

'Who votes?' asked Tang, the leather-worker.

'You do! And you, and you, and you. You all vote! Okay?'

This course was getting more and more peculiar.

'Who makes speeches?' asked Class Monitor.

'Well, I'm going to raise the issue and, Qiao, you can choose the speakers.' A nod of satisfaction from Qiao. 'The question we are going to discuss today concerns modern Chinese culture: why is modern Chinese culture so very poor?'

There was a quick rustle and then complete silence. What could Jake mean? Modern Chinese culture poor? Qiao looked around for possible speakers.

'Zhang!' he barked, but Spotty shook his head hard; so did Zhou and Tong and Cao, a trio of nonentities, as he tried them each in turn. Volley-Ball Lo refused too by means of her thin, supercilious smile.

'Oh, who will proposing motion then?' said Qiao.

Silence.

'Come on!' cried Jake. 'This is good oral practice. You can't still be shy!'

Silence.

'Qiao?'

'Please not! Responsibilities weighing . . .'

'Well, all right, perhaps none of you wants to criticise your own culture even in a friendly debate. I'll propose. Now, who is going to oppose me and my motion? We should have a few strong speeches here.'

Silence.

'What is going on? A big nose is going to stand up and tell the proud Chinese people that their modern culture is pathetic, a washout, and not one of you has a word against him?'

Fang's mind shuffled through 'culture'. What exactly was it? Art? A nice new sculpture of a pair of acrobats had gone up recently at the end of Harmony Boulevard. Theatre? There had been nothing on the stage since the Railway Workers' Song and Dance Ensemble's provincial tour in the spring. Should he mention that? Cinema? *Mirage*? You could call *kung fu* 'art' perhaps, but was it culture? Literature? He didn't have much need for books these days, except English ones and he couldn't really mention them. Music? Richard Clay . . .

Jake was barracking from the podium but still no one had spoken. Suddenly Fang remembered something from a few years back which might be counted as culture. Perhaps that would satisfy Jake. He stood up.

'Ah, Fang! Thank goodness for Fang!' said Jake.

'There were the Four Beauties in the Government's Campaign for Spiritual Civilisation.'

'Yes?'

'Beautiful Language, Beautiful Behaviour, Beautiful Heart and Beautiful Environ . . .' But by the fourth Beautiful Fang felt nauseous – as though he had spent a night alone in Interior Decor. He couldn't think of much to add; the campaign had been as brief as all the others; it hardly merited a speech; he couldn't muster much passion.

'Ah,' said Jake. 'I see . . .'

Fang reddened. 'That's all, Jake.'

'Okay. Well maybe we'll have another debate next week. I'd like to spend the rest of today doing some exercises on the complex sentence.'

'Right, Fang, I'm not going to let this thing rest. I may have to accept that the others never have a cultural thought between them but I'm not giving up on you. Or are you satisfied with your Four Beautifuls?'

They were walking down Peace Street together after class. Having accompanied them a little way Qiao had strode off for an 'immense' banquet with some Russian timber merchants. Fang now admitted he found the Beautifuls grotesque.

'What do you want of me, Jake?'

'To know if you're going to take me to the bookstore.'

'Now?'

'Now!'

Fang had been basking in some favour at the office recently. Coming down from his ivory tower a little, he had flattered the other clerks by managing to make them feel involved in the mixer manual translation (although he would make sure Sun knew where to place the real credit). Therefore he thought he could get away with half an hour off for shopping. But what did the bookstore have to do with culture?

'What's that supposed to be?' asked Jake.

The acrobat sculpture had appeared at the end of a vista to their right. Just before Heavenly Tinned Foods and Preserves blotted it out Fang noted that, from this angle, the granite figures seemed to be locked in sexual union; he thought suddenly of *The Golden Lotus*, an erotic novel Grandfather had occasionally mentioned along with some thrilling extracts. ('The need too urgent, they played the oldest, fiercest game: the Arrow through the Arch. Soon they were lost in the sounds and smells and tastes of battle. At the moment of his victory, which was hers also, Golden Lotus cried out from under him, "Darling, Darling!" It was her battle cry.') Prohibited in the seventeenth century, it had not stood much chance in the twentieth – and however many centuries were in store it would probably never be on sale in Yanzhou. *The Golden Lotus* stuck in the mind but was that culture?

He led the way past Eastern Market where a new delivery of fridges had the place seething with overheating matrons. They went down a side street and turned left into another, relatively quiet, where the shop stood.

'And what have we here?' said Jake, stabbing his nose at the window display. 'Translate for me, Fang.'

'Well, this one is *The Collected Works of Chairman Mao*.

Then, up there, *The Unification of China by the First Qin Emperor* and . . .'

'What's this one? I recognise the face on the cover.'

'This is by a Russian man,' said Fang. 'Sta Lin. Do you know him?'

'I have heard a bit about him, Fang! A tremendous body of work they say. But let's get inside. I sniff culture and I'm hungry for literature!'

Facetious, thought Fang. The word had always appealed to him for having all the vowels in alphabetical order, and now its meaning seemed to apply.

The only other customer in the shop was the Volley-Ball who must have come straight from class. She was browsing in the Science section which shared a shelf with Music, below Industry and above Minority Peoples. Of course, Jake understood nothing, but he bought a poster portrait of Zhou En Lai dandling some peasant baby on his knee. The severe and warty saleswoman was not amused when he loudly refused to take a poster of the Chairman in similar pose and she was horrified when he snickered at her other suggestion – the only English language edition in the shop – *Fundamental Issues in Present-Day China* by Deng Xiaoping. Fang led him out.

After work the next evening Fang dropped in at the department store to deliver the first Spring Festival invitation: Mother was inviting Old Liu! Rosy old romance could surprise them all yet. Although Fang feared the excruciating colours of the vases, their artificial blooms and odours, he dared to dash through Interior Decor because it was the quickest way to the stairs. He was shimmying to the left of a new display of plates with furry white cats' faces sticking out of their centres when he collided with another shopper. Qiao.

'What are you doing in this dreadful place?' he asked in Mandarin.

'Wedding present.'

'Who for?' Fang patted his pockets in preparation for the usual outlay to flatter another plighted classmate. 'Not the Podge?'

'No, Little Fang. Interpreter Li actually.'

'Ah.' Fang's wallet could relax. 'How nice.'

'Only it's late, you see. He was married a fortnight ago. Very small party. I've only just heard.'

'What did you have in mind?'

'About fifty yuan.'

'Fifty! He's not family, Qiao!'

'No, Fang, he's just a close friend of mine. Okay? Now if you'll excuse me, I've got some very important choices to make.'

He turned his back and thrust his nose into a dusty bunch of plastic peonies. Fang managed to catch the eye of an assistant and drew some derisory giggles from her, the perfect accompaniment to his own guffaw.

'Remember what they say, Qiao: the friendship of officials is as thin as paper,' he said and ran up the stairs.

twenty

'You can't do it!'

'Why not? Give me one good reason!'

'You just can't — it's not allowed!'

'Just because you didn't think of it. You wouldn't dare!'

'Belt up, you bastard! The Government is taking care of it — like Christmas.'

'He'll still have some free time, you know. Things have changed since Christmas. He *wants* to come to us.'

'You mean you've already—'

Their bicycles parted to avoid a tricycling granny.

'Yes, yesterday.'

'What did he say?'

Qiao messily bisected a pair of road-hog peasants and caught up again. ('Back to your paddies!' he shouted over his shoulder.)

'Yes! He said yes please!'

'It won't work, Fang. You won't be able to pull this . . .'

But Fang hung a sharp right down a lane, letting Qiao clatter straight on. If he wished to badmouth their Spring Festival plans he could do it alone.

Mother and he had decided they were really going to make something of it this year — the first ever free of censorious Fu. They were out to enjoy, enjoy. Of course Mother had to mix business with her pleasure for that was the only sort of pleasure she knew: she was going to present Jake with his socks at the lunch and Fang suspected she'd only invited Old Liu to the party in the hope that he would commission a batch of Jake-socks for the Menswear section.

Qiao could choke on his sour grapes: they tasted so very sweet to Fang. The presence of respected Liu would head off government disapproval. Besides they were being quite open about the invitation, fitting in with Interpreter Li's plans for another sterile Jake-junket in the evening at the Roast Duck.

Anyone could see the atmosphere had changed since the

warning about spiritual pollution at the opening ceremony. The door-lady's attitude, although extreme at both extremes, was really that of Yanzhou writ large. These days Jake was lauded and loved, applauded and approved. Ja Ke was OK.

But no one had ever invited him home. Fang had to acknowledge a slightly desperate strand in his thinking here. Being no stranger to the black mark – of black-mark stock and pretty black record – he felt there was nothing to lose. He might be riding a tiger but he was not about to dismount now. He was going for it – as Grandfather had advised – and going for Jake in particular. What else was there? In a way everyone was going for it too, with Deng Xiaoping's approval, but Fang felt he alone was actually getting somewhere, opening and reforming himself through Jake; Qiao and the others could hedge their bets if they wanted, but Fang wouldn't. He was putting everything on, going all out. He was all in for Jake.

It was not going to be a traditional family Spring Festival party. The Shanghai sisters had made it perfectly plain they would not be up again for a while, years even, and there had been no word from Father's brother or sister since the Cultural Revolution. Otherwise there was only the Yanzhou aunt, the one who had really suffered in the sword incident. Apart from the odd meeting with Fu, whom she fawned on, this insignificant woman had avoided them ever since. Clearly she was not about to put her ear at risk again now that it was working quite well, as well as could be expected.

But even if she didn't accept, the numbers were looking respectably large: in addition to Jake and Old Liu, Grandfather was being allowed to invite a couple of his friends (most unusual but Mother thought it might persuade him to give the tapir-face a decent reception in exchange) and Fang had thought this feast of dumplings and sea cucumber a good way to begin patching things up with Miss Ping.

Fang was reasonably amused that the (woolly) ball was back in Mother's court: now that he had got Jake's co-operation in the campaign she was having to knit like hell to finish the socks by Monday. His amusement did not survive the next two days, however, because her sock-work put the full weight of festival provisioning on to him.

Going downtown at this time he had no hope of playing

the lane game, nor of 'pedalling out'. The roads, even Harmony Boulevard, the widest of them all, were clogged. There was no way through. And so Fang had to crawl marketwards with all the other shoppers, clutching ration books and roaring about inflation.

Once there these dragons clawed and hot-breathed through the stalls. They all barged and mashed Fang's toes. And, quick as gunpowder, he too threw over a couple of millennia's civilisation to become a dragon for those terrible hours at market. He clawed and hot-breathed, barged and clomped. He hated everyone. Hate, eat, overheat.

After the first day of it he flung himself at the rice wine which Hong Wei had given Grandfather and, thoughtless of the repercussions, he gratefully sucked every drop from the bottle. He sat back on the floor by the stove to let his dragon brain absorb the mighty spirit. It carried him awhile, removed him and then dumped him back on terrifying cares (like what would he say to Grandfather, like life-after-Jake, like can I really get that scholarship?) and left him human again, with a primeval headache.

Back in the market the following day he soothed his general loathing by thinking of their Spring Festival plans and repeating to himself the great invitation.

Dear Jake,

We would be so pleasing if you could join us for meal over the coming holiday period. It will not be an extravagant get-together — just a few very close friends and simple fare. RSVP.

Sincerely Fang. (Nota Benny: lunchtime)

This had been deftly adapted from a Thanksgiving invitation featured in the VOA student life series: a smoothie called Hank, who had succeeded Jake in Chrissie's affections, was apparently confident enough in their relationship to invite the deposed Jake to party with them. Yes, after a six-week absence, Jake was back on the scene, as drawly and perfect as ever. But he'd been through a lot, this airwave Jake. All that rejection — it must be hell. Fang felt a sudden Ping-pang. What did she feel? She must really be hating me now. But she had accepted the invitation (through a go-between).

VOA Jake's return reminded Fang that his namesake would be leaving Yanzhou before long. He banished the thought, however, and smiled instead at the memory of Jake's acceptance, uttered so softly as they parted after the last class: another of those close, special moments they occasionally shared – and which never lasted long enough.

Hey, Jake! But Fang sucked back the shout. He'd spotted the yellow head bobbing about at the department-store entrance with another, brilliantined, too smooth, too familiar. But were they both wet?

Fastening his grip on the bags of pork fat, trotters and bean shoots, Fang let himself be dumped into the store by the wave of shoppers.

Qiao and Jake were thrashing along, halfway down the central aisle heading for Interior Decor which blazed with kitsch at the far end. Having skittered up there, Fang concealed himself amidst the clocks and scroll paintings and watched Jake buy a bunch of white funeral flowers. Qiao was nodding approval.

Although surprised by the choice, the assistant's eyes were rounding in pleasure as Jake laid out crisp Foreign Exchange Certificates on the counter (still using them – no business sense!). But then Qiao scooped them up and, in what seemed to be the same slick movement, calmly replaced the lot with grubby People's Money of the 'equivalent' amount. The assistant's eyes relaxed but in her slits there glowed a socket-fury matched only by Fang's own fire: a searing combination which would have grilled Qiao's liver, blistered his puds and boiled his brains.

Jake turned to leave and Fang ducked away. He had no wish to reveal himself. He was sure they had been together all afternoon, sure they had had a bath too, bugger it! Trying to muscle in so late in a day was unwise: he would have to give this one to Qiao. He wasn't a threat but any defeat niggles a man.

twenty-one

Where was he?

As Fang checked the woodshed again, Mother stepped back in through the gate, hugging and shrugging her shoulders. It had been just like lying in bed waiting for the alarm to ring: Spring Festival dawns and Grandfather goes off, regular as clockwork.

'He's bound to be back for his guests, don't you think?'

'Yes, Mother. Perhaps he has gone to collect them already?'

'Five hours early! No, this is a wander.' She darted into the kitchen and then came back to the door, shouting, 'And armed too! This is an armed wander! But I must have my sparrows! Oh!' She plucked at her apron.

Fang pulled Father's old air rifle out of the shed and dusted it with his sleeve.

'I had better get going,' he said, stuffing a small packet of pellets into his coat pocket.

'Good luck, Little Fang.'

He turned right out of the yard. Lying on the edge of the city the terrain quickly grew rough in this direction as the path left walls and moon-gates behind to become rocky, slippery and silent.

Gun a-quiver, Fang transformed himself into Communist guerrilla stalking Nationalists. Red-haters held no terror for him. He would prefer to handle a brace, even a dozen of them, rather than to meet Grandfather on this lonely track – Grandfather and sword!

His foot scrunched into a beer bottle hidden in the snow. Where the devil was . . . He froze at a rustling noise ahead. But surely Grandfather would have gone downtown, to the people and the attention he craved? But if not, if they did meet up here, how then would Fang explain the gun? There was no hope of Grandfather accepting the truth of the matter, that he had been sent up here by Mother to bag a few sparrows for today's guests. It seemed like a very tall story to Fang himself now. There would be no time for any stories, however, before the sword was sent a-swishing and a-stabbing.

But suddenly there was a sparrow to be had – fluffy and puffed up on a snowy bough. Fang crept forward and leant into a shooting pose. He fired – missed! A minute. Another ridiculous sparrow alighted, so close that Fang considered clubbing it with the barrel. He raised the gun. He was trembling so much he had to lower it again, to get a grip of himself. He fired. Hit! A truly great shot!

He scrambled over to claim the little victim, now plugged into the snow at the foot of the tree, its chest ripped open by the pellet, a weak flow of blood faintly colouring its grave.

But this would be the extent of today's carnage; there followed twenty freezing sparrowless minutes before Fang's adrenalin flowed again – and when that moment came he leapt into the air as though winged by a sniper.

'CccccccccccccccrrrrrrrraaaaaAAA!'

A massive expectoration from the other side of the spinney had Fang dropping into a classic leopard crouch. He waited. Footsteps. He wriggled even lower, deeper into the powder, soothing himself with thoughts of merry civil-war movies in which this sort of engagement was followed by lubricious peasant maidens giving themselves to Mao's victory boys.

He clasped the rifle tighter still as the throat clearance cracked around the trees again. Then two small boys came into sight. As they drew level with his hideout, Fang saw the outlines of about twenty sparrows in the polythene bag they swung between them. He was planning a desperate hold-up when the boys produced another long, proud Grandfatherly hawk and spat into the snow by his head.

Giving these scallywags a minute to get clear, Fang got up, colder than ever before, and trudged home with his kill. So much for Mother's Festival Sparrow Stew.

She was punching the dumpling mix in a tin basin when he got back into the fuggy room. Shaking her head miserably, she launched back into the squidginess: so Grandfather was still at large.

On the table lay the fruits of Fang's days at market: cabbage, masses of cabbage, bean shoots, the trotters and the pork fat, and a bag (so small!) of expensive sea cucumber. He cleared some space to rip out the sparrow's feathers and its tiny claws. Then he dropped it into a bowl of water where it floated, neck stretched, face startled, beak locked in a last tweet: their first guest of the Year of the Snake.

'I'll do a sweep of the city centre, Mother, just in case. Got to pick up the beer anyway.'

'Not too long, Little Fang. We simply can't let it distract us. I'll need some help stuffing the dumplings.'

Government dragons were clomping up and down Harmony Boulevard and loudspeakers on every lamp-post guffawed festive tunes, holiday exhortations, and good luck for the Snake. Most of the 750 million people said to be travelling about China over the Spring Festival seemed to be coming through Yanzhou – but not one of them brandished a sword.

After nosing into a couple of compounds and the Noodle Palace, Fang abandoned the hunt and cut through to Heavenly Tinned Foods (where Podgy's gatekeeping job had been firmed up, his uncle having taken very early retirement). As Fang locked the Pigeon he happened to see Volley-Ball Lo looking at him from the window of her office. He slipped quickly into the gatehouse, out of her chill stare, to find the fat man profiting hugely from the rapid turnover of cases of Qingdao Beer. Amazed to see such quality in Yanzhou, his clients were paying ridiculous prices for this last-minute addition to their tables. Clayderman was providing melodious backing to the steady fattening of Podgy's roll of bills.

'Cut it a bit fine this year – but my ship came in just in time!' He winked at Fang and, with one of his elegant and well-shod hooves, he shoved over a family-sized tin of Sunshine and Breeze mandarins.

'On the house, mate.'

'Thanks, Podge. I've got to run. Grandfather . . .'

But the King had turned away to berate someone for saying he could only afford four bottles. With the Qingdao and the Sunshine and Breeze strapped to his rack, Fang took another route back to the Baihao Hill Road. Passing the Roast Duck he noticed Old Fen in full flight through the restaurant, arms flapping. It must be like that on your busiest day of the year, thought Fang, and Jake due there with the Government in the evening.

Government Reception Building No. 2
Bright Future Street
Yanzhou

2.6.89 – Day One of the Year of the Snake

Dear Chrissie,

I've got to get this down as soon as possible and before I go and get tanked up again with the government boys tonight. I'm just back from the most bizarre occasion yet. What a way to see in the New Year!

I went to a real Chinese home for the first time – invited by that Little Fang I've told you about – Yanzhou's No. 1 English-lover. I'd heard a bit about his family from others, especially his best friend Qiao (I've mentioned him before too) but nothing could have prepared me for this lunchtime banquet.

'Do you think he enjoyed any of it, Son?'

'I'm not sure enjoy is the right word, Mother. You don't leave quite like that if you are enjoying yourself.'

'Well, apart from the . . . incident? What do you think?'

'He ate a lot. And drank. That was a good thing and must have helped him cope. Perhaps it will help him forget too.'

'Was there enough food?'

'It hardly seems important now, Mother.'

'But was there? I want to know.'

'Well, it was a good thing Old Liu brought those scorpions. And Jake liked the sparrow – I suppose that was worth the effort. But what a waste of sea cucumber. He must have got through twenty yuan's worth. It was lucky Grandfather didn't see that bit.'

My stomach amazed me, Chrissie. It took whatever they threw at it – and that means pretty well everything. I like scorpions! Get your Mom to fix some for May! I ate seven – all but the stings. One little bird was so tiny I ate half its ribcage without noticing.

There were a couple of things I couldn't manage though. Fang's mother brought out a specialty near the end of the meal – a metal-topped jar which she opened for me with her chopper. They were all watching as I poked around among the hunks of meat in jelly. 'Dog!' said Fang. I couldn't handle that. I retched – just as I was about to sink a chunk. How could I look Cindy in the eye again? It was totally embarrassing. Really, I didn't eat any.

I turned instead to what they call sea cucumber. Damn slippery. Do you know, I got six of them up to my mouth and dropped them all. There seemed to be nothing for it after that but to hit the bottle.

'Did he need to be so rude about the dog?'

'Well, Mother, VOA says they're part of the family in the West.'

'Don't be silly! Do you think Ja Ke got home all right?'

'I tried hard enough to catch him but he was away so fast.'

'Won't he be lonely now?'

'I doubt that, Mother. The Government is treating him at the Roast Duck.'

'Oh, how dreadful! Will they have anything left to give him? Won't you have some more duck, Little Fang?'

'I couldn't, Mother. I've had eleven pancakes already.'

They have these strange drinking customs at most banquets out here but 'at home' you can relax. I suppose I had had a couple of bottles of beer – large ones – and was beginning to feel a little more at ease when the most terrifying thing happened.

The door flew open and in walked a tiny old man with a vast sword dripping blood. Fang's Grandad! I knew he enjoyed something of a personality cult round here but I didn't really know why. Now I do! One of the guests, who hadn't said a word all meal, started screaming and ran out of the house holding her head. Fang and his mother managed to disarm him and take him into the next room. You'd have been proud of me! I didn't dare move! God, the shouting was terrific.

Apparently he'd gone off, as he is known to do, and gotten into the Roast Duck (where I'm due in an hour's time). The bloodthirsty old devil had slaughtered twenty ducks in the backyard before he was spotted. He chopped them up so badly that they couldn't be used for festival lunches.

The next thing to happen was that some friend of the family who works there as a roaster arrived at the door with a crate of cooked duck and a vat of red-bean sauce. He said he had just roasted the lot in a great mass of hacked up flesh, wished us Happy New Year and went off with his head in his hands.

It was great duck! I had seven wings and three pairs of breasts. God knows what they'll find for me at the restaurant tonight. Nothing I hope.

'Do you think Grandfather's friends were involved, Fang?'

'No, Mother, not at the massacre stage. But the next thing was definitely planned.'

'Never, ever again will I let him invite anyone to this house. I doubt we will ever see Aunt again.'

'And I don't think Miss Ping will be back in a hurry. Or her sister – she was terrified even before it happened.'

'Such a pity about Miss Ping – such a nice girl.'

Just when the old man had stopped screaming and spitting – awesome spitting – someone else rushed in to say there was an ambulance crew looking for the house. I thought they'd come for the grandad – I hoped they had – but in fact they were transporting two more guests, Grandad's cronies. They said they were late because they'd been caught up in a Dragon jam on Harmony Boulevard and Peace Street! At first sight these two, a man and woman, seemed to be more like I have always imagined old people to be out here – wise, peaceful and very, very ancient. The old biddy, as wizened as a passion fruit, was one of the province's top acupuncturists (they've even compared her to the great Cheng Dan'an!) and has got ambulance transport wherever she wants for the rest of her days.

Fang's mom tried to improve the rather tense atmosphere by producing plate after plate of cabbage, pork fat (Mao's favourite but not mine!), bean shoots, more cabbage, tinned mandarins and piles of duck. (Sadly they were out of scorpions!) And Fang was imploring me to drink more of the beer.

We must have been at it for more than an hour – Grandad still locked well away. The talk was typical, me having to field all those usual questions from the other guests – translated by Little Fang. I tried to tell them about my run-in with the amateur doctor – thought they might be interested but they weren't really. We moved on from beer to firewater, a toxic death spirit which makes you screw up your face as it grabs you by the throat. Everyone here pretends to like it and so do I. Same with the bamboo liqueur.

Also at the party there was an amused-looking guy who runs the department store (he brought me up a new knife and fork from his kitchen section as a present but these days I prefer chopsticks) and a stony-faced girl I'd seen at that dance, possibly Fang's girlfriend but he's cagey about that. She'd brought her young sister – about nine or ten, born just before the one-child law came in. This little one was very frightened of me and had to dare herself to look up from the cabbage even for a few seconds. I was pretty uncomfortable with my legs jammed under the low table but I tried to keep the old folks amused. They looked kind of pathetic without their playmate. The woman sat staring at me, chanting what I took to be some anti-foreign spell, but Fang said she was just running through the body's 365 acupuncture points – from *baohuang* to *zutonggu*, don't you know!

Then Madam Fang made a little sign at Fang and she disappeared next door – muffled screams; Fang whispered something about music to the girl, whom he calls Miss Ping (!).

'Miss Ping's quite a sensitive girl, isn't she?'

'Not specially. She just didn't expect to have the recital interrupted like that.'

'It was a nice idea to get her to bring her keyboard along, Son – could have been so nice . . .'

Then Madam Fang beckoned to me from behind the bedroom door. To be honest I was in two minds about following her, but the sword was by the sink and I discovered that they'd trussed the old killer up on his bed.

In there she handed me a small brown-paper parcel and told me to unwrap it. Once again I was really embarrassed because I'd only brought her a few silk flowers and they hadn't gone over that well.

'But why did you design them like that, Mother?'

'I just decided to at the last minute. The dimensions you

gave me for the feet seemed so big I decided to make the legs correspondingly long and since I had enough wool left over I thought I'd join them at the top.'

'I see . . .'

You won't believe what it was, Chrissie. A pair of sort of medieval leggings with pointed toes – or a multi-coloured romper-suit. As I held them up in amazement I saw that Madam Fang was almost weeping with pride: she'd knitted them especially. Do you remember that saga I had with Fang about the socks? Well, these were they. Some socks!

Of course I had to try them on. So I explained to her that I'd have to take my jeans off. She giggled and went back into the kitchen.

As I tugged them on, wearing nothing else except my Mao jacket and a dashing silk scarf I picked up some time ago, ol' Houdini was beginning to buck with life and I realised I would have to make my own escape from the bedroom – my entry into the kitchen – pretty soon. I could hear some sort of military march starting up on the electric organ in there. I opened the door.

'Where did they get them?'

'Oh, it's easy, Mother.'

'But so big and powerful? I thought that type had been banned by the Government.'

'Grandfather bought in bulk before the wedding, remember?'

'Of course I do! Just look at my walls!'

As I walked in, looking like some ballet star or grotesque sea bird (I don't know what sort of mess Fang had made of the measurements but they were long in the leg and longer in the foot), the two old folks started whooping and shrieking. I remember being surprised because they had been so quiet and benevolent until now. Then suddenly they produced fireworks from their laps, torched them with their cigarettes and started lobbing them at my feet.

With those things shooting off around me I had to hop about in my new role as sheriff under attack from trigger-happy gangsters. The bath-house was nothing compared to this for here was pain as well as terror – I kept treading on bits of duck carcass.

Little Fang tried to seize their supplies but there was now a dramatic escalation of firepower: Grandfather pogoed in, still turkey-tied, swiped a whole box of ammo from the acupuncturist and stuffed it straight into the stove.

From then on that kitchen became a bazooka range. Incredible noise and the crackers firing out of the stove, searing across the room and scorching the walls. Miss Ping dropped the organ and fled with her head in her hands. Everyone was screaming, me included. I snatched my overcoat to cover myself up and grabbed the basin from the sink for a tin helmet.

After about a minute of explosions and breaking glass there seemed to be a ceasefire. Very, very slowly, I peeked out. First thing I saw was the acupuncturist coming up from behind the table. This was no death mask – her features were hopping with excitement! A crazy grin which broadened and broadened till I thought the whole passion fruit would split; and her eyes glinted over the devastation.

Then the other old boy popped up his tufty little head next to her and nodded with satisfaction. Through the ceasefire silence I could hear sobbing from under the table but I never dared move to see who it was. Only the shop manager was looking at all composed, sitting by the window and holding the dumpling basket ready. Then suddenly Little Fang rolled out from behind the chest of drawers. He went into a lizard slither across the floor and bundled into my anti-flak tent.

Poor guy was gibbering with embarrassment and getting into the string of apologies which seem to be a normal feature of our expeditions when we saw appearing from behind the stove another box of firecrackers in that horrible scrawny hand. There was no time to intercept – we were just too far away to risk it – so we could only watch Grandad wham it into the burning coals. Once again that stove became the devil's own popcorn machine. This seemed to me pretty much like overkill. The first detonations could have been put down to aged high spirits – just – but now there was getting to be something really sick about it and all I wanted was to get out of there.

As new volleys of flak and stinger streamed across the room, I jumped up, rolling Fang out from the folds of my overcoat, and rushed for the door, holding my ears against the banging. Chris, I was halfway down the hill with the tails of my overcoat flying out behind the Forever before I realised I was still dressed like a court jester. But that's one great hall I'm never going back to.

Must stop here because the Toyota will be arriving in a minute. I love your letters and cling to them in the middle of this crazy wonderful insanity!

All my love,

Jake xxx

PS I need Hank's address in HK. I plan to go down there on my way home.

6 February 1989 – Year of the Snake
Carnage! Black Monday! Black Fang – blacker than ever! My ears are still ringing. My eyes sting. I shall resign everything – my place in Jake's class, my job. I'll get Xin to steal me some ping-pong-bat glue and take to the high road, become a tinker, pan for gold in Xinjiang, sell bean curd, nails, any sort of shit. Yes, that's it, I'll work as a night-soil spreader in the darkest countryside. I'll study Russian, Swahili, Serbo-Croat, learning to say each word backwards – I'll do anything to eradicate every bit of English I ever studied. Now, Fang, you must wrap your horizons around you, shut out the light and forget you ever dared to look over the edge of the world.

Fang shut his diary and looked at his watch: 7.03. He sneezed – a sure sign, Grandfather always said, that someone somewhere was talking about you. Fang had never felt readier to believe his stupid superstitions. Jake would have just arrived at the Roast Duck and be explaining to them all why he was dressed like a variegated gander.

He heard Mother shriek and something break in the kitchen. With the weary resolution of a war vet, he opened his bedroom door and went over the top again.

But he had been through the worst. This latest horror was just the sudden emergence, three hours after the other guests had left, of Miss Ping's sister, who had been cowering under the table like an abused kitten.

'She just bolted for the door. It gave me such a shock I dropped a plate.'

'Fled with her head in her hands, I bet. Didn't she even thank you, Mother?'

'Be quiet, Little Fang. If you can't be serious about this, then please shut up.' She bungled the lighting of another cigarette, her eleventh since the end of the Cultural and her seventh since the Snake had seen off the Dragon.

'I'm sorry, Mother. I'm not myself.' Whatever that meant now . . .

He tapped at Miss Ping's electric organ which lay on the window-sill like abandoned military hardware, the glass of a shattered pane all over its keys. He got nothing out of it. How could Jake have bundled me out of his coat like that? It seemed the grossest breach of trust and another shared moment utterly spoiled. They would be laughing about it now. Was Qiao there?

'These seem quite appropriate now, Mother,' he said, quite unable to stem his misery. He was flicking at the leaves of the silk mourning flowers which Jake had presented to Mother on his arrival.

'That was a poor start, wasn't it! Why on earth did he bring them, Little Fang?'

'I saw Qiao telling him to buy them a few nights ago in the department store.'

'Little Qiao? Whatever for? Why would he do a thing like that?'

'Competition, Mother. We are rivals now and he wants to do me down – especially since things have heated up.'

'Oh please no, Son. I can't go through anything like that again. What are you competing for?'

'I can't say, Mother. Don't ask me, please.'

But the pain was hers. Her head, now held in her hands like everyone else's that terrible day, would be filling with memories of the bitter conflict between the boys' fathers, of an era dreadful beyond belief. She had had to sit through some of the past already this evening – from Old Liu.

He had begun to talk seriously over a peaceful cup of tea once the ambulance had collected the old guard (Grandfather – and his firecrackers – had been invited to accompany the pin-pricker and her sidekick to a party at the PLA sanatorium).

Mother had been so affected by the day's disaster that she

had even forgotten to mention the Jake-sock idea to Old Liu, but he had appeared relaxed and most content to be back in Madam Fang's company after five years.

'I'm delighted to be here,' he said.

'I'm terribly, terribly sorry about everything, Old Liu. What a dreadful thing to have to put up with – so embarrassing . . .'

'No, not at all. I needn't tell you that I am hardly upset by a few fireworks, eh?'

'I suppose not.'

'You remember the night of my self-criticism?' Fang stood up to go. Mother signalled at Old Liu to stop, but he insisted 'And you can sit down and listen too, Little Fang. You should know about all this by now.'

'Why should he? It can do no good. I really don't think—'

'Please, will you let me speak?'

She poured more tea with head bowed.

'The night of my self-criticism – yes, that was firework night all right! They had taken every book, everything of any value in my house, out to a burning pyre in the yard, by way of a prelude. Then I was led to a hall, packed with people, all shrieking. The Red Guards made me build a pile of furniture at the front – desks and chairs and a couple of cabinets. As I stacked them up, the chanting grew wilder and the guards began dropping firecrackers at my feet, making me do the capitalist roader's dance, they said. After that they told me to climb, climb up the furniture. At first I was quite grateful to leave the scorched floor but then, as I got higher and higher, they started lobbing the bangers up at me. I suppose they expected the pile to collapse of its own accord but I had built it rather well and so when I got to the top they had to kick away the bottom desks to make me fall. And fall I did. Must have broken two or three ribs in the first tumble. The screaming hate-laughter intensified and still more when they told me to build it up again. At least this time I knew not to make it too high. They kicked it when I was halfway up – and down I came again, crashing to the floor. They made me climb that pyramid eight times that night, once for every year of my post-graduate study. They'd have been pleased no doubt to discover that I also broke eight bones.'

'Had you met Father then?' Fang ducked out of a fierce look from Mother.

'Well, I didn't know this at the time but he was at the back of that hall, and he was next up. Not so bad for him of course – he'd only been studying medicine for six years! I heard about it in the cowshed some months later. Yes, that's where I first met your father, in darkest Qinghai. Not the easiest of times. He was nursing his father's stomach cancer as best he could – he had only the most basic medicine and painkillers and he had to administer these in secret because the guards were especially vigilant about such rightist crimes as caring for a dying father – such a bourgeois and counter-revolutionary thing to do.'

Mother went to the sink and began washing dishes with deliberate clatter. Old Liu smiled.

'She was the only good thing to come out of those days. She had been sent down to a state farm near by and I think she started bringing bread or something, officially selling it to us intellectuals but never accepting the money. I watched your father fall in love with her – I watched them falling in love with each other. She was a beauty – still is!

'Once his father died, Little Fang managed to get a transfer to her farm – there was always a way for the really determined even in those days. In fact the back door as an institution really got going in the Cultural. They married, after a fashion, and I saw them often over the next few months, on the fields near our fence. We became quite expert at long-range communication! Very occasionally, when they were really close, they'd manage to pass food and notes through for a few of us. Those scraps and snippets made a hell of a difference. But those who didn't get them grew jealous and Fang had enemies anyway. He made enemies effortlessly, your father – he never could understand why and hardly noticed their malevolence. But they were to do for him after a while.

'A band of Red Guards was making a Western tour – "with Mao's personal blessing" they said, but their sort always had that! – to check on the re-educating being done in Qinghai's cowsheds. When they got to ours they found some hideous slackness: eggshells were "proof of our high living" and there were some parts of a radio. I think they also found a mirror!

The prison guards were replaced at once. But then, most horrible, they found two books under someone's mattress – Einstein's *Theory of Relativity* and a novel by someone called Jack London. The secret reader, a pathetic little man, was quickly exposed and the Red Guards took him outside to perform their punishment – "with Mao's personal blessing"—'

'No more, please, Old Liu. You've said too much – far too much.'

After some whispered words by the sink, he had been persuaded to leave. Fang had seen him to the gate and in the dark quiet of the alley asked whether the man to whom he had entrusted his scholarship application – Chen Ge of the Landu Municipal Government – was one of Father's friends in the cowshed.

'Yes, Little Fang, he was there – very young, very confused. Your father cared for him until they married and then I took him on. Chen was no more than a boy and he had a terrible breakdown. He should never have been in that place – didn't even have a bad record. He'd just been sent down to fill some bureaucrat's quota of rightists found. If they couldn't find enough real ones they picked out others to keep their bosses off their backs. Chen's come good now though – a really big fish in Landu. I only hope he can help you.'

'So do I!'

Old Liu kicked the back tyre of his bicycle and Fang backed through the moon-gate. A neighbour chucked out some slops a little way down the alley. Her pail clanked.

'Whatever your mother fears, I had a very good time to-day and I should think you've given that American of yours something to write home about! He seemed to be on the ball: the first to peep out during the ceasefire – except for me!'

'It was kind of you to give him the knife and fork.'

'That was just my way of showing support for Hu Yaobang.'

'Hu Yaobang?'

'Yes, don't you remember? He was the leader who campaigned for cutlery to replace chopsticks on hygiene grounds. He has some vision and he's done much to liberate our minds from Mao. He even got our bodies out of those Maoist straitjackets – he was the first to wear a Western suit. It was the worst news of the decade when Deng Xiaoping – his old friend – dropped him after the student demonstrations a couple of years ago.'

'Will he ever come back – be rehabilitated?'

'Never guess at the future, Little Fang: it's as dark as lacquer – remember? However, I will say that I may dare to come back here before another five years pass!'

'You must! We would like that.'

He rummaged in his coat. 'I almost forgot. Take this,' he said, presenting a small red envelope, the traditional Spring Festival money gift.

'Thank you, thank you,' said Fang, trying not to wonder how much it contained (that wasn't the point). 'Come and visit us again soon, Old Liu. Go carefully past the sand factory.'

He pedalled off. (Five yuan won't get me far!)

'Come on – please tell me what are you competing for, Son.'

'I will tell you, Mother, but on one condition . . .'

'That I tell you about Qiao's father?'

'Yes, Mother.'

'I've always said I never would.' She rubbed at an obstinate scorch mark on the wall with a cloth. 'Really thought it better you didn't know. But perhaps I'm being selfish – you have a right to know. It's hard for me too – perhaps we should share it . . . perhaps you have a right . . .'

'I think I do, Mother. A son has certain rights.' Sounded pi but it had to be said.

'Where shall I start?'

'Where Old Liu stopped?'

She was silent for at least a minute.

'They took the secret reader outside and, in order to cure his tendency to read, they drove two huge nails into his eyes. The man went mad with the pain and no one knew what to do. It would have been better to have shot him at once – but that was not the Cultural's style. They were re-educating him.'

'By going for his brain?'

'Yes. Anyway they were shouting for a doctor and no one came forward – perhaps there were none in the cowshed by that time, but it was never a good thing to admit anyway. But of course those people who were jealous of your father, jealous that he'd got out and also that he'd got me – yes they were! – they told the guards where he was and Old Liu was sent over the fields to get him. The pair of them returned and Father gave the man what little morphine he had left. But there was no way he could have taken the nails out under those conditions. They were rusty and hammered in deep. The man died that night but at least the pain had eased.'

'Where does Old Qiao come in?'

'Well, he was in the band of Red Guards, some sort of commissar, slightly older than the others.'

'Was he in charge?'

'Not exactly – no one would have dared discipline those "little generals" – but he had a certain influence and he managed to persuade them to commandeer your father there and then for their own purposes. In those days, you see, doctors weren't allowed formal training because Mao had declared that it was somehow better to pick up medicine in the field – you know, his "learn to swim from swimming" inspiration. Anyone with any sense, like Qiao's father, privately realised the madness of this and so they took Father away as a valuable asset – a qualified doctor. He was to keep them healthy so they could continue to "do revolution" on him and anyone else they happened to meet.'

'Was that it, Mother?'

'What more do you want? They just took him off. He spent his time patching up their wilder excesses. Nails were the band's speciality, you see, and they often got the balance between re-education and destruction just a little wrong. There was lots to do. Qiao was his master, personally responsible. They were always together and of course they talked. At any normal time they could even have been friends but then – well, their positions made it impossible and Qiao was responsible for much of the brutal treatment your father endured. Then Qiao himself developed cancer somewhere in southern China. Suddenly he was at your father's mercy. The nails were still being driven into rightists wherever they went. Fang tried to use Qiao's condition to bargain with the Red Guards. It was a mad risk and it failed. Qiao could perhaps have restrained them but he was thinking about his own pain of course. One night they smashed both your father's big toes with a hammer. They were about to start on his knees when he agreed to operate on Qiao. Evidently he chopped out this cancer in time – and of course some medicine was suddenly made available.'

'Did you know all this was happening, Mother?'

'Of course not. I didn't see or hear from him for three years. I thought he was dead.'

'They let him go eventually?'

'No, he escaped. Not his first attempt. But he did it eventually. Qiao may even have turned a blind eye – it was the least he could have done. And then we came down here to hide in 1971. That was possible then. The country was in chaos.'

'When did you see Little Qiao's parents again?'

'Two years afterwards – they came to live in Yanzhou too! Your father was hobbling down Harmony Boulevard when he spotted him. That jolted us! A few months later they actually talked. It seemed Qiao was in hiding too. The atmosphere was changing so fast. All sorts were having to lie low – so many people suddenly had so much to hide. You either persecuted others in order to hide your own past or else you lay low and, by this time, few people had the energy to go on persecuting and Qiao was not one of them. Mao may have said the Chinese had stood up in 1949 but within two decades they were back on their bellies. He was growing more and more senile of course as the Gang of Four gradually got going. Everyone was at risk with them around. And then one day you brought someone home from kindergarten. It was Little Qiao. You said you were best friends! At first I thought this was dreadful and I tried to stop you seeing each other but, you know, you were neighbours in class and got on so well. Your father said to me that this was the best way – the only way – to cope with the past. And, although we never spoke to Qiao or his wife – and I still haven't to this day – there seemed to be tacit agreement between us that you two could come and go through each other's homes, that this was the only way: forget about the Great Helmsman and adore the Little Emperors. Qiao even started calling me Aunty.'

'And I called them Uncle and Aunt too! But 1975, Mother?'

'There's nothing much to it.'

Her flow was suddenly checked.

'What did you find out?'

'Nothing. He just disappeared one day.'

'Do you know why, Mother?'

'No idea.'

'Was . . . Old Qiao . . . involved?'

'I've often wondered about that but I think I've decided he cannot have been.'

'Are you sure, Mother?'

'No, I'm not sure. Who can be sure? What is "sure"? That's enough of all this anyway. What about your side of the bargain?'

'Well, Little Qiao and I are going for the same scholarship.'

'What, this Landu agricultural thing?'

'Not exactly. It's to study English in Chicago – America.'

Mother looked away: she was not going to reveal her thoughts on this. There had been enough ruction and revelation for one day. Nor did Fang have to endure any difficult silence because the door opened and an ambulance man ushered Grandfather inside. The old devil was sooty and exhausted, as was Mother, and Fang wanted to go away and think. They each went to bed for the first night of the Snake.

twenty-two

As Fang woke the next morning his memory of the party quickly filled that space normally reserved for considering a day's potential. He was not usually a gloomy waker but the face he washed at the sink this Tuesday morning fronted a head full of black stormcloud.

Mother was back at the walls already, driving her damp cloth at the plaster; the duck carcasses had been collected from all parts of the room — most of them from under the table where Miss Ping junior had evidently coped with her hours of terror by scoffing furiously — and they were now piled high in the tin basin, the remains of the sparrow's ribcage being gruesomely involved with a half-eaten duck's head.

'We'll have to buy a new Tolerance, Son.'

'What?'

He followed her eye to the corner by the stove where there lay a blackened, crumpled sheet of calligraphy.

'Ah yes, Mother. Tolerance.'

The sweet smell of breasts, wings and red-bean sauce — plus cordite — was still strong enough to wipe out any desire for breakfast and accompany Fang into Grandfather's room. Healthy Balls in one hand and a Green Serpent in the other, Grandfather framed his greeting with such a leer that Fang almost ran from the task: but he knew he had to have some decent answers and that he must catch him as fresh as possible if this was going to be a worthwhile post-mortem.

People's Cement, Baihao Hill Road, Yanzhou

Febuary the 8th, 1989. Dear Jake,

Yesterday I spoke to my Grandfather for a long time about the terrible incident at the end of our Spring Festival lunch party. He has calmed down and told me some things which were going around inside his head when he was throwing the firecrackers at you Jake.

You may find these reasons hard to believe but I believe

they are the best ones available and knowing Grandfather they seem to make sense.

Although he was only thirty-four years-of-age when the Communists liberated our China in 1949, but his mind was formed in the traditional mould. This means he thinks all foreigners are bad people like the missionaries and business men who swaggered so much around old Shanghai.

The worst thing he believed is to invite a foreigner into the home of an elderly Chinese because he has heard that your Christian religion involves drinking blood and that the last rights are done by sticking a tube down the throat of the Chinese old person and sucking all his blood away. Like the Missionaries did with Jesus. Grandfather might have been in agreement with Mr RJ about missionaries no?

Grandfather is most worried about his old age because he thinks he missed youth due to historical circumstances and so he is always trying to prove he is still young even today. Which was why he did the massacre at the Roast Duck. Therefore he had arranged with his elderly friends to throw firecrackers to show you they are still in life's prime and don't want last rights. Perhaps you heard him shouting as well which translates as 'Tremble and obey', as the Emperors used to tell the embassadors from the West.

Quite frankly I believe there could of been another object to this display. He has told me many times about the beauty of the Golden Lotus, the quintessentially of oriental female beauty, and his saddest regret about Liberation was the final end of foot-binding in China. My grandmother was a Golden Lotus you see which means her feet were the most beautiful possible, the plantar just three inches long. He worshipped them and he made his three eldest daughters bind too although by that time it was not a very popular thing to do. Mother luckily was young enough to avoid it.

Now I say this because I think my Grandfather might have been made even more excited by Miss Ping's feet, which are in fact quite elegant. (I have noticed this even when she wears ordinary shoes.) At lunch party however she was wearing new high heels which even I have never seen before and these made her walk in that old Golden Lotus way. 'Teetering' is your word I think. Grandfather has told me that he became quite over-heated about the sight and could not allow a 'large-footed demon' to share it.

Indeed he considered your presence a great insult to a beautiful young Chinese girl. Of course I do not agree with that but I am just explaining the things going through his old mouldy mind.

Fireworks in our China have a long history beginning with the story of the stinking giant who lived outside a village and gave all the inhabitants malaria. One day a villager decided to light a heap of bamboo stems and the huge popping noise which resulted drove the stinking giant away. Since then, I'm afraid, making noise has always been a good thing to do in our China, a tradition which lasts up till today.

As I rite I do not really expect you to believe but Jake you must accept these words (so badly written I'm sure) as the explaination of my most latest insult to you.

Resting assured that I will not trouble you in the near future unless I hear word that you might possibly forgive me.

Sincerely Fang.

Reading through the letter for the fifth time, Fang had to admit that it was a little masterpiece – possibly his greatest work yet. But then, given the circumstances, nothing less would do.

There were few people in for the festival shift on Thursday, but Fang was one of them. This was the penultimate day of the New Year holiday, which now seemed like a personal reproach. He longed for it all to end and winced as every spluttering firecracker broke his concentration on the Mancunian cement mixers.

Important advice to supervisors: skin contact with the ingredients of low alkali cement (calcium silicate, aluminate and gypsum) can result in severe 'cement burns' with ulceration . . .

He had been told to finish his translation by the end of the month and, what with revising for Jake's exam, Fang felt under more pressure than ever before.

When dry cement becomes airborne, especially if mixed with air-entraining agents, workability aids, pulverised fuel-ash and granulated blastfurnace slag, it is especially dangerous to the eye, mouth and nose . . .

What was he supposed to do with a sentence like this? And yet, if Manager Sun was not aware of the lethal nature of the commodity he dealt in, then Fang must lose no time in presenting him with the correct Mandarin characters.

But the grief over what he had done to Jake would keep boiling over. He had left the letter, and the jeans and shoes, with the door-lady the previous afternoon. But there had been no reply – probably never would be.

He was gripping his head in his hands in an attempt both to block out the noise and to soothe the lobes of his brain, when someone tapped him on the shoulder. It was Wong.

'That foreigner, Ja Ke, he's here to see you, Fang.'

'Jake! Jake? Where, Wong, where?'

'Down in the front hall. The security man won't let him up.'

Fang bombed down the concrete stairs to find Jake examining the polystyrene model of the Guilin mountains now gracing reception in a large glass case.

'Hello, Little Fang. What are you doing here on your holiday?'

'What are *you* doing here, Jake?'

'Come to see you, of course.'

'How do you find it?'

'I went up to your house first.'

'You went back to there?'

'Well, not quite. I met your mother in the alley. She said you'd be here.'

Fang was amazed not only by Jake's boldness but by his skill in remembering the route to the alley and in conversing with Mother. Astonishing.

'But why? Why have you come here?'

'Don't you want to see me, Fang?'

'Of course, Jake. I'm terribly pleased. Just surprising, that's all!'

'I wanted to thank you.'

'*Thank* me? Thank *me*?'

'For lunch. It was an extraordinary occasion.'

'Extraordinary?'

'And wonderful.'

'What?'

'Well, once I calmed down and sobered up, I realised what a great experience it had been. And so I wanted to thank you – and apologise for rushing off like that. Yellow-bellied Yankee!'

'But . . .'

'Your letter was quite unnecessary, but very interesting to have an insight into the old fellow's thinking. How is he? If only I'd known that he thought I was set on giving him malaria and last rites and then sucking out his blood and fondling Miss Ping's little feet – if only I'd known I could have tried to calm his fears. But I didn't!'

'Nor did I! But nowadays he's fine. He's very okay . . . But I'm so pleased to hear you. Such a load off from my mind, I can tell you, Jake.'

'I brought this for your mother.' He went over to the bench where Fang had already spotted the dreadful Jake-sock on top of a khaki shoulder-bag. He was returning it. Hardly surprising. How would Mother take this blow? She certainly deserved it. 'I thought it would be better if you gave it to her from me. Otherwise she might be a bit embarrassed.'

But Jake pushed the sock aside and pulled a small package from the bag.

'You already gave her something – those flowers . . .'

'Don't remind me! I have never felt so bad in my life. It came out at the dinner afterwards – the Deputy Mayor mentioned you should never give flowers like that for anything except funerals. Qiao went white at the table and I gave him a real blasting afterwards. You see, he told me to get them for her. A calculated insult. I'm beginning to think there's some tension between you.'

Fang unwrapped the intriguing polythene to find a small plate with 'Wilmington, Delaware, USA' in gold letters around the edge. In the centre there was a detailed black-ink drawing of a small building.

'It's a souvenir of my home town. I brought a few out here as gifts.'

'How many did you bring?'

'What a question!' Jake laughed. 'Three – no, four, I think.'
Gave Qiao a blasting but has he given him a plate?

'Well? Do you think she'll like it, Fang?'

'Of course she will! What a question! Is this your house in the middle here? So big!'

'No! That's a mill on the banks of the River Brandywine. You see Wilmington was the first place in America to produce gunpowder – centuries after you guys of course! This building is a gunpowder mill.'

'So you know about fireworks, Jake?'

'I ought to. An ancestor of mine was one of the very first mill-workers. He got blown up with one of the mills. It was always happening.'

'Oh, I'm terribly sorry, Jake.' Everyone seemed to have explosions somewhere in the past.

'Don't worry! He was my great-great-grandfather or something. I'm not too upset about it.'

Trying to ignore this shocking disloyalty, Fang rewrapped the plate and held it against his chest.

'Well, I'd better let you get back to work,' said Jake.

'No, no . . .'

'I've got to go to another official thing in half an hour anyway.'

'Was your Roast Duck dinner success?'

'Didn't really feel like it actually – especially after hearing about the flowers. It was pretty tame compared to your lunch – and there wasn't very much to eat.'

'Did you . . . tell them about . . .'

'Hell no, Fang! I'm not that indiscreet.'

'But weren't you wearing those socks?'

'Of course I wasn't! I have got a change of clothes, you know!'

The needles pricking into Fang's cranium were being extricated one by one. The agony and the ecstasy.

'And you must thank your mother for this – I've finally solved the chill problem.'

He swung the bag over his shoulder and dramatically wrapped the Jake-sock round and round his magnificent neck.

'What do you think?' he mumbled through the wool. 'Goodbye, Fang, and thanks again!'

'Goodbye. And thanks.'

He watched Jake pedal out of the compound. I'll be jiggered. When the ill-fitting glass doors finally stopped thumping back and forth on their hinges, Fang was aware of the security man observing him from his box.

'Must be amazing that.'

'What!'

'Conversing – you know, in a foreign tongue like that.'

'Yes. Yes, it is.' Fang turned to go upstairs.

'And what about that thing round his neck?'

'That was a scarf. A new type of scarf. I think you can get them at the Sunday market.'

He beat a hand triumphantly upon the mountain display case and ran back up to the office.

twenty-three

Fang felt remarkably stable – almost calm – over the next few weeks. Although he saw less of Jake, who was now giving talks at the middle schools and any other institution boasting a few English-speakers, this did not agonise him. It merely marked a new phase of their friendship.

He had survived that wearing adolescent-passion stage; they had now reached full and confident friendship. They had been through so much together; there was no need for reassurance every day. The confidence was just there, and it was enough. Since the Spring Festival bomb party, Fang had even thought of Jake as a co-veteran, and of his Wilmington plate as a medal, as much long service as bravery.

Discreet inquiries showed that no one else had been so honoured – except the Mayor whom Jake had 'plated' during a formal presentation at the government offices back in November. A third plate was rumoured to be up as a prize for the best exam result – which would leave just one other to be accounted for. But such niggly uncertainties didn't really bother Fang these days.

There were other pressures, however. Manager Sun's reforms were beginning to bite throughout the plant and, to Wong's ill-concealed pleasure, Fang's translation deadline was brought forward sharply. Indeed, Wong had become an unexpectedly potent threat in another area: rumours were linking him to Miss Ping.

Fang had had no contact with her since she'd taken to her high heels from the hell kitchen; and in fact the only time he'd so much as seen her had been at a bicycle garage with Little Wong attending to the tyres of her Lady Pigeon. Fang blanched at the thought of that dullard, that non-being challenging him for the girl he – he what? Well, the girl he had always seen as his, as far as anyone was; deep down, he'd taken that as read. Especially after all that body language – dirty talk! – at the dance party. Surely that had meant something to her.

The cement-mixer manuals, which he now had to work on at home in the evenings, conspired with Grandfather to deprive him of revision time. The old fellow was requiring an especially huge amount of care: he had threatened to contact an old people's welfare group just started in Peking, to claim that he was being battered and exploited.

His post-festival attention-seeking was not unusual but Mother's decline was more alarming. She had become obsessed about abandonment: first Father, then Fu had gone and now Fang was considering his flight – to America. Only Grandfather, she said, seemed horribly constant. To soothe her Fang had been a little less sanguine – a bit more realistic? – about his chances of winning the scholarship. This lifted her out of the trough but dumped him right in it. However, in supporting his neurotic seniors, Fang felt filial, loyal and admirable; for the first time, he felt that he was perhaps becoming the Man of the House.

Relations with Qiao gradually improved now that he could no longer seriously aspire to friendship with Jake. For Qiao had taken the flower blasting very badly indeed and now barely mentioned him. This touchiness, which Fang felt typical of his repressed childhood, forced Qiao to see Jake actually as an enemy.

It was against this background that English Corner revived and in Qiao's room on the first Sunday in March Fang dared broach the other momentous subject – the scholarship – which had just begun to snag again on his general contentment. He was eager to revive this issue and by doing so in English he felt he might more easily tease information out of Qiao.

'Any new news from Landu?'

'Landu? Ah! I see, Frankie, Landu! Good question!' Qiao's grin was back; he was grinning like a possum. 'My father has heard that many many have applicated.'

'Oh dear.' Fang could only affect nonchalance by hiding his quivering lips in his tea – so hot that he had to swallow a yelp of pain.

'Not oh dear actually. These applications are made from residents of Landu only. From the rest of province very few.'

'Why, Charlie?'

'Lazy peasants, I suppose. Too stupid.'

'Or else never heard about scholarship?'

'Anyway I feel quite pleasing already.'

'Why?'

'Cannot tell you now – really cannot, Frank. But my plans are going according to plan – I'll put it that way for you?'

'Has anyone else from this region entered?' Fang knew he was being reckless and fishing for disappointment, but he was now back with his early fears about Lorryman Yang. So much of his contentment was due to the belief that his future was actually being worked out at last – and by the friendly Chen Ge. But if he had been hoping against hope all along . . . ? Could he coax some reassurance out of Qiao?

'I do not know in such details. But there are some others according to Interpreter Li. Why do you looking at me like that? I really do not know.'

'How is Interpreter Li, Charlie? Was he very delighted with your wedding present?'

'Not too delighted actually, Frank. The strange thing is – between you and between me – he seems not pleased with me, displeased. He even tries ignoring me.'

'I did tell you it would happen – a whitewashed crow does not remain white for long.'

'Be quiet. Could say the same about that Jake.'

'You were cut to quick by his comments in the Roast Duck, haven't you. Serves you right!'

'Funeral flowers were just a joke – might have gone wrong. But he really lost his cucumber. I have forgotten about him, but he made me lose face in front of all the Government Men. That's hard to forget. Anyway Interpreter Li is far more important for me. I'm worrieder about him.'

'Perhaps Li thinks you have been spiritually polluted?'

'Why? I am Class Monitor, remember! I *have* to contact with the American.'

'Not that. Remember you have also applied for a foreign scholarship.'

'But Interpreter Li write reference!'

'Makes no difference. You have still showed the Government your ambition. This is what matters.'

'Do you think so?'

Fang went over to stroke the dusty pate of the plaster

Chairman Mao which Qiao had always had on the bookcase (and was surely only keeping now on his father's instruction. Talk about over-filial!). 'It's like this fellow's Hundred Flowers Campaign in 1957, isn't it?' said Fang. 'He told all the intellectuals they could make their criticisms of the Party and then, when he knew who were his enemies, he gave them – as Jake would say – hell.'

Qiao laughed heartily at this. 'Interpreter Li is not Chairman Mao!'

'But he works for the same company, no?'

Fu's Spring Festival best wishes reached the family exactly one month into the Year of the Snake.

'She must be very busy,' said Fang drily.

'Oh, she is. And very happy too.' Mother was clutching the letter and speaking with a pride which should properly have been reserved for discussing him. 'She even has a maid from Anhui province living in.'

'Brother-in-law must be doing well.'

'Money hides a thousand deformities.' This was Grandfather.

'The maid's illiterate. Fu has to read her letters to her from the boyfriend in the countryside – and then write the replies! But she cooks very good spicy bean curd.' Mother looked up with a fatuous smile. 'The flat's beautiful now, she says. Electric fan in the sitting-room, dimmer switch on the light in the bedroom – and the whole place is carpeted! Imagine! Hong Wei's got an uncle who flies for CAAC and he got them some aisle carpet from an old Tupolev – aquamarine. They've done the whole flat in strips!'

'Sounds lovely, Mother, but what does Elder Sister actually do?'

'Well, she's been moved from the PLA san. They were short of nurses at the Capital Hospital so she's gone up there. Says they've even treated that leader, Hu Yaobang – he's got a dicky heart. Rumour is he collapsed when he went back to his home over Spring Festival . . .'

'Does she say what her Spring Festival was like?'

'Very grand, apparently. Hong Wei swept her off to see all the rich relations in the taxi.' She lowered her voice. 'The noise of firecrackers outside their block at midnight on the big night was recorded at 118 decibels. She says she actually missed "sleepy old Yanzhou" for a few minutes! She should have been here!'

'Grandson?'

'Oh, I don't think so, Father – not yet anyway. And there's a special message here for you, Fang. You'd better keep it to yourself.' She pushed the sheet across the table and Fang read:

> Lots of your Ja Ke Americas here. Husband says it's best to sting them on the way in from the airport when they haven't worked out about yuan! And there's an English Corner which attracts hundreds of students to a park every Sunday. When I see them I think of you. It's a different world up here. I've enclosed my paper place mat from Kentucky Fried Chicken. Husband took me there the other night. Fast food, I love it!

He sniffed at a splodge of grease on the mat. Mmmm, intriguing: distance seems to have made the heart grow fonder.

Fang dropped in on Old Liu a couple of days later in the hope that he had heard some news from Chen Ge. Ushered into the office, he was shocked to see such exhaustion on Liu's face, before it lit up in greeting.

'Come in, come in!'

'Is this a bad time for you, Old Liu?'

'No, no, no, not so bad. It's just that this job of mine . . . well, sometimes it's too much.' He pushed a jar across the desk. 'Here, take one of these, Little Fang. Know what they are?'

'They look like sweets – marriage sweets.'

'They are. One of the girls in this work unit – she works in the Musical Instruments section – got married a few months back. As manager I had to deal with all the paperwork and everything – a great hassle because she was a bit young and we had to press the authorities for the permit – you know the scene. She said love couldn't wait! And then I had to go off to the wedding and all, even though I scarcely knew either family.'

'And they gave you these?'

'And before I'm halfway through the jar the girl's name is back on my desk and I'm having to push through her divorce! Double Happiness has changed to Double Bitterness, just like that. It's ludicrous!'

'What is? Divorce?'

'Not divorce itself – I'm not against that, though it'll bring her problems with people not wanting used goods and that. At least she doesn't have a child – didn't quite have time! No, what bothers me is my role in it all – welfare bloody secretary as well as department store manager. I'm expected to expand the business to compete with all the new private shops – tycoons like your mother! – and, at the same time, carry through these outdated duties sorting out the personal problems of my employees. Sometimes I feel like chucking it all in and studying, like former Party General Secretary Hu Yaobang – it's said he spends his time now working on classical texts about court intrigue!'

Fang knew the girl, a former classmate, the bright one who'd got a bum job assignment. Her life was evidently going great guns. But Fang was here to talk about his own – and whether Old Liu liked it or not, he was a major player.

'Yes, I have been in touch with Chen. The whole thing has become predictably tricky – the infighting and the string-pulling. Actually he says he is delighted to have someone of his own to push. He was amazed to hear of Little Fang's son. And I don't know what you stuck in your application but it seems to have impressed Chen. Trouble is, as you're bound to know, what you write is only half of it. And now the Government is really belly-aching about the number of students who never come back from their foreign universities so they are insisting on ideological purity among the chosen candidates. Best advice I can give you, Little Fang – but don't get me involved in this! – is to find yourself a wife. They think that if you are leaving a little lady behind, then you are more likely to want to return. That's their thinking anyway!'

'I couldn't take a wife for a reason like that!' How odd that marriage should now be seen as the key to escape.

'One thing's for certain – Grandfather would enjoy another wedding in the family!'

Gunning the Pigeon back up the Baihao Hill Road, Fang

rather resented Old Liu's tone, which was a deal too flippant for his liking. Thoughts of the scholarship were pricking at him more and more.

Meanwhile, ten hours a week, Jake's English course continued. Attendance was still good but the institute director's idea that poor students be pulled up by the stronger was forgotten fantasy. Fang was relieved to acknowledge that human nature just doesn't work like that. (The Director had been as unrealistic as those desultory television reports of peasants presenting PLA soldiers with great fatted pigs in gratitude for all they have done for China. You just don't do that to soldiers!)

The barriers in the class remained. The reception desk, led by Pretty Pei, was the centre of unrest and dominated the likes of Ban, a weak soul from the flax mill, and the two leather-workers at the back of the room. Those trendy girls (all four of whom had bought Mother's scarves) still understood barely a word of English but this didn't stop their fun. They gossiped, tittered and passed cartoons (some quite good likenesses) of Jake.

For a time Fang had had to be part of the secret postal link connecting Pei and Ping-Pong-Bat Xin. At first it had been one-way mail as she kept her honour in the flood of lewd notelets and tiny keepsakes. But about a month ago Fang had started passing her replies as well and he had sadly accepted Xin's claim to have stormed her at last. The brazen addict even applied to Qiao for a change of desk so that he could be right up behind her.

Otherwise everyone was sitting unchanged from the opening ceremony. Fang and Qiao led the really serious contingent – comprising the four middle-aged students, Lin Hu, the trainee teacher, and the diligent Liu Wei. There were others, one of the most attentive being Miss Lo from Heavenly Tinned Foods. She sat apart and didn't contribute but took notes like a bloody bureaucrat and Fang was now sure she had been reporting back on the course to the Government Men. They must have placed someone and the idea of Qiao being a spy was ridiculous.

Jake presided skilfully. He'd deserved those night-school

honours: he could handle a class. Although the period of spellbound admiration had passed – he could no longer rely on the charm of his cartoon nose or his twangy accent – he was still in control. You could not afford to relax because he could suddenly turn strict and catch you out and make you feel stupid. For this reason, as much as any new linguistic trick he imparted, Jake compelled attention.

Fang still escorted him back from class when he didn't have to race off to a speaking engagement. After one lesson Jake mentioned that the students' pre-exam presents were coming in faster and faster, so Fang went on from Bright Future Street to the department store where he hurriedly bought a furry-cat plate from Interior Decor. (Jake would want something typically Chinese and this was *the* latest accessory.) From the bookstore he bought a card and, leaning on the counter, carefully wrote inside it:

My Dear Jake.

The Great Five things in our China are; Heaven, Earth, Prince, and Parent and Teacher. For me I can say that the fifth is the first.

Sincerely Fang.

That was the sort of thing.

He splodged some of the assistant's glue on to the envelope and pressed it down so the thin paper became satisfactorily soggy. Then he dropped it into a bag with the furry-cat plate, wrote 'Ja Ke America' in large letters on the outside and biked it over to the door-lady who said she would present it when he got back. In her fusty little box office she was contentedly stifled in the multi-coloured scarf which Fang had persuaded Mother to give her. He got back to catch the last ten minutes of Mickey Mouse. Grandfather never missed this new programme and tonight, as usual, he scoffed at the suggestion that his cheery little hero was American.

Fang got more entertainment (if that was the word) out of the real thing. Jake! He never ceased to amaze! Take the time he suggested they went for a 'walk in the country' – in the dirty, filthy, primitive countryside. Fang quickly put him off that wild idea!

Even in Yanzhou, Jake was perpetually tugging at him ('What now?') and seeking details of some ancient architectural feature. Remember how excited he got when, on the eaves of an old roof, he had spotted those Buddhist swastikas which some Cultural Revolutionary had tried to block out with little pats of cement!

And the turn of his conversation. That was something else! 'It sounds as if my Mr Bush made a boo-boo with your leaders the other day in Peking.'

'What? Boo-boo?'

They were walking briskly down Peace Street, Siberian gusts grabbing at them. Fang could hardly hear Jake, let alone understand what he was going on about now. They had just had the last lesson before the exam and Fang was almost tearful.

'I got a letter from a friend back home who said Bush invited that outspoken astrophysicist – your namesake – to a banquet during his visit last month.'

'Who?'

'Fang Lizhi – the most dangerous man in China, they call him.'

'Why?'

'Haven't you even heard of him? He holds some pretty wicked views about the Party and its doctrines. They expelled him a couple of years ago – just when that Hu Yaobang was dumped. Aren't you interested?'

'Yes, just very cold, that's all.'

Turning into Bright Future Street they were buffeted less.

'As Fang and his wife were going into the banquet a whole bunch of secret police headed them off. They weren't allowed in.'

Perfectly understandable, thought Fang. Who would want to sit down with his enemy? One speck of rat's dung soils a whole pot of rice.

'Amazing, isn't it?'

'Yes, Jake, amazing.' Now, are you going to invite me in out of this hellish wind?

'Hey, I never even thanked you for your cat plate – and the

card. Do you want to come up and see what else I've got?'

They clicked up the stairs and down the long corridor. Jake dug the key out from his massive overcoat and then flung open the door.

'Aaaaiiiieee!' Fang squealed. Kitsch! Jake's desk was arranged like a high-banked amphitheatre filled with representatives from the department store's Toy and Interior Decor sections. The colour flared on upwards too – he had stuck all his cards on the wall around that naked Renoir who seemed transfixed with horror on her couch.

Fang had to shield his eyes from the glitzy crowd: an alabaster monkey-king; his furry-cat plate; wooden building blocks painted in simplified Chinese characters; a plastic mandarin who wobbled from side to side when you wound him up so that his ear-pieces wiggled; a doll in a head-dress and pink marriage robes; another furry-cat plate; a rubber rabbit; two clockwork tin cars; a tank; glass ashtrays, one purple, one orange; Healthy Balls; a tiny jade Buddha on a plastic stand; fake silk peonies on bright-green plastic stems; a bag of sweet potatoes; yet another furry-cat plate.

'But where are your Wilmingtons, Jake?' It was important to keep track of them.

'In a drawer, Fang. They couldn't match this lot, eh?'

'So many!'

'Even Interpreter Li's out to win my favour these days. Look at my toilet paper supplies. These copies are pretty recent. There was one front-page picture which really made me laugh. I saved it for you.'

He looked through a pile of papers at the front of the desk and pulled out a *China Daily* cutting which he handed to Fang. 'It's from the end of January – this year!'

Smiling soldiers appeared to be playing pipes in the over-exposed photograph. The caption read:

Rounds of music – students from the People's Liberation Army Academy of Jinan Military Area perform to two elderly residents in a pre-Spring Festival PLA ritual of bringing joy to the lives of elderly throughout the country. The students have carried out their community-minded practices for the past two years. Kids, too, appreciate the sessions.

'What d'you think of that? One of these copies even comes from last week. It's bad news from Lhasa – you know, Tibet. My mom mentioned there'd been reports of some trouble in her last letter – yak-hair catapults against automatic rifles – but here's confirmation from your Government's organ.'

Jake thrust another cutting at Fang: Martial law imposed in Lhasa at midnight on 7 March. Eleven people killed and more than a hundred injured in violent clashes. Local leaders applaud PLA's intervention as a peace-keeping measure, designed to isolate the law-breakers and rioters. So what?

twenty-four

GRAND END OF TERM ENGLISH EXAM
THURSDAY MARCH 16, 1989
COMMENCING 8.10 a.m.
Instructions to candidates
  1. Write your Chinese name (in Pinyin) at the top of
     every sheet of paper.
  2. Dictionaries must not be used unless otherwise stated.
  3. Read the instructions CAREFULLY.
  4. There will be absolute silence during the exam (and
     no spitting).

'Is this all quite clear? . . . Good. Now when I say start you
can start.'

Interpreter Li was sitting at the front with Jake, supplying
the occasion with a gravitas quite alien to the rest of the
course. But now they were being assessed; if the Government
was going to issue proficiency certificates – and it undoubtedly
was – it had to be sure the American organised the exam
correctly. Fang had, as was his custom, put on new underwear
for the exam. He felt fresh and alert. There was fire in his
belly; he was out to win his family another Wilmington.

'Okay, START! Go for it!' Fang turned to the first question.

Rewrite the following passage correctly:

Once upon a time there was a little old english lady who
one sum monney in a national lottery. She called her childs
around her to say she was going to use her prise to go a
broad. They were all very surprising because in her hole life
she had hardly never left the town let alone the motherland
I want to visit America', she says. This worried them even
moor because they did not think America was not the place
for a little old english lady. She was insisting of travelling
alone. 'I'm going to Miami. Iv'e always wanted go their.'

At this they pretested even loudlier but she was determined to achieving her goal. In order to make them more

happier about the idea she agreed to stay in the citys' best hotel.

So the little old lady flew off. She had a loverly too weeks in Miami and visited all the sights including Disneywhirled. But all good things must come to an end and the last morning soon arrived.

She lift her sweet to take the left down to breakfast. As the doors open she saw to her horror that the only other occupants were two huge and ruff-looking men.

After everything she had being told about the violence of Miami, she was very frightening of them but she was a plucky old lady and she stepped inside never the less. It was only ten floors down after all.

As the doors closed on them one of the massive men said in a booming voice, 'Hit the ground, lady.' There was no point in struggle so she threw herself down on to the floor and waited for them to attack her. She waited and she waited but the two men did nothing except bursted out laughing. Then they picked her down and dusted her up.
'I'm sorry if I frightened you, madam,' says one of the men, still roaring laughter, 'But I only meant you to press the Ground Floor button.'

The little old lady graciously accepted their apologys and ate the break fast she had thought she would never see. After wards she return to her room to pack her bags but when she came to pay her hotel bill at the main desk the girl said, 'That wont be necessary, madam. A gentleman has paid for you already. He asked me to give you this envelope.'

The lady read the card inside: 'In gratitude. I havn't laughed so much in years!'

2. Tautology – as we know – is the needless use of words. This paragraph contains several tautologies. Rewrite it as succinctly as possible.

After a temporary respite the army was moving into even closer proximity. Among the rebels the general consensus was that they were now completely surrounded. Their leaders had always argued that past history would not be repeated again but even self-confessed optimists like them had now to accept the true facts of the situation: total annihilation was going to be the end result.

'Question Three will be a write-back exercise,' said Jake. 'You know the system – listen to the following and then write it back in your own words. Ready? This is an account of the weird scenes after the death of the Irish novelist Laurence Sterne. In the eighteenth century there was a great demand for corpses among doctors who were researching anatomy . . .'

Jake went on to maintain that this Sterne person was body-snatched from the grave and then returned by a student who recognised him on the slab during a medical lecture at Cambridge University. No easy story, thought Fang, and he wished he could feel more confident of the details.

Happily, the next two questions were 'drink and meat' (conditionals and relative clauses) and he rattled them off, eager to give himself maximum time for the last question which he had noticed was a free composition of some kind. He felt a little cheated that there had been nothing specifically on the gerund but was otherwise most pleased with the way things were going.

6. THIS QUESTION SHOULD ONLY BE ATTEMPTED IF YOU HAVE COMPLETED THE OTHER FIVE QUESTIONS!

We have worked on proverbs during the course and you have also been introduced to the extended proverb (or fable) which is used to put across a particular idea to the reader. In this question (dictionaries may be used) you have a choice:

> *Either*: write a brief story which illustrates one of the English proverbs we have learnt (you must make it clear at the end which proverb you are illustrating);
> *Or*: write a fable (you must make it clear what point you are making by writing the 'moral' at the end).

GOOD LUCK! Teacher Jake

Fang took another sheet of paper and began to write:

Proverb Essay
Once upon a time there was a farmer who had some cows. Now every day the farmer took his cows out of their cow-shed and let them grazing in his meadow. Now this fleet of cows was not at all stupid beasts. They soon discovered that the grass in the next meadow was much lusciouser and so they begin to eat it. Because however the

fence which is between the meadows was made off wire which has very sharp bits twisted on it periodically the poor cows cut their faces badly. The farmer decided to therefore climb over the fence himself one day before the cows waked up and to cut down all his neighbour's grass to give to his cows (well it seems to be going to wasteful anyway) The cows were very happy about this and they ate very much grass so that no mattering how fast the farmer cut down his neighboor's grass he couldn't provide enough for his cows. Even when the neghbour himself joined in (cheerily saying 'Don't worry I've got lots of meadows and want to help you') they still couldn't cut enough for the cows. Then one day the farmer decided they were getting too too fat, really overweighted, and so he stopped using the extra grass leaving them to graze on his own stubbly meadow. He even built a high solid wall so his cows couldn't see the neighboars grass. But early one morning the cows discussed matters in their cow-shed and when the farmer opened the door they put their plan into operation which was stampeeding at the new wall. Although some of the cows were very injured by the experience but most of the cows get through.

proverb employed: you can't shut the stable door after the horse has bolted to the grass on the other side of the fence.

Fang let an eye stroll over towards Qiao's paper, hoping this might provide some clue as to the spelling of 'neighbour' but Class Monitor snapped a protective arm around his work. Time was running out, so Fang glanced quickly down his own last sheet and, quite satisfied with it, launched into the other half of the question:

Fable essay
Once upon a time there was an ant-hill at the top of a mountain, which was covered in forest. One hot summer a fire broke out in the forest. The ants were very frightening of course by the licking of the flames which were spreading up the mountain towards their hill. So therefore as a result they called to a meeting and it was decided that they should combinate themselves into one big ball so that, by rolling down mountain through the fire, they could reach safely to the bottom. This was arranged, one of the ants in the middle of the ball shouted to the ants on the outside saying, 'I know

this is a good idea but I'm afraid you ants on the outside will being frazzled by the fire.' 'Don't worry comrade,' said the leader of the ants on the outside 'We may dead but the rest of the ants will survive for a brighter future.'

moral: in order for most people to get a better life a few people have to jump out of the frying-pan and into fire.

In the lift afterwards Xin and Qiao delightedly discovered that Fang had answered both halves of the either/or question. But he wasn't upset. He was too pleased with his little yarns. Jake had said 'Go for it!' hadn't he? Well, Fang had gone for everything on offer. And he'd never enjoyed an exam more.

twenty-five

Jake marked it in two days and that weekend the institute director, emerging from his office for the first time in months, arranged the course's closing ceremony. Qiao summoned the flock half an hour before Jake's arrival and they were obliged to obey his orders (his last!) to move the desks back against the wall, sprinkle them with boiled sweets, sunflower seeds and apples and await their teacher in silence. Once the Director had arranged a pyramid of tins of Sunshine and Breeze mandarins on the desk of honour, he too sat down and flicked his chisel-toothed smile to all parts of the room.

Interpreter Li arrived, nodded humourless approval and took the seat to the right of Jake's space. He could not look any of them in the eye; an outsider, catapulted so far above them all, he never dared face the envy he'd certainly aroused. They waited.

Fang welcomed the silence. He was most depressed now about the end of the course, though he had still not really come to terms with Jake's departure. This was to be staggered because he was going off for a couple of weeks (which was as long as his visa would allow) up the Silk Road; he would return to Yanzhou and only then pack up and – leave.

The Red Flag blared across from the clocktower on the hour and, three minutes later, Jake strode into the room. He stopped in surprise.

'Closing ceremony,' explained Qiao curtly.

'Ah, very good!' Jake nodded at the Director and Interpreter Li, taking his seat noisily between them. As he unwound his scarf with one hand, he pulled out the list of results with the other.

(Fang had had some difficulty in explaining to Jake that, of course, everybody must be allowed to pass.

'For otherwise they lose face and their managers will penalise. It will be for them', he had said passionately, 'a very black mark!'

'But surely there has to be a distinction between those who have made some progress during the course and those who haven't, Fang?'

'Pass mark?'

'Yes, a pass mark.'

'Just lower it, Jake. Lower it right down. No one wants black marks – you must give us diplomas, please, not black marks.'

Whatever Fang felt about his classmates, he could not wish black marks upon any of them – except perhaps Qiao.)

Failing to notice that the rodent Director was about to open the ceremony with a speech, Jake grabbed one of the mandarin tins, and beat it upon the desk to silence the excitement which had broken out since his arrival.

Briskly he gave the scores – out of a total possible of 372 – from the bottom up. Fang's guts began to writhe but his head remained cool enough to calculate that the reception desk had earned themselves a combined total of 68. Although there was a leap to the next score – an effortful 109 for Liu Wei – good ol' Jake gave no indication that anyone had failed.

Soon he had passed the double century and Xin was pegged at 222 – an extraordinary score in view of the state of his brain and the thrust of his attention during the course. He really had some talent, Fang had to admit it. And Spotty Zhang shot a remarkable 229.

Then, delaying slightly, Jake increased the tension (Fang's colon was now sidewinding through his trunk) for the final three: Qiao at 271, Volley-Ball Lo, 289, and Fang . . . a glorious 333. He accepted the Wilmington plate and glowed orange. Another of those moments. Beautiful! His snake guts stilled and his mouth slid into a grin as he began to digest each of his marks. 333!

Ratty leapt up to speak but nothing he said over the next ten minutes could disturb Fang's drowsy contentment and he only really woke up when Qiao called three cheers for Jake. When Interpreter Li insisted on saying his bit afterwards, Fang got away with some gentle hissing, taken up by his quick-tongued friend on the left, Python Xin.

The Director closed the ceremony by handing out diplomas for all. Fang spent several minutes gracefully acknowledging his fellows' congratulations and then left the classroom. Qiao caught up with him on the stairs.

'I'll say well done but you must admit it was very much your sort of exam, Little Fang.'

'What do you mean, Little Qiao?'

'Well the questions weren't exactly "mainstream" were they? They were hardly suitable for students of a more practical, relevant English.'

'I suppose you are referring to your blessed Business English?'

'Yes, I'm afraid Business English has lost out very badly during this course. I'd say many people have been betrayed by Jake's deliberate shift of emphasis towards—'

'Towards what the English call logodaedaly perhaps?'

'Perhaps, Little Fang, perhaps – very clever, I'm sure. Of course I should have called a halt to it at the start but with that gerbil of a director I could not be sure of the institute's total support – otherwise I'd certainly have taken Jake on over this. Instead we have all had to watch a precious opportunity dissolve into frivolous irrelevance. If I manage to get to America then I shall be able to make up for lost time but if not . . .'

Fang sympathised completely with the nervousness which now shimmered across Qiao's face. The traces flitted away so soon but how gratifying to see them at all!

'He has humiliated us.'

'Don't be ridiculous, Qiao! The classmates love Jake. You heard the cheers. He is a stimulating and imaginative teacher who has become a good friend to almost everyone. Once upon a time you would have been the first to claim that.'

'I would not! My association with Jake was purely formal. I had to meet him about class matters—'

'And have a bath with him, and take him to watch circumcisions and—'

'Shut up, Fang. I was acting in accordance with government guidelines: by being helped to relax the foreigner is able to work efficiently and thus we gain maximum profit from him, drawing deeply on his intellectual resources.'

'I don't believe I'm hearing this, Qiao. You'll be talking about bourgeois liberalisation and spiritual pollution soon.'

'Well, if anyone's been exposed to those, Fang, then it's you! Who else has invited Jake home, eh? Tell me that!'

'You know perfectly well it was cleared with the authorities. You're still just jealous.'

'Now who's being ridiculous? I wouldn't have him in my home for all the . . . for anything! He's what the Americans call a bum.'

Qiao was very worked up and Fang feared the conversation, which had taken them down to the entrance hall, was now about to explode on to the pavement – and that he might not be able to refrain from escalating his attack with the new weaponry of their grim family backgrounds. He was relieved, therefore, when the 'bum' emerged into the sunlight and Qiao skulked away.

'Are you pleased, Fang?'

'Delightful, Jake. Very pleased.'

They bicycled off together, Fang hoping to be invited up to flesh out the brief post-mortem – sweet death! – with which Jake had rounded off the exam results. But it reminded him of another post-mortem and, as they pedalled down Peace Street, he suddenly remembered a rendezvous at the acrobat sculpture.

'I have got to meet my grandfather now,' he shouted over the wind; Jake waved and accelerated on. It turned out to be the last time they were to see each other before his Silk Road trip.

Fang had agreed to share the exertion of giving Grandfather a trip around town and was going to use the time to buy a new bottle of rice wine. The consumption of the last had been discovered and, although alcohol was not a central part of his life, Grandfather had seen scope in the affair for kicking up a stink, which was.

As he approached, Fang could see from the power of Grandfather's hawk and the cast of Mother's face that the pair had had problems.

'You're late.'

'Only a couple of minutes, Mother.'

'Every minute counts – you'll see. Goodbye, Father. See you later.' And she was off.

'We should be able to get you a nice bottle at the Friendship

Store, Grandfather,' he said, watching him pick open a pack of Queen Bee cigarettes.

'Should hope so too!'

Fang had already made sure that Podgy would be there so some sort of deal could be struck with the flexible shop assistant.

They bicycled the short distance, Fang noting with approval Grandfather's control of his rickety machine: Queen Bee a-glowing, he took a bullish line through the traffic and, on three occasions, cut people up quite beautifully. They parked in the official rack outside the shop and Fang had to ladle a few cents into the hand of the attendant who came up to them with an enthusiasm which suggested he was on his unit's shortlist for a Model Worker Award.

Podgy was chatting to his friend at the counter as they entered.

'Hello, Fang – and good morning to you, old sir,' he said.

'Hi, Podgy. How's it going?'

Grandfather had already gone straight off to a new motor-cycle parked at the other end of the shop which he was caressing as though it were a thousand tiny Lotus feet.

'The ultimate idea, Fang! Came to me yesterday. Tell me what you think. You know the peasants round here are ob-sessed with having baby boys, not girls?'

'Yes, of course.'

'And that they get so desperate for boys they'll buy them for masses of loot?'

'Yes, I've heard that too.'

'Well, it seems to me that if you went into that line of business you could quite easily pass off girls as boys! Those peasants may be rich but they are as thick as pig shit. All you need to do is stick some fake equipment on the front of the baby girls and they take one look and think they got themselves a little man. By the time the cock falls off you're miles away.'

So Podgy had graduated from risking his own genitals on the pea-processing machine to hawking babies. If this was enterprise culture, bringing Marx into the marketplace and all, then Fang was happy to be an 'intellectual'. Tycoons can get carried away so easily.

'Count me out,' said Fang, trying to mask his disapproval.

'It seems you need to put a bit more thought into this one – like how do you make false penises and where do you get the baby girls in the first place?'

'There's masses of families out there still bumping them off. It would be too easy to offer to take the babies off their hands.'

'And sell them as boys in the next village?'

'That's it! Brilliant, eh? Oh, come on, Fang, I'm not really too serious about it right now. But it just occurred to me as a possibility.'

He winked at the assistant, who leered back, clearly in cahoots.

'Anyway, what was it you wanted for the old codger? Motorbike?'

'No fear. And keep your voice down, Podgy. I just want a reasonable bottle of rice wine to replace one I knocked back the other day.'

'That all? What can we offer him, Zhou?'

'You can have this for fifty.' Scarcely moving, Assistant Zhou flicked a bottle up from under the counter. Clearly this was staple trade.

'He's paying People's Money, not Foreign Exchange Certificates, remember, Zhou.'

'Oh, in that case I'll want seventy-five, call it seventy – still the best deal in town.'

'Done.' Fang passed the notes and rammed the bottle into his coat. He was about to go when Podgy's eye of avarice caught him full beam and forced him to remember the other term of the trade.

'And a bar of CDM for Podgy.'

The motorbike had stayed upright through the Gobi Desert from which Grandfather claimed to have just returned. Fang managed to lift him off as he was discovering the horn.

'What d'you get me then?'

'A nice bottle of Lily and Brimstone Wine, Grandfather. How's that?'

'I suppose it will have to do.'

Out on the pavement his insides reacted to the exertions on the big bike in their usual way and he angled a spectacular jet of bile at the feet of the parking attendant who immediately summoned a policeman. He took out his notebook to set about fining Grandfather the standard two yuan. With a speed and savagery which appalled and thrilled Fang, the old gobber whipped out four yuan and shot another geyser on to the pavement between the officer's feet.

'That'll pay for both,' he said, thrusting the notes into the man's jacket. 'Come on, boy! We're out of here!'

They mounted their Pigeons and flew away like bank robbers, the rice wine in Fang's coat knocking against the Wilmington plate as he followed Grandfather's getaway route through the dense lunch-hour bike rush.

Pondering the exam in the cement office that afternoon, Fang marvelled again at the emergence of Volley-Ball Lo. Her score of 289 had shattered the Frank and Charlie duopoly and immediately made her a major player on Yanzhou's English-speaking scene. She was an unwelcome arrival.

A rhinoceros on the volley-ball court, where Fang had first encountered her, she was a fish when it came to human contact, a clever red mullet. Even Jake had said he found her quite the most unapproachable in the class – not surprising in view of her spying.

Fang's finger went faster and faster around the rim of his plate as he woke up to the horrible likelihood of her having applied for the scholarship as well. He could imagine one of her first debriefing sessions in the Education Department three months ago.

'Thank you, Miss Lo. An invaluable report.'

'It is no more than my duty requires, Interpreter Li. May I go now? I have to attend a volley-ball training session.'

'Yes, of course. But I have something which might interest you.' (Lo sinks back into plush Hong Kong-designed chair.)

'What is that, Interpreter Li?'

'Class Monitor Qiao asked me to write a reference for a scholarship application he is making to study for a year in America. Of course, he was eager to keep it a secret to avoid any competition from the likes of that cocky Little Fang. But I am happy to be able to inform you of this opportunity and do all I can to help your application.'

'Thank you, Interpreter Li. This is generous of you.'

'As you know, Miss Lo, it is our duty to help one another

according to the rules of loyalty laid down by the Party leaders. So, let me give you the details . . .'

The bunker mentality!

Ling came over to say that Manager Sun had summoned him and the thought of praise from this enlightened quarter soothed Fang's troubled brow as he clicked down the concrete corridor.

twenty-six

Dear Little Fang,

I hope this reaches you. I've copied out the characters
you wrote in my address book as neatly as possible but I'm
worried they might still defeat the postman.

I know you don't understand why I wanted to go up the
Silk Road and I must admit that for the first few days I was
wondering too. The only train ticket I could get was straight
through to Urumuqi so most of the best sites just went right
on by. But I was dead set on reaching Kashgar and that's
what I've done. Sitting in this bar right now I'm very pleased
I made the effort. Don't worry – I'm not going to sing the
praises of a city you would find disgustingly primitive and
an embarrassment to the Motherland. But as I said, you
just have to accept that these backwoods do appeal to a
Westerner – especially after a few months in your China of
the Four Modernisations.

Getting here from Urumuqi was no disco – three days
and three nights across the Taklamakam Desert in a bus
that wouldn't be allowed to do the school run back home!
I sat next to a huge 'minority person' in the front row. Best
for leg room but unfortunately the stairwell by the door
was used as men's-room, women's-room and kids'-room.

My neighbour's tobacco, smoked in twists of newspaper,
knocked out most of the smell – so did the hen she had on
her lap. We were at loggerheads though for the first day,
each trying to claim a few extra millimetres of the double
seat. But then the second morning she offered friendship –
a cigarette and a slurp of raw egg, as fresh as ever an egg
has come. I was left feeling guilty that I hadn't been big
enough to make the first move. By the end of the trip we
were sharing everything – she loved Leonard Cohen on my
Walkman and I was allowed to fondle her hen, a charming
bird.

These Uighurs have got good noses on them and I feel much more at home. Lots of Hans are said to have been transplanted into the region but I don't know where they can be – probably shut away in the corridors of power. Out on the streets it's more like Turkey.

That journey! There's no way I'm taking the bus back. It's the plane to Urumuqi for me. You wouldn't believe the places we slept on the road – oasis towns. But they were wised up: charged double for foreigners and refused to accept my worker's card so I had to pay in FEC. (Thanks to you, I'm now pretty reluctant to use those any more than is absolutely necessary.) I woke up the third morning covered in sand – in my mouth and ears even. A storm had blown through town and through my window in particular!

I've met some fellow-Americans here. In fact they're Californians which means they seem as much like my 'fellows' as the Uighurs and the Tibetans must seem to you! We are all holed up in this wild old building which used to be the British Consulate and is now a cheap hotel. The night before I got in some British guy had flown the Union Jack from his room window, reclaiming the building for his country. The Public Security were in pretty swiftly though and marched him down to the station to write a self-criticism! I suppose the police here have to be careful – we are just a few nuclear testing-grounds away from Tibet after all and they don't want foreigners encouraging the minorities to stake claims to territory, do they?

These Californians came in from Pakistan and, I'm sorry to say, they breached your borders with a great rock of opium. We smoke on the consul's terrace as the sun goes down each evening. They've even managed to find some trollops (look it up!).

I'm aiming to be back in Yanzhou by the end of the month or early April so I can then get down to Peking, spend a week or two there before flying home via Hong Kong. I have to be back in the US by April 21. Looking forward to seeing you and telling you more about my travels when I return.

Best wishes to your family.

Yours,
Jake

The letter arrived at People's Cement on 3 April and Jake was seen stepping off the Baihao minibus late the following afternoon. Fang called on him that very evening, eager to hear more about these adventures, the opium and the 'slatternly draggle-tails who accept money in return for sexual intercourse'.

'Oh, and I've got another cutting for you,' said Jake at the end of his account. 'More excitement in Tiananmen Square – March 29.'

It was another front-page picture – this showing three Western women with long legs standing in front of the Mao portrait on Tiananmen Gate. The detail was poor but their smiles were clearly supercilious.

'French fashion models pose in front of Tiananmen,' ran the caption. 'They are part of a modelling team which has come to Beijing to present the first Paris Fashion Night to local citizens.'

'Mmm, very beautiful, Jake. So long legs!'

'Those Frogs go everywhere in the name of fashion. From what I've seen of your ladies, though, I don't guess they'll be too impressed. But a Chinese backdrop will probably boost sales in France.'

Fang thought of Fu and her legs. How wrong Jake was! Suddenly it occurred to him to give Jake her address in Peking. If she had mellowed as much as her last letter suggested, it couldn't do any harm, and from what he had heard of the capital it did not sound such a big deal to have a foreigner in your home there. He wrote down the address in Chinese characters and Pinyin for Jake, whose immediate delight made the suggestion worthwhile, even if the meeting itself proved unsatisfactory.

'I should say she is waspy girl, Jake, but I think improving now.'

'Right, Fang, I'll take it easy and give her every opportunity to avoid meeting me if she doesn't want to. I'm very grateful.'

'Must go,' said Fang, with a fake yawn. He didn't want to leave at all but it was the only way he could think of introducing his latest new word. 'You see, Jake, I'm utterly ramfeezled.'

To Fang's disappointment, Jake was not impressed – merely bamboozled. If only he would spend a few minutes a day with an English dictionary, the quality of his life would improve greatly. Anyway, the thought of Jake visiting Fu did something to ease the break of his departure in a few days' time, which Fang had still not come to terms with. At least he would be keeping him in the family up in Peking.

Jake's train ticket had been arranged by the Government – the only means of getting stress-free travel – and they were also laying on a car to Baihao station. Uncertain as to the best way to say goodbye, the classmates had decided to see Jake off from the government reception building on the last morning, even though he was due to leave at six. Fang had thought about a private farewell but in the end he had not felt up to it.

As he pedalled towards the building at a quarter to six he saw about fifteen students loitering by the door, beating their arms and stamping feet against the cold. The snow had left for the year but the cold would stay awhile.

'What's the problem?' Fang asked Liu Wei as he joined the group which included some kids from the middle school. 'Why aren't you waiting inside in the warm?'

'Oh, can we go in?'

'Of course!' Fang realised that he was the only one of them familiar with the Jake protocol: these others had not risked more than one or two visits over the past months. He noted Qiao's absence – and that Miss Lo was present.

As he led the group into the foyer the door-lady clapped her hands in dismay.

'What do you lot want, Little Fang? Not to say goodbye to Ja Ke America I hope!'

'Of course we do!'

'But he's gone!'

'Gone?!'

The students muttered and groaned.

'But it's not six!' said Spotty.

'They said he was going at six!' said Pretty Pei.

'You mean we've really missed him?' said Liu Wei.

'They arranged it late last night. He went at five. Apparently the Baihao Road is bad today.'

'Well, that's great!' said Fang in disgust.

'He won't think much of us lot, not turning up for a last farewell, will he?' said Xin. 'I bet the bloody Government switched it deliberately!'

'He knew you were all coming,' said the door-lady, 'but there was no way he could tell you about the change of plan. He asked me to say goodbye and tell you he will come back in the future.' Did she sniff a little?

Fang felt sick. The students began to shunt back outside. As he turned to follow, the door-lady hissed at him.

'Little Fang, come here! Ja Ke America asked me to give you this.'

She lifted a small package out of her box and Fang pushed it into his coat.

'Thank you. I shan't forget all your help over this time — and when my Mother brings out next winter's range I'll drop something in for you.'

'Sssshh!' She turned back into her box and Fang saw Miss Lo by the door. He tried to get outside, but her rhino mass blocked him; her fish face demanded an answer.

'What's that, Little Fang?'

'What's what?'

'That package in your coat?'

'I don't know. I haven't even opened it yet.'

'Shall we have a look?'

'No we shan't! You smarmy little bitch. Get out of my way!'

He unlocked the Pigeon and pedalled off faster than he had ever pedalled without even giving her the satisfaction of looking back at her scheming smile. He mashed his ankles with the flying chain, threw the bike into the junction of Bright Future Street and tore up Harmony, past the acrobats, whom he circled at terrible speed, into Peace Street and down past the institute on Liberation. He didn't look at the building but headed on and on up the Western Hill and only when his frustration began to lose out to exhaustion, when the first sweat prickled on his forehead, did he chuck the bike down, pull the package out of his coat and sit against the street lamp to see what Jake had left him.

Government Reception
Bright Future Street   April 9, 1989

Dear Little Fang,

I feel very bad not to have said goodbye to you in person – so bad, in fact, that I damn nearly rode up to your house in the small hours but I didn't want to risk another war.

I must tell you that I regard you as my best Chinese friend and I'll never forget my time here. Although the language barrier occasionally intruded, I think we saw eye to eye in the end. We are always hearing about the 'profound differences' between our races but what about the similarities? Sense of humour, hospitality, sympathy and ambition – they are the similarities and they are interesting because they are human. The differences, the ones that make for tension, they are imposed from above, from your system. And that's why I once said I admire you all so much – for being so similar yet having to seem so different.

I can't imagine anything better than getting you over to the States for a visit – I'd give you a hell of a time back home. I only wish I'd had the presence of mind to tell you about a scholarship to Chicago which our esteemed Class Monitor applied for months ago. He swore me to silence and, in those early days, I didn't have any idea you'd be interested. I even assumed there'd be plenty of other opportunities. By the time I realised what a unique thing it was for you people I couldn't bring myself to reveal what you'd missed and so I am now doing it, like a coward, by letter.

Unless the Mayor of Wilmington suddenly decides to build his shopping malls in Yanzhou cement, I guess the only chance of my seeing you is by coming back to Yanzhou again. This I *will* do – but how damn sad you can't come out.

Till then, til we meet again Fang, we must write each other. Okay?

I enclose another Wilmington plate – your family's third I believe. There's no one I'd rather give it to. And also the key to my Forever – give to your grandpappy with best regards from the blood-sucking, foot-fondling missionary.

All the best,

Yours,
Jake

PS I've enclosed one last *China Daily* picture for you. Perhaps there will soon be so many foreigners passing through Yanzhou that it will be on sale, but I think there is a while to go before that day comes. Who knows? I'll be pleased to get back to two-ply tissues myself.

The picture, from a 6 April edition, showed hordes of children.

Some 10,000 Young Pioneers gathered in Tiananmen Square in Beijing yesterday – the day the Chinese pay respect to the dead each year – to take part in memorial services sponsored by the city's Youth League Committee and other departments. The activities, with the theme of 'I love the Five-star Flag', included laying wreaths at the Memorial Monument to the People's Heroes, taking oaths and paying tribute to the country's revolutionary martyrs and visiting Chairman Mao Zedong's Memorial Hall.

Fang went home. There was nothing to say that evening. He arranged all the Jake-plates around Father's portrait on top of the chest of drawers and looked at them for several minutes. Grandfather's speechlessness on being given the Forever provided enough amusement to leaven Fang's misery – but only briefly. Mother was sensitive enough not to bang on too much about the new fridge (flamingo pink) which she had bought with some of the wealth still deriving from her scarves. Instead she quietly drew his attention to an article at the bottom of page five in the day's local paper.

American Mr Jake Elliot has arrived in Yanzhou to conduct a Business English course for new graduates. Trained in Wilmington, Delaware, Mr Jake will stay for three months at the invitation of the People's Municipal Government which has extended a cordial welcome and lodged him at the luxurious Dong Lan Hotel. A spokesman for the Education Department said: 'We are pleased to greet Mr Jake in the spirit of reform and openness and we will soon be drawing on his intellect in order to speed the development of our city's export business, which is already a high-growth area. When not in the classroom, Mr Jake will be organised by the Government which has arranged a tight schedule of visits to factories and installations in the region.

Once *Yanzhou Daily* gets hold of a story, it's really over.

twenty-seven

The thought that Jake might visit Fu in Peking did ease the pain of separation but, everywhere he went, flashbacks to the time they had spent together exploded in his face. Now that the course no longer ate into office hours, work loomed larger, but it hardly occupied his mind: there was nothing more to translate except the glances (glances of victory?) which Wong kept firing from his desk. It was back-invoicing and production figures, back-invoicing and production figures, all week.

The Yanzhou Syndrome seemed more virulent now (as Fang had predicted) and he found that he swiftly transferred all his desperate hopes from Jake to the scholarship. This agonising subject came up in an unpleasant exchange at the wash-house one evening. Number Three was not a government haunt and Fang thought it Quite a Coincidence when this particular head rose above the low partition between beds.

'Well, good evening, Little Fang.'

'Hello.'

'Good bath?'

'Good bath.'

'Good exam result.'

'Thank you, Interpreter Li.'

'Good course?'

'Yes, good course.'

'You saw Mr Elliot off the other morning I suppose?'

'No, actually, we missed him.' Fang farted.

'Oh dear. No message?'

'What do you mean?'

'Did Mr Elliot leave you any message?'

'Yes, Mr Li, he did as it happens – and a package. I think you probably know a bit about this . . .' Only a worm holds back from battle.

'I don't know if you realise, Little Fang, that such exchanges are not appropriate.'

'What do you mean?'

'That you were unwise to have taken that package and, might I say, generally unwise in your familiarity with Mr Elliot – from the very first. Remember? Perhaps it would be useful to remind you that the "special relationship" is over and that any further communication between you – postal communication – may be monitored in accordance with government policy.'

'I don't think I need feel guilty about any of my contacts with Jake. I do not even need to deny that he became a good friend of mine. Times have changed, Mr Li.'

'Yes, Little Fang, I wonder if you know quite how right you are. Times *have* changed and perhaps they will be changing even more . . .'

He dropped out of sight. Fang's heart beat in its cage. Lo's cover was blown to pieces anyway. And they had nothing on him. But still his heart beat like hell. Li's head reappeared, its hairs slicker than ever.

'An interesting scholarship entry,' he said.

Now Fang's heart actually stopped. He shook himself and leant up on one arm so as to face Li over the partition. As he spoke it started beating again.

'What did you say?'

'Your scholarship application, Little Fang – it was interesting and has drawn some comment – some favourable comment – from some quarters.'

'How do you know? Have you seen it?'

'I know, Little Fang.'

They were so close – not more than three inches apart: Li was all eyes, all-knowing, and Fang decided to profit from his dreadful omniscience.

'What about Miss Lo. Was her entry deemed "interesting", Mr Li?'

'She did not enter. She feels there is much to be done here before she goes abroad to study the West. But there are other entries.'

'Qiao?'

'Qiao?'

'Class Monitor Qiao.'

'Ah, yes, Little Qiao. Maybe.'

'When do they decide?'

'Oh, I should think they probably have.'

'But when do they tell us, Mr Li?'

'When the time is right, Little Fang. Pleasant talking to you. I must be getting back.' He fell away and Fang thumped down on to the mattress.

The next day, Sunday, Fang decided to call on Qiao, to try for the first post-Jake English Corner. He knew *he* would have to make the effort: it was always him.

But to his surprise Qiao pulled him into the flat with real urgency, evidently panting for English conversation.

'Okay, okay, Charlie, be cool,' said Fang (such phrases coming easily now).

'Forget that, Fang.' He spoke in Mandarin. 'This is big news, big Chinese news.' He hurried back to his room and Fang followed to find the Qiao parents sitting on the bed staring at the radiogram.

'Hu Yaobang! He's dead – died yesterday morning,' said Qiao in a loud whisper. Fang's first thought was for Old Liu. This news would really cut him up. It was only when the radio began to whine and bleat in ill-tuned sympathy that Fang realised they were listening not to a Chinese news broadcast but to the VOA bulletin. He had associated VOA with the student life series alone for so long that he had quite forgotten about its Chinese-language news broadcasts. The American reporter seemed to be trying to get across the point that none of the official expressions of regret had mentioned Hu's fall from grace after the demonstrations of December 1986. But the whining was winning and Old Qiao leant across to fiddle with the channel knob.

'We should be able to pick it up on another band. I'm afraid the Government are trying to jam it.'

Qiao looked proudly at Fang. No flies on my father. But Fang knew he was only affecting interest because his father said the news was significant. Retard.

'Technique we picked up at the end of the Cultural,' the old bastard continued. 'You know, when it all went haywire – VOA and BBC were all we had. The Americans were much better jam-busters even then.'

But on every band VOA seemed lost for words and the BBC sounded utterly drunk.

'Bloody old radio! Dust in its guts, I'll bet. Come on, dear, let's go and watch the box.' The boys followed them through to the living-room where the great Japanese screen beamed pictures of two beautiful big noses cavorting under a waterfall – another advert for Chinese fridges. Then, fortunately, some news appeared. But this was CCTV, of course, and the bulletin was devoted to the launch of yet another government campaign ('Morality, Security and Culture' was the latest arresting slogan from the Party's copy-writers); it wound up with some more stuff on 1.1 Billion Population Day which had been declared in Peking on Friday.

Fang was so little affected that when Mother asked him at home whether he had heard the news he barely responded.

'What, another hairy baby born to delighted parents in Inner Mongolia?' What's for supper? Cabbage? Yes, smells like it.

'No! Hu!'

'Who? What?'

'Hu, Fang! Hu Yaobang!'

She's smoking again.

'Oh that! The young may die, the old must die . . . so what?' he said, noticing Grandfather a second too late. But he had switched off too.

'*Listen* to me, Fang. Old Liu picked up some news from one of those Western channels. There's demonstrations going on in Peking – in our great one-hundred-acre Tiananmen Square.'

'Demonstrations?' He could imagine the chanting: 'Ja Ke! Ja Ke! Ja Ke America!'

'Old Liu knows about these things. He was brought up in Peking – he's political. And he says there's something big starting up. He says it reminds him of '76 when Premier Zhou En Lai died and the mass shows of grief were so large the Government had to break them up by force.'

Fang listened but failed still to focus on the events so many miles down the railway. Instead he found himself tying this curious passion of hers to a love for Old Liu. Perhaps he was winning her at last.

Over the next couple of days other people mentioned the death and Fang even saw a couple of old fuddy-duddies wearing black armbands.

Then, just after five o'clock on Wednesday, that little shit Wong said there was a phone call for him. Fang knew he would be deliberately passing on an order for a heap of shingle or sand or something because Fang hoped to get off down to the wash-house early.

'Are you sure it's for me?'

'Positive. Long distance.'

Fang grabbed the receiver. Scholarship news?

'Yes?'

'Is that Fang?'

'Yes. Who's this?'

'Little Fang, it's Fu – Elder Sister.'

His grip on the orange plastic relaxed and then tightened again. What did she want?

'Hello! How are you?'

'Fine. Listen, I can't talk for long. I've been trying to reach Mother all day. The lines are so busy. Impossible. Anyway, at least I've got you. I just *had* to tell . . .'

Fang could barely hear. She seemed to be screaming down a 400-mile drainpipe.

'Tell what, Fu? Jake? Have you met Jake?'

'He came round, yes, but I wasn't there. He met Hong Wei – they tried to talk. But listen, I was down at the hospital at the death—'

'Hu Yaobang?'

'Of course. I was on duty. You wouldn't believe what's happening here now. The students – your English Corner types – they're marvellous. They're out there in the Square, mourning Hu, calling for the Government to clear his name and . . .'

Fuzz, fuzz.

'. . . morning they were outside the leaders' residences, Zhongnanhai, shouting for Li Peng to resign. The wrong man has died they said!'

She was really excited. Did it take just two months of this Peking air to make activists out of the vainglorious? She sounded like she'd had one too many of those Molotov cocktails.

'But, Fu, why are you telling me this?'

'You've got to know. No one else is going to tell you lot down in the sticks. Tell Mother – tell everyone, anyone.'

'Thanks for your letter and well done with that carpet. Mother is really pleased you are getting the place so . . .'

But the fuzz was victorious and killed the line. Students telling Premier Li Peng to resign? Impossible. What *was* this? Mourning is all very well and traditional but 'Li Peng resign'? That sounded quite different.

One might have thought the rhythm – the drip, drip, drip – of Yanzhou life would reassert itself after Jake left. It did in a way, but the beat was new: a psst, psst, psst of whispered rumour about the death in Peking and, still more important for Fang, the decision-making in the Landu Trade Bureau.

Fang was surprised to see more and more people, young and old, wearing black armbands for Hu Yaobang. But as April's final days grew longer and warmer there were greater surprises. The gentle bubbling of excitement among the classmates uncorked them one by one and Lin Hu, Liu Wei, Xin, Spotty and Wong all admitted to having applied for the scholarship. Pop, pop, pop, pop and pop. It was incredible. Even though each knew his own chances were made slimmer every time another bottle burst, they all seemed relieved to discuss their dreams and by bringing them into the open, to make them seem real.

Fang didn't know what to think. He was a little put out when a couple of them said they too had dreamt of great white campuses: it amused him to speculate on the contents of Spotty's essay and self-taught Wong's; he was pleased because, of all the applicants, he was the best speaker; but he was worried that each person who had applied must have strings of varying strengths running in through the back doors of Landu and he prayed that Chen Ge would have the strength to beat off every challenge. He slept badly, ignored sword and flail and, with each morning, he pumped his iron more desperately.

Though excluded from their excitement by lack of English skills, Podgy was clearly delighted to welcome them back to his gatehouse and they started meeting every evening to amplify and discuss the latest whispers. This was the Yanzhou Spring, a merry confusion.

Fang said he believed Interpreter Li's assertion that the Volley-Ball wasn't entering; Xin said he was going to Peking to see for himself what was going on; Fu rang Fang again and talked of more massive marches and the sound of breaking glass at night: the people were shattering bottles in protest at Deng Xiaoping whose name sounded like the Chinese for 'little bottle'; Lin Hu said his mum had caught some television footage of Hu's widow actually shooing Deng away when he tried to commiserate at the official funeral on 22 April; Liu Wei said his friend in Landu had hinted that both the provincial scholarships were going to Yanzhou people; still no one knew when it would be announced or how; rioting was reported in Xian, a city considerably less far down the railway (Fang had been there once), and people were being arrested; there were demonstrations in Changsha, hundreds of miles in some direction or other, the city where Mao had been to school; even Old Liu blew into the gatehouse one night for a few minutes' ranting about the official treatment of Hu Yaobang.

On Tuesday, 25 April, they gathered around Podgy's radio for a broadcast which was going to be published as a *People's Daily* editorial the following day. Now the mourners were suddenly accused of 'planned conspiracy and turmoil'. This seemed way off the mark and, sitting round the stove which hadn't been dismantled since winter, the indignant graduates took one of Jake's 'votes'. Thus they decided to express tentative solidarity with their 'classmates' in Peking (even Fu had said they were being rather splendid). Podgy was pelted with his own nuts when he suggested the protesters listen to the Government and go back to school.

The next day Fang read the editorial in the *People's Daily* which was always on public display under glass outside the department store. The 'essence' of the demonstration, he read, 'is once and for all to negate the leadership of the Communist Party of China and the socialist system.'

Fang's surprise turned to confusion when the Motherland's radio news the following night revealed a very different 'essence':

Peking college students in several tens of thousands, holding
streamers and banners and shouting slogans, took to the
streets in a parade here today . . . The paraders shouted
'Support the Communist Party', 'Support the Constitution',
'Support the Four Cardinal Principles', 'Eliminate
corruption' . . .

This might be what the editorial called a 'serious political
struggle' but both sides seemed to be campaigning for the
same thing.

That Saturday night, in the gatehouse again, it suddenly occurred to Fang that tomorrow's English Corner had become
ideologically unacceptable. Nowadays it seemed elitist, exclus-
ive and undemocratic. He had a quiet word with Charlie and
persuaded him, without much difficulty, that they should
throw it open to the classmates.

'But what will my parents think? There won't be room.'

'Well, we could do what they do in Peking.'

'Which is?'

'My sister mentioned that the students there hold a huge
great English Corner in a park once a week. We could go to
Moon Park.'

'Good idea but . . .'

'But what?'

'Then what do we do?'

'Well, how should I know, Little Qiao? Just talk English I
suppose, like we do at your place every Sunday.'

And so at 2 p.m. the next day a few classmates met in a
corner of Moon Park. Yanzhouers taking the spring air noticed
them and word got around so fast that middle-school students
and others arrived to swell the numbers to thirty or forty.
Soon anyone who'd ever said 'How are you thank you disco
disco' was out there nattering away.

Fang had been holding a dozen youngsters (not bad-looking
some of those middle-school girls) quite spellbound with an
account of the Wilmington club scene when he decided to take
stock for a moment. A proud moment. He felt chuffed, as
though this were his congregation, his flock. Qiao's power-
kick as Class Monitor was well over now. Ever since the exam

Fang had enjoyed a mild celebrity in English-speaking circles and today – well, it seemed clear: his time had come. Obviously he would be expected to say a few words and he was preparing something (condolences for Hu's family pepped up with a couple of new idioms he'd gleaned from the office dictionary that week) when he noticed Interpreter Li sitting on a bench a little way off – and next to him, Volley-Ball Rhino Mullet. They were watching. That anti-establishment shudder racked him, the same he had felt on seeing Lei Feng, the ridiculous wax PLA soldier, wearing Jake's coat in the department-store window so many years ago; the same he had begun to feel lately during the television news.

He looked around at his English Corner, now in full swing, and then back at the bench, the Party Bench. Interpreter Li was staring straight at him, shaking his head slowly from side to side. Fang felt angrier than ever before. He overturned a full litter-bin and jumped up on to its base.

'Students!' he cried. But he couldn't help looking across at Li and Lo once again. Now they were up on their feet too. And in the seconds it took for the students to focus their attention upon him, these two skewered Fang. His nerves started popping. It was not embarrassment, but just a burning nervousness about what exactly he was doing, about precisely how much he was risking. He decided, in the last second available, that he would not say another word. He dropped down into the mess of eggshell, apple peel and paper arse-wipes and hurried out of the park.

twenty-eight

The extraordinary events of the big cities continued to reach Yanzhou over the next week – just. Liu Wei picked up a certain amount from a friend of his in Baihao whose wife's sister worked on the 340 train – up and down to Peking twice a week. Everyone got more practised at picking up VOA and the BBC and shared the findings. Fang almost got Mother to buy a decent Japanese receiver (his own Chinese-made transistor had no short-wave band) but at that very moment their television spluttered its last and she decided it was more important to put her money into a new Hitachi. (With prices of foreign goods increasing even faster than everything else, they couldn't wait for Brother-in-law to honour his word.)

In fact the Government's newshounds were slipping their muzzles on both television and radio to report an increasing amount of the unrest and, in order to maintain the popularity of his gatehouse, Podgy had rigged up a screen on the filing cabinet. Incredible to say, Clayderman was ousted from number one by the radio news bulletins at the top of every hour. It was a ham's paradise down there at Heavenly Tinned.

But some of the most detailed information – as first-hand as any they had had – came in a letter which landed on Fang's desk on Thursday, 4 May. The envelope was written in naïve style and its contents ran as follows:

Qiaoyuan Hotel, Peking   April 27, 1989

Dear Little Fang,

I've just got back to my room after the most incredible scenes on the streets. You wouldn't believe what's happening here. There's been about 150,000 students going through the city all day. When it comes to mass demonstrations the Chinese have it! They just marched through all the police blocks chanting for dialogue with the Government. The cops looked so bewildered. It was bewildering because half of the marchers were yelling 'Long live democracy' and the other half, 'Support the Constitution'! I was just swept along and could see over the top of them all. The atmosphere was great, everyone cheering from the side and offering food and drink! I hardly know what caused it but some say this latest march was prompted by the *People's Daily* editorial written, it is said, by Deng Xiaoping's own hoary hand. If that's it, then this was some reply – definitely not the reply of a 'tiny minority of trouble-makers'. Another thing which got the students going was when, last night, the police suddenly took down all the tributes to Hu Yaobang from that obelisk in the middle of Tiananmen Square (the Monument to the People's Heroes I think it's called – practically the only landmark I've had a chance to see here apart from the shrivelled Chairman in his display box!). Peking's been chaos ever since I arrived – so exciting that I've delayed my flight twice.

I managed to drop in on Fu but she was at work. Her husband (Wei Hong?) was there in his underpants, cooling off. Thank God you'd told me he was a driver because I was able to start some sort of conversation on that. (I now realise how absolutely you people stopped me learning any Chinese in Yanzhou. It's still complete baby-talk! Whatever happened to those lessons you once offered?!) Wei was friendly enough to start with but he got very agitated when we heard some procession go chanting by on the street below. 'Students! Students!' he kept saying. 'They'll ruin everything!' Fortunately I didn't have the words to argue with him. After about ten minutes he offered to drive me back to my hotel in the south and then when we arrived he surprised me by charging. I took out my foreign worker's card and paid him in People's Money which made him extremely annoyed. He stalled three times trying to get back into the traffic.

Tomorrow I have to drop down to Hong Kong. A college friend is working there and I'll also be trying to pick up a compact-disc player and a video camera. Can't decide which to give my parents for their anniversary! I wish I didn't have to leave but I've got to be home by May 4 and anyway I think the students will settle back down again now. They've made their point after all. And even the octogenarians will have taken it on board. The sound of bottles breaking! Every night I hear it in the alleys round the hotel.

I enclose a cutting from a real paper, the *Washington*

Post, which I picked up in the Peking Hotel. They do okay sundaes there too. Write me at that address I gave you in Wilmington.

Take care.

Yours
Jake.

Washington Post
April 21 1989

To the disquiet stirred by the pause in economic reform in China has now been added a burst of unrest over the lag in political reform. Students and others numbering in the tens of thousands seized on the occasion of the death of Hu Yaobang, the reformist Communist Party leader dismissed in disgrace two years ago, to go into the streets in Beijing waving the democratic banner and (some of them) heaving rocks. The police have escalated their responses, and beatings are now reported. The scale of the protests and the extent of the government's distress are at this point not to be exaggerated, but already these events are taking a place among the larger known outbreaks of public disorder since the Cultural Revolution convulsed China two decades ago.

Once senior leader Deng Xiaoping's heir apparent, Mr Hu may not exactly have fully earned the rather Jeffersonian image in which the protesters have recast him. On the Chinese spectrum, nonetheless, he was unquestionably at the liberal end. Challenging the reigning reform orthodoxy, he made no secret of his view that economic reform could not succeed without political reform as well. This seems to be the fundamental point that the demonstrators are making now. In so doing, they are pressing on the most neuralgic point of the Chinese reforms: the stunted progress on the political side. Mr Hu was ousted in a power play arising from his reluctance or failure to suppress pro-democracy student demonstrations in 1986–87. A broad historical record indicates that street protests and official responses to them are a principal medium in which politics takes place in countries that do not provide a democratic arena where different forces can legally contend.

It is often observed that the democratic spirit is sweeping the world, touching in the Soviet Union, in Eastern Europe, in Latin America and now, and not for the first time, in China. We hope it's true, but we think that what is really happening in places such as China is the collapse of an arbitrary, cruel and unworkable political order – communism. The institutions and legal procedures of democracy may not be available to those searching for a way out, but they turn as a moth to a flame to the symbols and slogans of democracy in order to establish accountability for power that has been abused. Governments under this sort of siege will be judged by whether they accept the challenge as legitimate, and meet it.

The letter had taken a week to arrive, in which time Jake had gone shopping in Hong Kong and crossed the world to his motherland. This silver wedding anniversary, was it taking place today or tomorrow? Was Chrissie invited? What would they eat? What would they do? Fang tried to imagine the scene in 1237 Abraham Lincoln Drive and failed completely. Briefly it thrilled him to think that he might be able to walk up to Jake's front door later in the year and say 'howdy' – but such speculation soon grew painful and he stopped thinking about the scholarship.

The news that night covered celebrations in Peking to mark the seventieth anniversary of the May Fourth Movement, an earlier flowering of optimism whose slogans had been 'science and democracy'. Fang had also heard that Mr Gorbachev, the Russian leader, was coming to Peking in a few days and that in October there would be more partying for the fortieth anniversary of the founding of the People's Republic. Clearly it was a good year to have moved up to Peking and, but for awaiting the scholarship news, Fang thought he would probably make the journey there with Xin. With people deciding your future in their own good time it was impossible to plan anything.

When he caught the headlines of *People's Daily* on the board outside work the next morning he noticed a front-page picture of student demonstrators in the Square. It was the first he had seen. How odd to see something *un*official going on in the Square – something popular. Something messy within its awesome geometry! How very odd to find these people pictured on the front of the Government's main newspaper – next to a procession of Youth Leaguers marking the anniversary with clean-cut, customary enthusiasm. The account of the students' march accompanying the photograph dripped with none of the editorial's bile. Could it have been written by the same hand? – for where there had been rebuke there was now almost sympathy. In fact Fang realised that these hands were wrestling with each other – and yet they were writing in the same paper.

Upstairs Wong was telling everyone that he had picked up the figure of 30,000 demonstrators on VOA's or the BBC's reports of yesterday in the capital, and, he said, journalists had been spotted on Changan Avenue waving banners in support of the students' demands. Without wishing to show interest in anything Wong had to say, Fang noted this and praised Jake's China-watching: he was right – the number of protesting students had fallen considerably and they would get back to their campuses soon.

Leaving Moon Park on Sunday, Fang related some of the letter's contents to Qiao but he hardly listened. Numbers at the Corner had doubled that day but Fang had again held back from addressing them. The graduates' good-natured discussion of their American dreams which had followed the revelations of mass scholarship applications had certainly been heady; but they had deflected Fang only momentarily from his goal, which was to win the award for himself. Nothing must block this. Qiao gave the impression of hiding a similar angst, intensified in his case by the painful end of his classroom power. He had been especially edgy all week.

'Come on, Qiao. What's up?' said Fang as they mounted their Pigeons.

'Huge decisions, that's what. They drain a man.'

'What huge decisions?'

'I'm getting married – in a fortnight.'

'What?' Fang swerved.

'Married! I'm marrying Bo, Little Fang.'

'But that's . . .'

'Wonderful, eh?'

'No, Qiao, that's . . . cheating!'

'Cheating? What do you mean?'

'You're just marrying to enhance your chances of the scholarship, aren't you? Go on, admit it!'

'Certainly not! What a mind you've got, Little Fang!'

'Everyone knows you're more likely to get out if the Government sees you've got a family to come back to.'

'Oh, rubbish!'

'What are you going to do about a kid? Could be tricky – did you hear the news this morning? They've just passed a law to improve population quality – prohibiting imbeciles from having children!'

'Very funny.'

'But of course you could cheat on that one too by picking one up for a couple of hundred yuan from Podgy.'

'Bloody lucky I'm on my bike because otherwise—'

'Serve you right if they snip your cock!'

Qiao stuck one finger up at him (a gesture learnt from Jake though Qiao would never have the grace to admit as much) and forked off right, leaving Fang to lean into the Baihao Hill Road. It had to be the reason. Lin Hu had just announced his marriage too. Xin had left for Peking but it was well known that he had Pei pretty well lined up. The way the rumours were going, Fang would be lucky if Wong didn't make off with Miss Ping. As he strained past the cinema he winced at the immorality of them all.

twenty-nine

The next few days did not bring much thrilling news from the capital. Ministry of Agriculture officials met students from Peking Agricultural University and Peking Agro-Engineering University but the tens of thousands of other students, with their less agricultural, more general complaints, received no satisfaction. A few thousand of them took to the streets by bicycle to continue the protest; although this time they came out of the campuses in nothing like the previous numbers, Fang was still pleased to picture Hong Wei seething at the wheel, his saloon snarled up in the bike flow.

But otherwise things seemed calmer: Fu didn't ring and even VOA had little to say except that Gorbachev was due the following Monday. This historic moment in Sino–Soviet relations did nothing for Fang's private chaos. He was in turmoil – his head churned like a cement mixer – expecting daily to hear about the scholarship, his future, his life. It was, of course, more than he could bear even to see Qiao, let alone speak to him. Two tigers cannot live on one peak, especially when they are hunting the same buffalo.

Evidently Qiao felt this too, because when Fang dropped in at Podgy's after a large, fridge-fresh supper on Friday night, his rival left immediately.

'Whooo ooo oooh!' said Wong, jiving his eyebrows quite intolerably. 'The competition getting to you, is it, Fang?'

For a horrid little second Fang thought he was referring to their own issue, the Miss Ping affair; Wong's confidence was inflating by the day and he was quite likely to say anything. How Fang wished him jammed back into the bin where he'd spent his early years!

Fortunately Wong's banter was not taken up by anyone else (evidence, Fang felt, of his own standing) and the general chatter resumed – lively and quite amusing. But Podgy was unusually silent, rotating slowly on the chair behind his desk. He had made several attempts over the past fortnight to get the classmates interested in marketing babies, but had been shouted down every time. Fang could always read his mind – it was a simple book: You lot go on and on about democracy and freedom of speech – but you never give *me* any. I know precisely what I'd say if you did: don't bother! Who ever made a buck out of democracy! With money you're a dragon, without it a worm – it's as simple as that!

But today Fang thought the Podge looked exceptionally boot-faced. The reason was soon apparent. Liu Wei had distinguished himself again by picking up some exciting news on the foreign wavebands. He hoped to be able to confirm this with his railway contact when he went over to Baihao tomorrow but it seemed the students in Peking had started a 'hunger-strike'.

The suggestion had been made, before Fang's arrival, that the classmates escalate their vapid expressions of sympathy into co-action. And this had made Podgy very worried indeed. He couldn't win, the tycoon would lose either way: if he refused, the classmates would abandon the gatehouse as they had done before; if he joined in, well – he'd simply starve.

Fang decided immediately to intervene: 'I'm not sure it would do any good down here in the sticks,' he said, uncertain exactly why he was counselling caution. Perhaps he felt he could only cope with the scholarship news, whichever way it went, on a full belly. At least that firebrand Xin was no longer here to argue with him; his opinion should hold sway in present company.

'Quite!' said Podgy very quickly. 'Fang's right. Who the hell would notice us down here?'

'Yes, it might take a while,' said Ling grabbing at some of Podgy's flesh.

'But aren't they asking for the right sort of things?' Spotty said. 'Less corruption and privilege, more money for education and a retraction of that editorial . . .'

'Yes, Spot, you're right,' agreed Fang, turning away from the gust of bad breath to address them all. 'And *they're* going about it brilliantly. The world always looks at Peking. Did you know foreign journalists *live* there? Just looking, China-watching. And now others are arriving because of Gorbachev. It's their hour – in Peking. Go there like Xin if you want to,

Little Zhang, but don't kid yourself that by pushing away your mum's noodles in Yanzhou you'll make a splash. All you'll get for that is a line of black marks. Splodge! Splodge! Splodge!' And three times Fang stamped his foot to emphasise the point – and to warn anyone against declaring any other view.

'Ah yes, the black mark!' said Ling. 'You should know about that!'

'Well, yes . . .' Fang nodded modestly.

But then Wong wrecked the moment by accusing him of 'selling out'.

'You just haven't got the bottle have you, Little Fang? You never go through with anything.'

'What the hell do you mean by that, pox-head?'

'You know! Since this scholarship fell on to the scales you've been a greasy little toe-rag!'

Fang leapt up at the dirty, filthy slander and grabbed Wong by the neck. He was planning to impale him on the corner of the filing cabinet when Ling and Liu Wei separated them.

'Calm down you two! You've got it wrong about Fang, Wong. He sailed pretty close to the wind when Jake was here. They'll have noted that down at the black-mark centre.'

'Dead right, I did, Ling. And where were you all that time, Wong creep? In the bin where you belong?'

'No actually! Down at the pictures with Miss Ping! And back at her place . . .'

Fang reared again, now quite insensible to the reasonable charge that he was losing face by losing his temper. But this time Podgy's impossible bulk blocked him.

'. . . and,' Wong yelled on, 'that's another thing I know you haven't managed to go through with!' He shrieked victory but it was the nervy laugh of one uncertain of his support. To Fang's relief it had been alienated by this last, rancorous comment.

'Let's get him out of here,' said Podgy.

'You bet we will! Really shouldn't talk like that,' said Ling, who obviously relished the heavy role. 'Piss off!' And with that Little Wong was thrown through the gates of Heaven.

Although Fang really didn't fancy hunger-striking – and genuinely believed it could do more harm than good – he did feel a mounting sympathy with the Peking students and he admired them for getting the demonstrations going again just as they had appeared to flag. One of their demands in particular occupied his mind: the notion of dialogue (the dictionary called it 'an exchange of views in the hope of reaching an agreement'). Jake had mentioned it in his letter and it seemed to have been taken up all over the country: over these days the authorities were reported to have talked to student bodies in Shaanxi, Gansu, Lanzhou, Hainan, Jilin, Xian, Shanghai – even in medieval Qinghai.

The idea obsessed him because it was just what they needed in Yanzhou – a bit of dialogue with the Municipal Government. Then perhaps they could discover what was going on over this scholarship.

It was not entirely pleasant to acknowledge his train of thought, especially with Wong's charge of selling out tagging along still; it did seem rather that he was trying to use the demonstrations to further his own cause. But was there anything wrong in that? Wasn't he just going for it – like the classmates in Peking: for ambition, the right to life satisfaction, a fair crack at individual success? Wasn't that, at bottom, what a democratic society was all about? Wasn't he just making the most of a bat's squeak of a chance to escape from the dead weight, the minimal expectation, of a provincial Chinese life?

Besides, it seemed such a little thing to ask: 'Will you tell me who has won two scholarships offered by the Landu Trade Bureau?' Such a little thing, and yet he could imagine the uproar in the Education Department if he did demand this tiny clarification, this chink of openness. 'They'll tell you when the time is right, Little Fang,' Interpreter Li had said. Pah!

He could ask Old Liu to make some discreet enquiries. But why should he have to do that? Old Liu was in a hell of a state anyway, and it seemed feeble to go through him every time.

Perhaps the spring had emboldened Fang; perhaps his wash-house summit with Li had exposed deeper fury; perhaps the success of his English Corner was too heady: but whatever it was, Fang felt he should demand satisfaction. Now. And, if the decision went against him, he might just ask how they had reached it and who the judges were and . . . well, suddenly there were so many questions: yes, that's what's needed – a bit of dialogue!

He tried to discuss the general situation with Grandfather, whom he found chuckling on the bed that evening as usual. Round and round in his palm went the Healthy Balls. 'Bah! Don't talk politics to me, boy. My generation, and your mother's, gave that up as a bad lot years ago. Fools' talk! What possible good can it do? No, I'm following another issue – the Muslims out in the minority areas. They're furious about a book called *Sexual Habits*. Couple of Han fellows got the Shanghai Cultural Publishing House to print it but the Muslims have kicked up such a fuss – even marched in Peking (don't know how they found any road space!) – such a fuss that the Government's just destroyed 90,000 copies. Damn pity if you ask me. Might have been a good read – supposed to be about rumpy pumpy between pilgrims and female camels. But how the authors are 'suspended for examination' and *Sexual Habits* seems to be going the same way as *The Golden Lotus*.'

Fang said he would see if Podgy couldn't swing a copy through his publishing contacts. He pondered the issue: these Muslims did not appear to have used dialogue. They had just declared their displeasure and got their own way.

Pumping iron the next morning he thought a little more about his scheme (the good thing about dumb-bells is that you can do them without having to concentrate on some ancient philosophy). If the boys liked it, the plan would have the added effect of confirming his reputation as a leader at the gatehouse. This had not received a serious knock but Fang looked forward to renewed admiration when he told them what he had decided to do. For a moment he considered unveiling it tomorrow, Sunday, in Moon Park, but he feared this would be dismissed as a mere publicity stunt and anyway he still doubted whether he could play the demagogue. Much better to gather only those who had actually applied for the scholarship and, *en masse*, to demand dialogue with the Education Department. But would he get the support? Qiao probably wouldn't co-operate; nor would Wong – which left him a back-up of Spotty, Liu Wei and Lin Hu (who had said nothing in the Year of the Snake so far): not the most inspiring troop but loyal certainly.

The first step, making contact with the Education Department, brought the first problem: how? Fang had never heard of anyone applying directly to Government for information. It had never seemed right – until now. Now it seemed a right.

But how? Apart from Interpreter Li, the rising, shooting star who moved so easily through every department, Fang could only think of the two Government Men who had attended the opening ceremony. But they were unlikely to open any doors, to shed any light; they would fence, obfuscate and dodge – anything to defend their inner circle. Mother might have suggested someone else from her teaching contacts but Fang was unwilling to set her thinking about the scholarship again. He decided to call on the Director; although he would have no direct access he would probably know the network of tunnels.

'Why do you want to talk to them, Little Fang?' he said, bunched up on the chair behind his desk, nose wrinkling absurdly. Hadn't anyone ever *told* him he looked like a rat?

'Well, Director, a group of us graduates applied for an award many weeks ago and now we really need to know whether anything has been decided – otherwise we cannot make any plans. The waiting is putting our families, especially our elderly relatives, under great strain.'

'Yes, I see. But surely the Government will let you know in good time?'

'This is what we were led to believe, Director, but it does not seem to be happening. Now is the "good time". All we want is a meeting with someone from the Education Department to let us know what is going on. The rumours are getting terribly unsettling. It's bad for our health. We have a right to know, don't you agree?'

'Well, I'm not sure about that. You speak like a Peking boy! Why don't you go through Landu for the information?'

'With respect, Director, I would say that is not practicable. Not only is it hard for any of us to find the time and money to get there but, even if we did, there would be no chance of actually meeting any of the officials in Landu. Surely it must be easier to seek this information from our own Municipal Government?'

'If they have it . . .'

'I think a decision must have been reached by now. Interpreter Li has even hinted as much. And if our Education Department has not yet heard, they need only book a phone call to Landu and they would know within hours. Time is passing, there are formalities to go through – visas, passports – before the American term starts.'

'America?'

'Yes, didn't you know, Director? I assumed—'

'No one tells me anything round here – I just run the institute, that's all.' Squeak, squeak.

'The award is a scholarship for a year's study in an American university.'

'Well, I really don't know about this!' The Director sprang up. 'It's hardly the time to be going off there. I think you'll find we've had quite enough America here. You've all got your diplomas. What more do you need! It's time to knuckle down and do some work for China. Eh? No, I certainly can't help you with this. Interpreter Li – he knows the scene. Go to him if you really must go to someone. Goodbye.'

'Goodbye, Director. I shall seek satisfaction elsewhere.' Enough of these Mickey Mouse officials.

He ate a large supper of cabbage, dried beef (chilled) and rice in front of the box. Gorbachev had arrived for some dialogue with China. Deng Xiaoping was shown reminding the Russian that China had first sought the meeting three years ago, passing the message through his old pal, Comrade Ceausescu of Romania.

Deng said his feeling was that 'there could be a turn or a solution to the arms race between the USA and the USSR and that confrontation could be turned into dialogue.'

When the announcer concluded with 'Dear viewers, the meeting is still going on, but our live report will end here, thank you,' Fang went to sit at Fu's dressing-table to write to Li. He didn't bother with any flowery language; he simply explained what the undersigned wanted to know: have any of us won the scholarship? Yes or no? Then he hurried down to the gatehouse where he was surprised and pleased when Qiao stayed to listen as he explained the petition. Wong, now back in the bin, seemed so cowed that Fang had to flatten a pulse of pity. It was okay, these guys were okay: they were behind him.

The signing was grave – moving even, as Fang had hoped. Lin Hu, Liu Wei and Spotty put their names under Fang's and shuffled back from the desk. After a brief silence Qiao stood up.

'It's worth a try,' he said quietly (he who would try anything!). 'I'm in.' Below his bold characters, Ling added his even though he hadn't applied for the scholarship.

'Just want to express support,' he muttered, sucking up another volley of lychees from a Heavenly tin. The atmosphere had also penetrated Podgy's hide. Having seen the signatures added on the far side of his desk, he reached out for the paper and wrote his own.

'Better this than some stupid hunger-strike.'

They took to their bicycles and headed for the Education Department. Podgy came too, on his brand new Tiananmen Transporter, a flat-bed tricycle truck, and as the classmates waited on the forecourt by their machines Fang strode through the gloaming and up the marble steps. At the door he turned to look down at their intense faces (so young!) and, just before the moment could go melodramatic on him, Fang rammed the little envelope through the letterbox.

thirty

People's Cement
Yanzhou
China   Wesneday 17th May, 1989

Dear Jake,

I hope silver wedding party was good. Which did you give, compact camera or video disc? We all miss you here, especially me. Our own Voice of America! Thank you for your letter of April 27 from Peking, Qiaoyuan Hotel. Very interesting actually confirming our impressions of the chaos. Sorry about Hong Wei. He can be a twerp. Ask Grandfather! He is thrilling with his Forever and says he looks back to Spring Festival party as one of his life's favourite days.

Now, as you said to us often – I have got some bad piece of news and some good piece of news. Good first: I *did* apply for the scholarship. But I kept just as quiet about it as you kept. Bad news second: We *still* don't know who has won it. I try to keep cool but these are difficult times for us Chinese and we were encouraged by our 'classmates' in Peking to apply for our own little meeting with Yanzhou Municipal Government. Clarificatory meeting you know. It is our right. This is our strongly held belief. Monday I sent a petition from all the people who applied for it (there were others apart from our esteemed former Class Monitor). There has been no reply but maybe today later.

Demonstrations are all over our Motherland. Gorbachev is here you know, they met him at the airport not the Square. There is a hunger-strike. How many students? 2,000? Maybe, it's possible. Rumours everywhere. 200 or 600 have fainted. Little Xin – do you remember him? – has gone to the Square. He will tell us the truth when he returns. Last night I saw a big character poster (this is traditional type of Chinese protesting) outside People's Cement. 'Bomb the Headquarters!' it said. A very, very brave person must of wrote it.

Best wishes to your dear parents, and Chrissie and the dog.

Sincerely Fang.

When he requested a stamp for America the postal clerk disappeared for ten minutes.

'What's the problem?' asked Fang as she lifted her buttocks back on to the stool at her desk. 'Do you have to have a summit meeting every time someone asks for a foreign stamp?'

'Watch your cheek, young man! You might find these hard to come by before very long.'

The radio that night broadcast a message to the hunger-strikers from the All-China Women's Federation:

Fellow-students, you have actually achieved your main objective already. Do you not want to talk to your mothers? Your mothers have heard your voices. Fellow-students, love your lives! The way ahead is still long. Come home children!

They didn't hear from the Education Department on Wednesday, or Thursday, or Friday. As leading ironist (self-appointed), Fang explained the perversity of the situation to those sitting in the gatehouse on Friday evening. For they had just heard the news that Li Peng, prime minister of the Middle Kingdom, had called a meeting with the student leaders in the Great Hall of the People on Tiananmen Square. It seemed that *they* had got dialogue at last!

'Premier Li will talk − but Interpreter Li's lips are still sealed,' said Fang with telling force. 'What do we think of these two different ways of dealing with students, eh, boys?' There was a chorus of loutish jeers.

Actually the events of the past three days in Peking had been so gripping that Fang now realised no decisions would be taken about anything until the turmoil was resolved. No one would dare pitch camp before they knew which way the bush fire was rolling.

Old Liu agreed, saying the Landu cockfight would go on at least as long as the one in Peking. Chen Ge was still very much in the pit but . . . Old Liu would say no more except that the hand of those wishing to cancel all overseas study trips or send only the 'ideologically very sound' could have been strengthened during the week. This was because Party general secretary Zhao Zhiyang might yet have to take the blame for the total loss of face opposite Gorbachev and the China-watching world. And if he went – well, the ruins would be back, careering down the corridors in their foreign wheelchairs and skittish behind their Zimmer frames.

Fang felt nowhere could have been China-watching more carefully than Yanzhou. News was now being broadcast from loudspeakers on all street corners and workers and cadres craned out of every open window to catch the latest. Televisions lit up the homes of all but the very poor and, once again, even *People's Daily* was having its say. In the evening there were so many people on Harmony Boulevard that it was almost a march.

On Wednesday the press reported there to be more than a million people out on the streets of Peking. On Thursday it was a million again and that evening, by popular demand, they were treated to the Chat Show of the Century, hosted by Li Peng and starring twelve top student leaders. Dialogue! Live!

They watched enthralled, automatically feeding on sunflower seeds and firing the husks on to the floor. Spit, spit, spit. Students wearing headbands (and one called Wuerkaixi in pyjamas!) were talking to the Chinese premier, the emperor's heir! And he was talking to them! Pyjama-Kid versus Emperor-elect! Fang was thrilled.

But on the way home, as he waited for a convoy of sand lorries to get out on to Baihao Hill Road, he realised that for all the 'exchange of views', no progress had been made. The Government must know the issues now – and yet they still did not seem to understand. There had been no step forward in Peking. He felt angry for Wuerkaixi and later, lying hot and naked on his bed, he felt angry for himself too.

thirty-one

Ling seemed to be spending more and more time with John, squatting in the doorless booth, reading the *People's Daily* which he now bought (rather extravagantly, to show his political awareness) on the way to work each morning. And he could get away with his slacking quite easily because the cadres were in almost permanent session discussing Manager Sun's now stumbling reform campaign.

'Anything good?' Fang grunted from the porcelain hole next door, holding his bowels so as not to miss the reply: just a tremendous rush of excrement from Ling and a sigh.

'Naah! Nothing much today. Still just bubbling along it seems.'

Back in the office Wong said there had been a call from the Education Department. 'They are inviting us to attend a meeting this afternoon.'

'A meeting? Well, that's something. But of course you know what their idea of a meeting is, don't you? A damn lecture – with a fat chance of us chipping in. Dialogue's what we want . . .' Fang dropped his voice at a scowl from a typist trout in the corner.

'Who did they get to ring, Little Wong?'

'Some bureaucrat – didn't give a name.'

'Who else is invited?'

'All of us I should think, wouldn't you?'

'Hmmph!' But excitement vaulted in Fang's stomach. The scholarship! He would know!

The meeting room was festooned in the Government's own awards for education: swathes of red cloth praising this middle school and that kindergarten. And there was the Mayor's own Wilmington plate, damn him!

Daintily covered easy chairs had been arranged in an oval; they were separated by small tables, each of which bore tea equipment and a pack of cigarettes in an orange glass ashtray.

Thermoses of hot water stood under the tables. Backed by tall windows and net curtains, three men were seated at the far end of the room. As the classmates muddled in, they rose and Fang quickly identified them as the two Government Men who had taken part in the opening ceremony and Interpreter Li. These genial hosts smiled and gestured to the seats. Fang quickly took the one at the end of the oval shape, directly opposite the trio who had already sat back down at the other end. It displeased him to see the others fussing about, deciding where to go – as if it mattered where they sat: the lead actors were in place.

'Welcome! Welcome!' said the main man. 'We are delighted you could come to this meeting.'

'Er, excuse . . .' But Fang swallowed his objection and rode the speaker's stare. It was too much to expect to hear that the petition had been acknowledged – though registered it would most certainly have been, and filed, and fingerprinted. . .

'It is a bright day outside and, looking around at your apple complexions, your young and vigorous faces, I suspect you would prefer to be kicking a ball around in Liberation Stadium.'

Polite laughter.

'But you are here precisely because today is a bright day – a bright and glorious day for Yanzhou. We have some excellent news to relate, some news which should make your young hearts thrill with pride in your city.'

Fang was surprised to find that amidst all his excitement he was still annoyed to notice that the cigarette packs were only half full, a calculated insult. He decided, for the first time in his life, to smoke one. By the time he had got the thing alight (a stale Leaping Lizard), everyone in the room was watching him in silence and the hosts were smiling like wicked step-mothers. Admittedly, he had been coughing quite a lot but he didn't need this attention.

'As you know, the Landu Provincial Government's Trade Bureau granted certain terms to a private university, Goodfellow, in Chicago. The conditions were struck with the best interests of our youth at heart. They comprise a scheme whereby Goodfellow admits three young scholars from the province to one of its business courses and sends three newly

graduated teachers over here to help with our modernisation
– three Mr Ja Kes, you might say!'

More polite laughter: his pronunciation had not improved.

'Another condition is that only one student from Landu
itself should be allowed to go to the States, the other two being
selected from diligent students all over the province. Therein
lies our pleasure!

'I am not unaware of the keen speculation and excitement
this scholarship has aroused and I have been delighted with
the sheer number of you who have tried your luck. Believe
you me, you are guiding lights for all those youngsters in
Yanzhou who desire to follow in your studying steps.'

Podgy nodded sagely and helped himself to some apples
which happened to be on the table nearest him.

'Rumours have reached even into the department that both
these awards might have gone to Yanzhouers.'

Frank and Charlie shared a glance. Do I look as ill as him?

'Rumours should sometimes command respect, even
attention . . .'

Get on with it!

'. . . but, in this case, the rumours were unfounded. Nevertheless, I have said we have reason to be proud and reason to
be proud we do have: one of these awards *is* ours. One of you
will be America-bound in a few weeks!'

He stopped again. For applause? Yes, Li and the other
flanker started the clapping. Happy days.

'Now I would like to go through with you the reports I have
received from our comrades, the judges, at the Landu Trade
Bureau. I shall be brief because I am aware that you want to
know who has won. Right . . . Mr Lin Hu. Is he here? Do we
have a Mr Lin Hu? Ah yes, and, let me see, Mr Zhang –
present and correct? Good. Now you two young fighters made
valiant bids but the judges decided your present level just
excludes you from really handling a full course in English.
They suggest you try next year.

'Mr Wong? I am to compliment you particularly on your
calligraphy. A fine hand they say. But your syntax, oh
dear, your syntax let you down! Where did you come in the
exam?'

'Nowhere. I wasn't selected for the course in the first place.'

'Ah, I like that! The self-taught entrant! Marvellous, marvellous. Keep it up. Now then, you are . . . ?' He looked up.

'Peng, sir, Little Peng.'

'I don't seem to be able to find your name on my list.'

'I didn't enter, sir.'

'Ah, well, why are you here then?'

The flanker muttered something in his ear.

'Ahaaa! I see. And Mr Xin?'

'Absent,' said Fang.

'Absent?'

'Visiting relatives.'

'Mr Ling?'

'I didn't enter either.'

'Right, well, who else have we? Let me see, Mr Liu Wei. A plucky entry this but again I'm afraid it's a "try again next year" for you too, which leaves Messrs Qiao and Fang. You boys have quite a reputation – for your English. Good little speakers, I hear, and it seems from this report you can both write a bit too. Your essay, Mr Fang, especially interesting and perceptive. It found much favour among the examiners who are pretty fed up with naïve fantasising about the West. They were the first to be saddened when, in the end, it all boiled down to one detail – a small one, but a crucial one, picked up at the last minute by an attentive clerk. Can you think what that might be?'

'No!'

'The entry fee, Mr Fang, ah yes, the entry fee. Five yuan may not seem very much to you youngsters – the cost of a haircut perhaps! – but for the Government it is a useful little defrayer of expenses and when an entrant doesn't pay it, well – as they say – it don't look good!'

Fang stopped listening. At first he lane-gamed through his memory, trying to recall whether Qiao had told him about this fee – or had Lorryman Yang pocketed it? But any malice he felt was quickly diverted. His knuckles whitened on the chair-arms. He saw through this bastard scheme straight away. Suck on another Lizard and concentrate!

'And so to Mr Qiao. You too have reason to be proud. You too wrote intelligently and, in your essay, showed what they have called an "aptitude and passion for business" – which you have probably been developing in our Foreign Trade Bureau, eh?'

'Yes sir!'

'In the course of time you will, no doubt, gain the opportunity to represent one of our products abroad, but for now you will be able to continue your training here.'

Fang stopped listening again. The world and the future were somersaulting through his guts. In chaotic embrace they wheeled, and up through the fumes of his third cigarette. He wastefully suppressed a huge belch and fought off a wrench of manic laughter as he caught Qiao's face: the mouth muscles had collapsed, the eyes had flopped shut, all his hairs had fainted and even the tops of his ears seemed to be drooping. With money and contacts, Qiao had failed too. Even Charlie Qiao!

In this jiving spin, pressed hard against the back of his easy chair, Fang surveyed the flipping oval. The main man was talking on and on: Fang focused his ears again; pricked up his eyes. The main man was smiling and talking at the same time. Clever! And now his voice rises. He is turning and shaking the hand of the other Government Man, the political commissar at his side – no, no, it is Interpreter Li he has turned to. Fresh-faced Interpreter Li is smiling too. The main man is clapping, the other man is clapping, Interpreter Li is clapping – who? Himself! Great Buddha, he is clapping, we are clapping, all clapping Interpreter Li.

'Thank you, thank you all!' said Li. 'This is a great opportunity for a provincial Chinese and I am delighted to have been offered it. I hope I shall be a credit to Yanzh—'

'Hang on!' cried Charlie.

'Yes, wait a minute!' shouted Frank, even louder because he was annoyed to have been pipped at the detonator.

'Excuse me!' said the main man. 'Perhaps you two fellows would be good enough to wait—'

'No, we've waited long enough,' said Fang, standing up. 'We should be allowed to speak.'

Qiao leapt to his feet too: 'After all, this was supposed to be a . . .'

'Dialogue!' They shouted together.

The three hosts fell back against the dainty doily headrests, raising their hands. But all the classmates were up and shouting the word, the one, great word: 'Dialogue! Dialogue! Dialogue!'

Eventually Fang motioned to the phalanx, his team, to be seated. Qiao dropped back down too. Fang went on.

'We sent you a petition five days ago demanding to know the result of this scholarship which we felt was long overdue. You then "invited us to a meeting". We accepted. But now it's your turn to accept something: in accordance with the healthy mood of apple-faced youths all over China, we now demand dialogue with you over this decision – in order to discover how and why it was reached.'

'But the decision was made in Lan—'

'Don't give us that!' Qiao was up again. 'You were involved all along. You're all in it. We don't need a hint of openness to know that much.'

'It's not true, simply not true,' said Li, livid Li.

'Yes it is!' said Fang. 'We know the system and its tunnels and we've run you to ground over this one. I'm not about to be fooled by your five-yuan entrance fee. It's my two-bit black marks, isn't it! But let's hear about Charlie here, Little Qiao. What was he picked up for, eh? Come on, let's hear what the interpreter's got that none of us have, eh?'

'Enough, enough. I refuse to—' the main man blustered.

'Sir, if you'll excuse me, I would like to say a few words. I feel the charges are beginning to take on a personal tone and I would like to give an explanation. As a young man myself, perhaps I can make them understand.'

'Do you think so, Interpreter?'

'Yes, sir – and as the scholar I feel it falls to me.'

'Well, I suppose it's all right.' He looked at his henchman. 'What do you think?'

'It might be appropriate in view of the passion of—' But the classmates were chanting again, 'Dialogue! Dialogue! Dialogue!'

Li raised his hands. 'Fellow-students, you must be calm. You don't need me to tell you about the turmoil in our Motherland's capital. This is common knowledge widely reported through official channels of the media. What you may not be so clear about is the effect the turmoil has had in such large cities as Landu – reaching, I'll be frank, even behind the doors of office. The Trade Bureau there and educational administrations all over the country have for some time received information about the distressing tendency among our young graduates sent abroad to stay away indefinitely.

'This tendency has come under even closer scrutiny since the mourning of Hu Yaobang was hijacked by unscrupulous elements who used the mass emotions to cause chaos and turmoil. This we know. But in dealing with this question we should pay great attention also to the quality of the love professed for the young of China by senior statesman Deng Xiaoping. He said in his broadcast of May 3 – I happen to have the words here – "the growth of the young generation is precisely the dependable hope for developing and succeeding in our cause . . . The young people's initiative to demand that their potential ability be put into play and that their own value be turned into reality should be safeguarded . . . the value of young people lies in that they like to think deeply and dare to explore new knowledge. Without thinking, how can young people make progress? . . . The future belongs to young people. The younger generation that stands astride these two centuries is shouldering a glorious and arduous mission. The Party pins its hopes on you."'

Yeah, yeah, yeah, and the rest! Keep it coming! Fang started coughing quite loudly.

'And so we know that when Deng Xiaoping sees the glorious youth of China being sucked into the materialist vacuum, something has to be done. With typical speed and force the Party has implemented a policy of sending abroad only those who have proved themselves unstintingly loyal and who will therefore return. It was to my great surprise and pleasure that my own humble application was deemed to be suitable.'

Fang's fury flared again, pure fury.

'And who's to say we would not come back, eh? Who has made that decision!'

'I appeal once again for some calm, Little Fang.'

'Answers are what we want, not calm!' said Qiao, just stopping Ling and Podgy from rising into another 'dialogue' descant.

'Well, shall we just say that your conduct during Mr Elliot's stay gave us cause to worry.'

'No, let's not "just say" that! We know what you think about Little Fang and his – excesses,' (Qiao had the grace to look at Fang for permission to continue; Fang the grace to grant it) 'but what about my own case? I'm getting married now, you know? And you should be giving me a decent pres—'

'That is quite irrelevant. You, too, overstepped the mark.'

'How? Go on, tell me! As Class Monitor?'

'You were too liberal in your dealings.'

'What dealings?'

'The excursions.'

'What do you mean?'

Interpreter Li spoke more softly now. 'You took the foreigner to all manner of sensitive areas.'

'Where? Telephone factory? Tyres? Nails and Screws? Heavenly Tinned Foods? The Government sanctioned all those trips and sometimes came too. What do you mean? Please tell me!'

'The hospital.'

'Yes, the hospital? What about it? I took him there often for his back trouble.'

'No! The operating room . . . ' Li looked down.

Explosive dialogue this! Fang looked at Qiao and Qiao met his eye. Together they understood – and to each other they mouthed 'snip cock!' The others were quite lost. A sublime moment, even here, even now. Qiao's fall from grace had begun that day – oh terrible day! – when Interpreter Li was spread on the slab, his groin full of pins. Joy!

'Circumcision!' shouted Fang, eager to be emphatically open about this matter at least. 'Qiao took Jake to watch the interpreter being circumcised. But embarrassment and your loss of face and foreskin aside, do you think, Mr Li, that your circumcision constitutes a state secret? And that by showing it to a foreigner Qiao has compromised his reliability utterly and completely – and for ever? I put it to you this way: should his life, his future, his ambition rest on your penis?'

Uproar. Podgy was practically on the floor farting horribly. Everyone was in states of horror or mirth depending on his position in the oval. Fang let them writhe for a minute and, a demagogue at last, he then quelled the helpless yelps.

'Circumcision, you know, Mr Li, is not a Chinese speciality. Millions of people around the world go in for it, I'm told. Indeed, I remember even Jake was—'

'Enough! This is intolerable!' said the main man. 'It's an outrage! Get out, all of you! Now!'

Li was slumped, sapped: the other two shooed them away like radioactive geese. Fang managed an insolent saunter nevertheless, casually pocketing Leaping Lizards from each table as he went down the line.

He swaggered out of the door and clicked along the corridor with Podgy at his side. As they turned to descend the stairs, Miss Lo started to come up from the hall. The boys went down as a pair, as a wall, and for all her muscles Miss Lo had to squash her rhino rump against the banister as they passed her.

'Half an hour,' she hissed. 'Remember, Comrade Peng!'

'What was that about?' Fang asked him outside the building.

'Oh, nothing – nothing to worry about. See you tomorrow.' The fat man squeezed back on to his Tiananmen and rolled away. Fang exchanged defiant looks with the others as they came down the steps but no one said a word. They bicycled off on their separate ways through the hot and crowded streets. Dialogue! We gave them dialogue all right. But the scholarship? They had kept that.

thirty-two

As Fang passed through the kitchen the next morning to collect the sword, Mother caught his arm.

'They've declared martial law in Peking,' she said without looking up from the screen. She was gripping him with dreadful force. Fang's bowels shifted.

'Why?' he murmured and his arm fell against his side as she released it.

'So as to check the turmoil with a firm hand,' replied the presenter, 'maintain Peking municipality's public order, protect citizens' lives and property, and protect the Party and state organs and the Peking Municipal Government doing day-to-day official business.'

'Will Fu ring, Mother?'

'The lines will be too busy now.' She sounded flat but the screen was pulsing as never before, beating out support for Li Peng's announcement, support from units, commissions, academies, institutes, army personnel regions and Liberation veterans across the Motherland.

The Pigeon flew down to the gatehouse. But it was locked. Locked? Fang cut straight over to Qiao's. There were fewer people on the roads than in recent days but he lane-gamed where he could, terribly fast. Old Qiao let him in with an affectionate smile. The young man of the moment was sitting by his radio semi-dressed, trying to get VOA.

'I don't believe it,' he said. 'What is happening?'

The radio buzzed its non-reply. Fang found himself speaking English. The room always had that effect.

'Had you better not get ready, Charlie? You know, red tie and etsetterer.'

'What a day for wedding! Just can't believing it!'

'I want to apologise about what I said about your wedding and—'

'No worry, Frank – that's all over. I don't thinking about it. Actually it did cross across my mind that a wife might help when I asked her but I told myself that no one would be so . . .'

'So what?'

'So, how do you say, cynical to think I wed because of that.'

'Cynicous, Charlie, the word's cynicous. Yes, I'm sorry, I guess I am rather like this nowadays. But perhaps it is best . . .'

'Perhaps – but where my wife comes into it, no! She's a beautiful person, good and kind and sexual.'

'Sure, Charlie, sure.'

'One thing is for certain – whatever is happen in Peking – that here in Yanzhou Charlie Qiao loves Betty Bo.'

'Betty Bo! Oh, she'll like that, Charlie.'

'I think she will.'

'Well, I wish you the best of British lucky. But you should count your stars – some of us is still a loner.'

'What about Miss Ping?'

'That Wong . . .'

'Biff him, Fang, biff him. She's your girl. Anyone could seeing that at flax dance.'

'You think?'

'I know! Biff him and . . .'

'And what?'

'Give her one!'

'Charlie!'

'It's the best thing. What else is there to do now anyway? Make sexual not war. Perhaps this *is* a good time to be getting marrying after all. We don't have to be secret about it now – openness. You should get in there.'

'Stop it – but I suppose you're right. As my famous grand-father says, we Chinese, when going gets tough, we should internalise.'

They filled the flat with such gales of ridiculous, nervy laughter that both parents came in to tell Little Qiao to get on with his dressing. It was almost time.

Fang walked slowly down the stairs and stroked a cat on a landing. He was relieved Qiao and Bo and their relatives had opted for a no-guest affair in a private room at the Roast Duck. He didn't have the stomach for celebrating. Marital, martial – he played with the words and thinking then of

Charlie's advice, he suddenly whinnied with mad excitement again.

Off Peace Street he saw a Tiananmen going round and round the acrobats. It was Podgy – in a daze like so many others today.

'Terrible, isn't it?' said Fang, skidding up to a lamp-post near by. The King of Wind kept circling. He was weeping.

'That won't do much good, Podgy.'

'You don't know what's happened.'

'Course I do – everyone does!'

'No, here! At the gatehouse, to me! I'm out!'

'Out?'

'They've sacked me. I'm going to court. Corruption, embezzlement, bribery . . .' He was wheeling faster and faster, tipping the Tiananmen dangerously.

'Steady on, old man. Look, how about stopping that and coming here? What's happened?'

He came over, a huge, fat baby.

'Lo – the volley-ball – she rumbled me. You know she works at Heavenly Tinned? Well, apparently she's been watching for months and noting and they hauled me in after the meeting last night and . . . well, that's it. I'm done for.'

'Well, Podgy, that makes two of us – no, all of us, all the gang are in the shit.'

Rather than start blubbing too – though he felt he might – Fang told Podgy to go and get himself married like Qiao. 'It's by far the best thing to do these days – the only thing. And don't worry about the court case. When this "political struggle" is over they'll have hundreds of even bigger fish to fry. You'll be all right!'

He thwacked the great rump and pedalled home. But Podgy (the little minnow) would be sent down for sure. That's the way things were going. Down.

The television was still pouring its stuff into the kitchen but there was no one there to receive it. Mother must have been trying to get through to Fu from the school telephone. Citizens of Peking were building barricades of furniture and traffic dividers across the vast road intersections. Students were still occupying the Square but the hunger-strike was over.

Fang crammed an apple into his mouth and shoved open

the door to Grandfather's room. He was smoking a Burmese Bamboo. Evidently it had been a good morning for bile.

'Grand to see you, boy. Hell of a business, eh?'

Fang nodded and perched next to him.

'Just been thinking what a fine fellow that tapir-face was. What's his name?'

'Jake.'

'Yes, well, I thought I might write him a letter.'

'A letter?'

'Yes, get you to translate it, just to thank him for the bicycle. What do you think?'

'Good idea, Grandfather. I'll be writing to him later today to tell him about the . . .'

'The what, boy?'

'The . . . bat's squeak, Grandfather.'

'The bat's squeak?'

'Yes, do you remember telling me once that my generation had a bat's squeak of a chance?'

'What about it?'

'Well, it's squeaking its last, don't you think?'

'Nooo! Don't be such a drip! You young ones! Ain't seen nothing! No, this will sort itself out. Just sit back and let it flow over you. Grand opportunity for some sword practice, I'd say. Not much going on at work I shouldn't think, eh? Take it easy. Enjoy the television! Big screen. Those Japanese dwarfs can really make a decent screen, eh?'

Thus the days went painfully by; days of watching and listening. Fang spent more time than ever with Grandfather, preferring his increasingly deranged patter to anything the 'sane' could offer. Mother could only crow about the scholarship result — when she wasn't gawping at the television. There was no word from the Education Department, but they would pounce when they had finished having banquets for Interpreter Li.

On Sunday journalists at Xinhau, the government agency, denied that soldiers were occupying their newsroom but the content of their bulletins now suggested otherwise.

Fang visited the young marrieds, who were living in Qiao's bedroom temporarily and having to delay their trip to the photographic studio in Landu until the railways got back to normal (there were still rumoured to be as many as 20,000 young people going into Peking every day). Qiao deeply embarrassed Fang by telling him again to storm Miss Ping – and in front of Betty, whose knowing smile further confused him.

On Monday Mother finally got through to Fu, whose comments hardly squared with the excited tone of the previous calls. The maid was having difficulty getting fresh vegetables and they could smell the Square from their flat but otherwise there was nothing to worry about; Hong Wei was at her side. Mother said at the end of the call she had added, somewhat hurriedly, that shouts of 'Down with Li Peng!' were still being heard in alleys and dark corners; that bottles were still being smashed.

An army chief went on the air declaring that the people's army belongs to the people and therefore must never shoot at the people: 'To prevent the situation worsening, troops must not enter the city.'

On Tuesday the radio said there were nearly a million people in the Square which, against the background of the past days, seemed an extraordinary figure. When they met in Harmony Boulevard that evening Old Liu suggested that perhaps someone in the media was trying to exaggerate the unrest to boost the students' morale – not that it could be all that low if they were prepared to march through a city under martial law! He added that he had heard there had been protests in eighty other cities.

Fang also bumped into Spotty, who said the Peking students would probably now hang on for the capital's next great event – some committee of the National People's Something-or-other due to meet on 20 June. Liu Wei had suggested they might wait for the Party's own fortieth birthday celebrations in the autumn. Or maybe for the Asian Games in 1990. Everyone brandished opinions and rumours.

There was the odd fact to cling to: the number of traffic accidents in the Motherland was down on all previous weeks this year. Only six people had died on the roads. And here was another fact: three people had thrown eggshells full of paint at Mao's portrait on Tiananmen Gate.

Fang came in from the office to hear Grandfather in hysterics about this. Summoned to the bed, he tried to calm him with the offer of a Leaping Lizard, but to no avail.

'Bah! Bureaucrats' baccy! Get it out of here!' And with his deft right hand which he claimed could still punch the eye out of a mosquito, Grandfather snatched the pack and stuffed it into the stove which heated the brick-based bed. 'Admirable blokes, those paint-chuckers,' he continued. 'Should have done it long ago! We have to rescue ourselves from the Great Rescuer. Debunk him! But who dares? Irony is you can't even quote Mao these days. Take that "Bomb the Headquarters" poster stuck up down the road the other night. They've gone barmy about that. A witch-hunt's already under way, I hear.' He chuckled. 'But it should be a wizard-hunt!'

'Grandfather!'

'What you staring at *me* for, boy? Cheeky little blighter! Go and empty this!' He thrust the jar at Fang and once more set his Balls a-clinking.

On Wednesday Fang skived off work and stayed in bed all day, trying to avoid the news and his incredible grandfather. But he could hear the television proclaim Lhasa utterly peaceful; messages of support had been sent from Tibet to Peking. It was only after he'd heard the bulletin through the wall four times that he remembered Lhasa itself was still under martial law.

Wrapped in the quilt despite the heat, Fang worried about Fu, and Little Xin. He tried to 'write Jake' but could not; Grandfather had forgotten his desire to do so, too. He wondered idly when Manager Sun would be told about the 'dialogue' and whether the rumour that Sun was himself about to be sacked could be true. That evening it was announced that a new portrait of Mao had been hung on Tiananmen Gate.

On Thursday Li Peng was seen receiving the new ambassadors of Nigeria, Mexico and Burma. He told them that 'foreign friends have always been unable to see the situation in China clearly' and that there was no harm in watching a little longer, 'before making a judgement'. Leaders were shown visiting 'PLA fighters who were beaten up by some lawless elements while enforcing martial law'.

The cement mixer arrived from Manchester. Fang could see that he would be needed to help get it going and so he spent a day examining its gleaming parts. Any fool could see that half of the engine was missing but Fang wasn't telling. That evening he returned to find Mother transfixed by the screen, window-blinds down. She seemed to have shrunk in comparison. Perhaps it was bigger. But the news was the same: everyone cherishing the PLA; the PLA cherishing everyone.

On Friday Mother did not go to work either. They both stared at the screen – and the PLA seemed to be in the kitchen with them all day.

One charming bulletin had the soldiers watching Peking children dancing in the streets and then giving hand-to-hand combat demonstrations to passers-by, cleaning windows, and watering flowers.

> A unit of the Chinese PLA that has come to Peking in order to enforce martial law has carried out extensive educational activities aimed at cherishing the capital, the people and the young students . . . They also took some time from their schedule to do cleaning work for the people, following Lei Feng's example. In great delight the masses cried: Lei Feng has come to our city.
>
> Army–people friendship activities were carried out. The unit gave military training demonstrations for local people and students, while children sang and danced to entertain their PLA Uncles. The leaders, teachers and students of a local school presented a colour television set so that the fighters may watch television by way of recreation. In addition local shop assistants delivered goods to the unit to serve its needs. All these activities, which fully manifest the close fish-and-water relationship between the army and the people, are welcomed and appreciated by the commanders and fighters.

On Monday a propaganda cadre was officially declared to be a Revolutionary Martyr. He had died while enforcing martial law when he was knocked over by onlookers and crushed by passing vehicles (presumably military ones). That same day an eighty-seven-year-old leader called Peng Zhen declared: 'It is now quite chaotic ideologically . . . we should and must unify our thinking.'

On Tuesday they heard that the national image had been 'vilified by the so-called statue of a goddess' in Tiananmen

Square. Grandfather whooped when Mother passed on Fu's description of the white statue which had been put up overnight to stare straight into the eyes of the fresh, new Chairman, with her torch held aloft. But Fang had thought only of Jake's disco stab at the flax-mill dance party.

On Wednesday the screen screamed news of an anti-student demonstration and an open letter from the elders of Daxing County to the students: 'You should study knowledge for building up the Motherland, instead of doing stupid things that sadden our own people and gladden the enemy.'

The masses, it was said, were suffering badly from the frightening acts of youths on motorcycles who had formed bands called the Flying Tiger Team and the Iron-Riding Guard Team. Fang liked to think of Little Xin, high on ping-pong-bat glue, roaring away from the lights on the Avenue of Eternal Peace.

On Thursday came official denial of the rumour that Deng Xiaoping had been hospitalised. Fang was more worried about his own grandfather, who was now in state of perpetual excitement, twanging around the home like a knot of gristle, quite unable to settle, lunging for the sword so often that Fang had had to keep it down his own bed.

He was still the most engaging thing around and Fang felt he would go mad himself if he no longer had this crazy fellow to monitor. When he delivered a mighty concoction of ground reindeer horn and ginseng to his bed that evening he was treated to further revelations.

'Sit down, boy, stay awhile. I'd like you to cast your mind back to Spring Festival time.'

'Yes?' said Fang warily.

'Well, you probably don't remember this but I was in fact absent for the first few minutes of our little celebration.'

'Yes. I do remember your absence, Grandfather – and your gory arrival.'

'Ah yes, you do! Good. Well, I just feel like giving you a bit of background to that one, because it's all a bit important to me right now, you know, state of mind sort of thing . . .'

'I don't understand.'

'Let me explain. For a long while now I have wanted to get my own back – symbolically like – by giving the name Mao

Zedong to a chicken and then cleaving off its head. I wanted to do it with my sword on one of the weekly birds your mother gets us but since I was barred from it after – after the incident with your aunt, I have only had the chopper to deal with. Well, the chopper is a most ungainly weapon but there has been another much more important obstruction to this ambition of mine.'

'Yes? Drink up, Grandfather.'

'Some sort of loyalty to the Helmsman, some perverted ancestor worship if you like. He wrecked my life for sure but somehow I just couldn't take his head off. Anyway, that day I decided to do it once and for all – down at Old Fen's restaurant. I sneaked into the yard with the sword and in order to get me going I started off calling each of the ducks after each of Mao's Cultural cronies, the Gang of Four – get the idea? Chang Chun-chiao, CHOP! Chiang Ching, CHOP! Wang Hung-wen, CHOP! Yao Wen-Yuan, CHOP! Absolutely no problem with them. Bloody great blows they were, meticulous! But when I tried to call the fifth one Mao Zedong I just froze – couldn't do it, boy! I'd take the head off all right but by then I'd have called it Chang Chun-chiao again! Chop! And so I'd have to go through the whole lot of them – chop! chop! chop! I'd taken out five Gangs of Four like this – twenty bloody ducks! – when suddenly I felt a new force inside me, never felt anything like it before. I knew I could do it. I screwed my loins or girded up my courage or whatever the hell you wordsmiths say you have to do and I raised the sword high above my head in preparation for the fulfilment of a lifetime's ambition. And do you know what happened, boy?'

'No.'

'Nothing! Absolutely nothing. I couldn't bring the sword down at all because Old Fen had snuck up and grabbed me from behind – grabbed me just before the swipe of my life! Imagine! The Chairman was just there – as close as you are to me.'

Enough. Fang fled to his bed to check that the sword was still hidden. This old man was going, going.

He drifted into work late on Friday morning. Wong and Ling, who had once made things difficult for him there, were now his desperate allies. They all expected the repercussions of the Education Department 'riot' to break over them at any time. A fortnight had passed and still they had heard nothing.

But, as Fang quietly pointed out to Wong by the clapped-out Korean photocopier, there was no hurry: none of the graduates was going anywhere. Time was the Government's ally.

'The uncertainty's getting to me,' said Wong. 'It's worse than waiting for the scholarship result.'

He can't really have set many hopes on that, can he? Fang was unwilling to swap depressions with Wong, whom he would never really trust nor respect, but he saw here a chance to impress and this he could never resist.

'Yes, Little Wong, they are certainly playing with us. They consider our lives to be – what is that rather splendid English word? – floccinaucinihilipilificated. Is that how you see it?'

If Manager Sun had been told about the meeting, he did not alter his courteous manner towards the three graduates. Or perhaps he sympathised with their fight. Sun's own determination not to bow to the conservative cement-heads had certainly inspired Fang over the last two weeks and this alone kept him from withdrawing his labour entirely.

He was pleased that afternoon to have the opportunity to speak to a German who was considering building flyovers with Yanzhou cement. Over apples and tea they made some progress towards this goal despite the German's execrable English accent, and afterwards Sun invited Little Fang to dine at the Dong Lan Hotel where the company was treating its guest to a farewell banquet.

But as they exchanged pleasantries over the rich food Fang grew sad again. This funny little German had enjoyed his trip to Yanzhou, and he would take some merry tales of China back to the Fatherland. But did he realise what his decision on the flyovers – which he said he would reach 'in a week or so' – meant to Manager Sun? How could he know what swords hung over their necks?

As Fang translated the German's procrastination, he saw fear grow in Sun's eyes and it was only by busily licking up the last eight sea cucumber, in a thick sauce, that he could quash another surge of his own fear.

The next morning was another bright one and Fang had to carry a heavy rice-wine head into the office to help Sun draw up a few final papers before the German was whisked away. Then he went to his own desk and tried again to write a letter to Jake. Still he could think of nothing to say, however, and shoved the old office dictionary away to reveal Fu's telephone number which he had scratched into the metal desk-top some days before.

Collecting the orange phone from the other side of the office he carried it back to his desk, tugging the extension lead through gaps in the furniture. To his great surprise, his dialling was rewarded within minutes by a loud ringing – and then by Fu's nasal 'Hello?'

'It's Fang, Elder Sister – Little Brother . . .'

'Hello.' Her voice flattened noticeably.

'Well, how is everything?'

'Fine. Fine, thank you.' Now he thought he could hear another voice in the background.

'The demonstrations?'

'I can't really . . .'

'What? Why?'

'Everything here is fine, Fang,' said Hong Wei. 'There is fresh food in the shops, the weather is fine, the air is good. The situation is back to normal, everything is fine. Thank you for ringing.'

'No, thank *you*, Brother-in-law.' Fang looked at the receiver and replaced it carefully.

He headed home, hoping to take in the television news, but as he entered their alley he ran into a gaggle of neighbours. They were examining a patch on the wall but on seeing him they turned as one and started clucking disapproval.

'He's done it this time, Little Fang!'

'Vandalism, that's what it is!'

'Political crime, I'd say!'

'Your lot had better watch out!'

Fang said nothing, deigning only to glance at the wall as he pushed firmly through. The 'crime' related to a faded Cultural Revolution mural of the Great Helmsman, which Fang had passed every day of his life and had not actually noticed for years. But today it had changed: where Mao's plump face had beamed for so long there was now an ugly hole in the plaster. Grandfather had hacked it away with his chopper.

Mother was in front of the television, watching *The Sound of Music*. (Continually repeated by the arbiters of television taste, the film was pitiably dubbed, but it was effective escapism and just what Mother needed.)

'Where's Grandfather?'

'In his room. Been there all day.' She didn't look up.

Fang peered round the door. He was snoring softly but there was dust on his old cloth shoes and the wire had been wrenched off the window catch. Fang left him be.

'What's the news, Mother?'

'By their concrete deeds of ardently loving the capital and the people and the young students, officers and soldiers have demonstrated that the PLA is forever the people's own army,' she declared.

'Ah, right,' said Fang looking at her quizzically. 'Well, that's something, isn't it?' He sat in front of the screen and wished he was an Alpine cow.

thirty-three

Fang lay in bed the next morning and dozed. He had slept well – better than for several nights. Why? At first he couldn't tell but then he suddenly threw his sheet to the floor and searched the bed urgently. There was the explanation: he had not been sharing his bed with four foot of tempered steel. The sword was gone. And then from the yard came dreadful confirmation – a long, mad scream.

Fang jumped to the window just in time to see Grandfather execute a violent, magnificent stroke. He swept the blade through a perfect arc, catching the sun and taking the chicken's head clean off. The bird ran in two tight circles around his feet and then, blood squirting from its neck-stump, hurtled towards the foot of Fang's bedroom wall to collapse under the window. Leaning on the sword, Grandfather looked up from the chicken and met Fang's astonished face still pressed against the glass. His own seemed to be forming a smile of triumph when it suddenly crinkled into another long, crazy yell.

Fang fumbled into his track suit and canvas shoes wondering how best to disarm Grandfather this time. In the kitchen Mother was already back in front of her television. She looked tiny. She didn't even say good morning. The screen seemed to be blotting out Fang's existence and, much more surprising, the sound of the screams.

With his hand on the door latch, Fang glanced up at the presenter who was wearing black, unusually, and apparently refusing to look at the camera.

. . . in order to defend the tranquillity of the capital and the prestige of the Motherland, to defend the leadership of the CCP and the socialist system, to defend the fruits of the revolution and construction and reform, to defend the life and fundamental interests of the workers, peasants, intellectuals and other citizens of society and, by carrying forward

the spirit of fearing no fatigue and sacrifices, they are suc-
cessfully smashing the counter-revolutionary riot.

Riot? What riot? Fang's hand slipped from the latch.

Their heroic acts and the glorious exploits have won fervent
praise and strong support from the masses of students and
citizens. They are worthy to be called soldiers who are sons
and brothers of the people under the leadership of the Party,
and worthy to be called the staunch pillars and iron wall of
our socialist People's Republic of China.

Fang went out into the yard with his hands in front of his
eyes. The news. The sun. The riot of brightness. What would
Grandfather have to say? But when his hands fell away he
faced an empty space and a moon-gate which hung open on
its ancient hinges.

Fang could hardly have cared less. If the old sword artist
had found peace at last, then why the hell shouldn't he go and
declare it in the marketplace? But what about me? Fang pushed
his bicycle to the end of the alley and began to freewheel
downtown. What about me?

In his distraction he failed to notice the articulated sand
lorry which had pushed itself rudely out into the bicycle flow.
By the time he did, it had straddled the whole Baihao Hill
Road – and stalled to blow its bulbous nose. He was going
far too fast to stop. A swerve was impossible even for the King
of Shimmy and instead – somehow – he shot through the
waiting flock of Pigeons. Then, with an agility he would never
be able to explain to his grandchildren, he ducked below his
handlebars and flew under the lorry's oily belly.

He hit Harmony on a high – genuinely pleased to be alive,
delighted now to be a man and not a cow – and shot through
the milling masses who were out in the sunshine discussing
the counter-revolutionary riot. He took himself automatically
to Qiao's block: it was Sunday. But he met the parents on the
first flight of stairs. They told him Qiao and Bo had gone to
Landu first thing to have their wedding photograph taken.
Fang turned on his heel, pushing the Pigeon away and jumping
on to it as he ran, eager to avoid small talk with the benevolent
bastard and his wife.

Where to now? The gatehouse. There must be someone there today. There was: the new gatekeeper — the one who had turned them all away at the gates of the Dong Lan Hotel on Jake's first night. Like some crack war correspondent he always seemed to be sent to the front's most sensitive areas.

'Can I help you, Mr Fang?' he sneered.

'No!'

Fang rocketed up Peace on fury fuel, set now on the reckless idea of declaring himself to Miss Ping. Stop talking about it: Act! Storm! Dialogue was out of fashion already; declarations were the rage. If the Government could spout canting kitsch as their tanks rolled through Peking, there was no more fitting time to give her some propaganda about love (Miss Ping, I declare I will cherish you for ever!) and then take her at last.

But going past the market he spotted Podgy's ponderous Tiananmen disappearing down a narrow lane. Eager to hear any news there might be on Little Xin in Peking, he changed his plans again and clattered after Podgy.

He had just paused at a crossroads, uncertain which way Peng had gone, when a bicycle came hurtling towards him from the direction of the bookstore. It was Grandfather on Jake's Forever, legs flailing and bloodied sword straight out in front of him, something crazy in his eyes. Fang tried to hail him but he shot past; and his manic scream, like the siren of some police van which flashes by, went with him.

A radio loudspeaker on a lamp-post was regaling them all with the latest derring-do of the PLA. He swivelled his bicycle and headed back to Peace Street. His mind crackled with a hundred different ideas, on a hundred different wavebands. Yes, virginity had to go. But shouldn't he catch Grandfather? Or call Fu? Or find Old Liu? No, first he needed noodles.

He thought of Qiao, probably now squeezing into a tired old tuxedo, Bo at his side in her hired silk train and veil; the studio photographer would be asking them to choose between his 'natural' background of purple mountains, a river, huge great herons winging off left and right and, over here, the 'interior set', furnished Hong-Kong style, against a tasteful string of Roman arches, pink on purple. He thought of Sundays past with Qiao and then Jake's voice blurted in on him, indistinct. What was *he* doing now? Fang wondered, too, about Herr Flyover who would be back in Munich already.

As he waited – uncharacteristically – at the lights on the junction with Peace Street, the clocktower declared one o'clock with a protracted dong which triggered the electronic tones of the Red Flag in celebration of another hour of socialism. The loudspeakers raged against this music: audible or not, they were not to be outdone today. The lights changed. As Fang absently sought the pedals for the short run over to the Noodle Palace, someone tapped him on the shoulder and he started. It was Wong and, on the other side of him, Spotty Zhang. They were saying something, but what? Fang could hear nothing against the Red Flag and the radio.

He noticed Interpreter Li emerging from a small door opposite. Fang stared at him. The clocktower had fallen silent and the radio announcer was able to reassert himself. He was speaking in English. This was unusual. Ignorant passers-by, unfamiliar with Sunday's English service from Radio Peking, looked at the loudspeakers in surprise. But Fang stared on at Li. This is what that announcer said:

> Remember 3 June 1989. A most tragic event happened in the Chinese capital, Peking. Thousands of people, most of them innocent civilians, were killed by fully armed soldiers when they forced their way into the city.

Interpreter Li stood gripping the door handle still. At last he had caught Fang's beam.

> Among those killed are our colleagues at Radio Peking. The soldiers were riding in armoured vehicles and used machine-guns against thousands of local residents and students who tried to block their way. When the army convoys made a breakthrough, soldiers continued to spray their bullets indiscriminately at crowds in the street. Eyewitnesses say some armoured vehicles even crushed foot soldiers who hesitated in front of the resisting citizens. Radio Peking English Department deeply mourns those who died in the the tragic incident and appeals to all its listeners to join our protest for the gross violation of human rights and the most barbarous suppression of the people. Because of the abnormal situation here in Peking there is no other news we could bring you. We sincerely ask you for your

understanding and thank you for joining us at this most tragic moment.

Frozen astride the Pigeon, Fang looked quickly around at the people moving about so uncomprehendingly, buying their pork fat and their cabbage, pork fat and cabbage. He glanced too at Wong and Spotty who had sunk to the pavement at either side of him, both covering their faces. Then, clenching his fist and thinking he might even raise it in defiance, he looked across the busy street again. But Interpreter Li was gone.

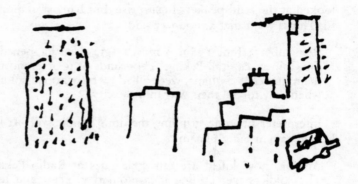